The
Leipfold Files

The Leipfold Files

Leipfold Mysteries • Book 3

Dane Cobain

Encircle Publications
Farmington, Maine, U.S.A.

Encircle editor: Michael Piekny

Cover design: Christopher Wait
Cover photograph © Getty Images

Published by:

Encircle Publications
PO Box 187
Farmington, ME 04938

info@encirclepub.com
http://encirclepub.com

Introduction

JAMES LEIPFOLD is a complicated man, a complicated character with an interesting backstory that hasn't been explored. Until now, at least.

The stories in this collection are written in such a way that you should be able to enjoy them whether you're new to the Leipfold series or not, although it'll certainly help if you've already read *Driven* and *The Tower Hill Terror*. Many of the cases in this collection have been referenced there, at least in passing. And if you've read those two books, you'll also know that Leipfold served in the army, spent some time in jail and eventually formed his own private detective agency. You'll get to see how that pans out in this collection.

The goal of these stories is to shed a little light on Leipfold's London and the background that led to him starting his detective agency. Some link together and others don't, but they all show a different side of Leipfold that we haven't seen from the novels.

This collection also includes "The Game," "Leipfold Inc.," and "The Marshall Stack," three tales that were originally imagined as side stories in *The Tower Hill Terror* but were removed for the sake of brevity and clarity[1]. They found their new home here and offset Leipfold's past with a little glimpse of the future.

I'm not going to go on and on because I'm sure you want to get started, so I'll leave you in the capable hands of the young James Leipfold.

And who knows? You might even see a familiar face or two.

Enjoy your visit to Leipfold's London.

---

1 Note from Pam: And for your editor's sanity.

CONTENTS

Three Hoodlums

"OI, MATE, YOU GOT A CIGARETTE?"

Fourteen-year-old James Leipfold flinched as he heard the words, then bowed his head and increased his speed slightly until he was half-running, half-walking through the underpass.

His mind was working overtime as he tried to analyse the situation without turning his head. The easy confidence with which the request had been made, coupled with the timbre of the voice and the slight inflections of the dialect, put him in mind of a spotty seventeen-year-old, probably one of the other kids from the estate. He could hear the click-clacking of bicycle wheels and amended his mental picture to include a couple of accomplices, probably wearing Doc Martens and leather jackets and looking pissed off at the world.

"Oi, I'm talking to you," the voice said. It was closer this time, and Leipfold was still thirty feet from the end of the underpass. Like most of the estate, the underpass had a bad reputation. Drug deals, solicitation, mugging and murder. If it could lead to jail time, it happened there. Leipfold was so busy wondering what the walls would say if they could speak that he didn't register the screech of the bike's tyres until they skidded to a halt.

Leipfold stopped dead in his tracks and then risked a quick glance behind him. His assumptions, for once, were incorrect. The man on the bike was in his early thirties, and the two of them were alone in the underpass. The bike was built for comfort and not for speed, and the man had short black hair and a sharp suit that would've looked more at home in a bank or the Houses of

Parliament. He wore patent leather shoes and a platinum wedding ring on his left hand. He stared at Leipfold.

"What's the matter with you?" he asked. "You deaf or something?"

Leipfold shook his head but didn't say anything.

"Well, whatever," the stranger said. He put a foot to the ground to steady himself. "You got a ciggie?"

"Why?" Leipfold asked. "You don't look like a smoker. Your fingers, for a start. Immaculate, never chewed and no nicotine stains. If I give you a cigarette, will you need a lighter, too?"

"Huh?"

"Perhaps you're having problems at work. Shouldn't you be in the office right now? Or maybe it's to do with the wife? Did she catch you—"

Leipfold was cut short as the man's fist connected with his cheek. It wasn't a hard punch, but it took him by surprise and sent him reeling.

"You horrible little shit," the man said. Then he boosted himself back on to his pedals and rode away. Leipfold spat a little blood and laughed himself silly.

Must've touched a nerve, he thought.

Violence was a part of life for Leipfold. Though his nose throbbed and his eyes were watering, he savoured the pain like a connoisseur. He'd never been good with people. Either that or he was *too good* with them. He knew what buttons to press to get people going, whether they were friends and relatives or total strangers in the underpass. He liked to make them uncomfortable, to disrupt their narrow-minded view of the world and to push them until they snapped and did something that they wouldn't normally do. And in spite of the shiner he'd be sporting once the swelling died down, he felt good about himself. He felt good about the man on the bicycle, too.

Hell, Leipfold thought. *Maybe he'll feel guilty enough to patch his life up. One minute you're hitting a kid in the underpass, and the next you're trying to figure out where it all went wrong. Like a wake-up call but with a fist to the lips.*

Leipfold walked out of the underpass and along the street for a couple hundred yards before sitting down on a low wall and lighting a cigarette. He watched as the traffic rolled by and wondered whether the man he'd just met had stopped to call his wife. In his (admittedly limited) experience, women were perceptive creatures of a seemingly different species, simultaneously more observant and less likely to encourage confrontation. But he'd be willing to bet a monkey that the man was having an affair, a ton that his wife already knew, and a pony on him being so shook up that he'd come clean and she'd forgiven him. And a deep sea diver said he'd goaded a stranger into punching him for no real reason other than that it was a cheaper thrill than a hit of cocaine or amphetamine.

Leipfold's train of thought was interrupted by a familiar *click-clack-click-clack* sound. For a brief moment, he thought the man on the bike had doubled back to apologise. Then he started laughing again when he realised it was three teenagers—three hoodlums—tearing along the path like they were racing Croydon's equivalent of the Tour de France.

"Move out of the way, dickface," one of them shouted.

Leipfold recognised that voice, and he wasn't enough of a masochist to antagonise it. It belonged to a kid called Jimmy Squires who shared the occasional class with him on the rare occasions that they were both at school. Squires himself had no grudge against Leipfold, but a couple of his cronies did. So instead of saying anything, Leipfold bit his tongue to help him to hold it, then lowered his head as they approached. The leader of the pack popped a wheelie while the three of them hooted and guffawed their way past. Leipfold watched them with lazy antipathy as they disappeared towards the inner city.

Leipfold finished his cigarette and flicked it to the ground, and he was about to get up and go about his business—mostly taking notes on the locals and getting himself into trouble—when he spotted a policeman hobbling along the path towards him. He was a tall man who walked with a slight stoop and who cut his scruffy black hair short and wore his uniform with the same kind of reverence that an army veteran has for the medals he's earned. Not quite imposing and with a baby face that betrayed his inexperience, the policeman still exuded an air of quiet confidence and authority that persisted despite the scowl on his face and the perspiration that had pooled around his temples and started to dribble inexorably down the sides of his face.

"Excuse me," the policeman said, slowing to a halt in front of Leipfold. "I don't suppose you saw a bunch of kids going past on bicycles?"

"Might've done," Leipfold replied. "What's it worth? And for that matter, who the hell are you?"

"It's worth a bloody great deal," the copper said. "And the name's PC Jack Cholmondeley. I caught the little bastards spraying my car and then they rode off before I could get a good look at them."

"What were they spraying?"

"I think it was supposed to be a pig," Cholmondeley said. He took a closer look at Leipfold, and the young man could feel the eyes focussing on the side of his head, which was starting to swell from the sucker punch he'd caught from the man on the bicycle. "Let me guess, you walked into a door."

"What?"

"Don't play ignorant with me, young man," Cholmondeley replied. He pointed at the red patch under Leipfold's eye. "Looks like you're developing quite the shiner. A nice fresh one, too. How did you get it?"

"Oh, *that*," Leipfold replied. He briefly thought about telling the policeman about his altercation with the man in the suit and then decided against it. "Yeah, I saw the kids you're looking for. They went past a couple of minutes ago. You'll struggle to catch them on foot, though."

"I thought as much," Cholmondeley replied. He looked gloomy and downtrodden, like a man in a shabby suit who'd just been splashed by a passing car. "Did you get a good look at them?"

"Not really," Leipfold said. "One of them had a mole on his right hand."

"*Fantastic*," Cholmondeley replied. "Now I just need to track down a guy with a mole in a city of—"

"No need," Leipfold interrupted, gesturing for the policeman to let him speak. "I recognised the mole."

"You recognised the mole," Cholmondeley repeated.

"Yeah," Leipfold replied. "You need to find a kid called Jimmy Squires. He has the same mole in the same place. It has to be him."

"You're sure about this?"

Leipfold shrugged. "We go to the same school."

"And you checked his hands for moles?"

"It's hard to miss it," Leipfold said. "The other kids call him Jimmy the Mole, and not because he can dig a mean tunnel. Besides, he called me dickface. It was just like sitting in front of him in assembly."

"Good enough for me," Cholmondeley replied. "Do you know where the boy lives, this Jimmy Swires?"

"*Squires*," Leipfold said. He shook his head. "No, I don't. Sorry. And I didn't get a good look at the other two, either. Anything you can tell me to narrow it down? I, uh…know the circles he moves in."

Cholmondeley considered this for a moment and said, "One of them had a limp. He could've been faking it, but I doubt it. I'm a policeman, you see. I know when people are lying."

No, you don't, thought Leipfold. *If you did, you would've called me out on it.*

Out loud, Leipfold said, "Mark Flowers. His dad runs the Fox and Hound. He's tight with Jimmy, and he walks with a limp. Tells people he was knocked off his bike, but everyone knows he was sick when he was a kid."

"Interesting," Cholmondeley murmured.

"You said there were three of them, right?"

"I did indeed."

"Good," Leipfold replied. "You might want to have a word with Donnie while you're at it."

"Donnie?" Cholmondeley asked.

"Donnie Flowers. Mark's older brother," Leipfold explained. "Those two are inseparable. They're like twins, except for the limp and the fact that Donnie's eight inches taller. If Mark was there, so was Donnie."

"How do you know all this?" Cholmondeley asked.

Leipfold laughed, and then he winced as the pain in his face flared up again. "I watch people, Mr. Policeman. It's what I do."

Cholmondeley nodded absentmindedly and scribbled the names down in his notebook. "Thanks for the help, young man," he said. "Would you mind if I take your name and address so I can get in touch if I have further questions?"

As a matter of fact, young James Leipfold *did* mind. It wasn't good to be seen talking to a copper, especially on an estate like his. Talking to him even there, just past the underpass where there were no nosy neighbours to keep tabs on them, was bad enough. A policeman turning up at his door in uniform would be tantamount to social suicide, unless they cuffed him and bundled him into the back of a Black Maria. So Leipfold gave Cholmondeley a fake name and address, then made his excuses and went about his business before the policeman could ask any further questions.

Leipfold's eye darkened over the next couple of days, but his mood didn't. As the only child of a working-class mother and father in an underprivileged estate on the edge of London, he was left mostly to his own devices. His mother had accepted his story about a bogus game of rugby, and if his father noticed the big bruise on his son's face, he didn't mention it. But then, Charles Leipfold had been involved in his fair share of scuffles over the years. Only last month, he'd come home from the pub with bruised knuckles and blood on his shirt. When his wife had asked where the blood came from, he'd simply shrugged and said, "From people's faces."

Leipfold spent his time keeping an eye on Jimmy Squires's place with his father's Bausch and Lomb binoculars. He'd told the cop that he didn't know where the three hoodlums lived, but that had been a lie. Leipfold's memory verged on eidetic, and he made it his business to know other people's business. But he also wasn't a grass. While he'd been happy to help the policeman by pointing him in the right direction, he wasn't going to do his job for him.

As for why he was taking an interest in the first place...well, it was personal. And it turned out that while he thought he'd gone about his business unobserved, someone had been watching the watcher.

*   *   *

Leipfold was woken up the following morning by a torrent of angry cursing and a loud slam as his bedroom door swung open and then bashed against the wall. His father, Charles Leipfold, looked haggard and bleary-eyed. He hadn't shaved, and he was wearing a threadbare dressing gown with a couple of cigarette burns on the arms.

"Have you got something to tell me, son?" he asked. There was a steeliness to his tone that suggested he had a hangover, and there was a mean glint in his eye.

"No," Leipfold said. "Nothing."

"Get up."

Leipfold did as he was told, shuffling out from underneath the duvet and standing shivering in his boxer shorts, his bare feet on the cold, hardwood floor.

"Look at me."

Leipfold did so.

7

"Who have you been talking to?"

"No one," Leipfold said.

"No one at all?" his father asked. "The police, for example?"

Leipfold cast his mind back to his chance meeting with PC Jack Cholmondeley and an answer leapt into his mouth automatically. "No, sir," he said.

"Liar." The old man's hands went to his waist, unbuckling his belt and pulling the faded strip of leather out from the loops in his trousers. He folded it in half and hefted it, testing its weight in his hands. "Someone's sprayed the word 'snitch' on our front door, lad. I'm no snitch, so it has to be you. Unless you're trying to tell me it's a case of mistaken identity."

"No comment," Leipfold said.

"Do you know who did it?"

"No," Leipfold lied. His old man sighed.

"Okay," he said. "Bend over and touch your toes."

Leipfold gritted his teeth, but he did what he was told and waited for the sting of the belt. Whatever happened, he wouldn't give the old bastard the satisfaction of crying out. He took a dozen blows in silence. Then his father put his belt back on and stormed out of the room.

Leipfold washed his wounds and dressed as quickly as he could. His father had left for a job on a building site by the time that he left his bedroom, and so he took some time to check out the graffiti. He hadn't seen the graffiti on PC Cholmondeley's cop car, but he would've been willing to bet a fiver that it was similar to what he saw across his front door. It was an amateur job, graffiti from a thug and not an artist, and it spilled out from the front door and on to the front of the house, stopping just in front of the bay windows. And although he didn't know if it was even possible, he could swear he recognised the handwriting.

He was late for school, missing assembly altogether and going straight to his double science lesson, but his mind was hardly on the task. Leipfold's teacher, a Scotsman called Mr. Owen, was a tough but fair man who cracked down with a vengeance whenever one of his pupils pointed out the sweat patches beneath his armpits when he reached up to write formulae on the chalkboard. Leipfold was one of his favourites, not because of his attitude but for his aptitude, but the young man was in a world of his own today.

"Something wrong, Leipfold?" Mr. Owen asked. He had one eyebrow raised in an effort to look hip, but he couldn't pull it off and it just left him looking concerned—or worse, on the edge of a stroke.

"What do you mean, sir?"

"You're not paying attention to a word I say," the teacher replied.

"Yes I am," replied Leipfold, silently thanking whatever it was in his genes that gave him his near-photographic memory. "Iodine, element number fifty-three on the periodic table. It's used to disinfect wounds."

"Hmm," Mr. Owen replied, thoughtfully. "Very well. But next time I look up, I want to see you taking notes and paying attention, young man."

"Yes, sir," Leipfold said. That wouldn't be too much of a problem for James Leipfold. He was a born multitasker.

The rest of the science lesson passed by without incident, as did break and his third period English lesson, where the class was reading *Lord of the Flies* aloud by going round the classroom, one person at a time. But then it was lunchtime, and that was when the bullies struck. The three hoodlums cornered him round the back of the science block while he was smoking a crafty cigarette.

"Oi, dickface."

Leipfold sighed, put the sandwich he'd made the night before back into his lunchbox and turned to look at the hoodlums.

"Hi, Jimmy," Leipfold said. "To what do I owe this pleasure?"

"I need some money," Squires said.

"You always need money."

"Don't try and be funny with me, dickface," Squires said. At his sides, his cronies leaned forwards menacingly and made it clear that they were there to block off any escape. It was the same old drill, and Leipfold was sick of it. As Squires himself leaned forward with an outstretched hand, like Oliver Twist begging for more food in the workhouse, Leipfold grabbed the fingers and suddenly twisted, turning his back on the bully and bending the hand with him. There was a sickening crunch and a horrible second or two of silence, and then Jimmy Squires screamed.

Leipfold kicked backwards, and his boot connected with Jimmy's knee, sending him tumbling to the ground with his wrist curled protectively in front of his stomach. Leipfold turned to Jimmy's two henchboys, daring to hope they'd make a run for it, but instead they moved towards him as one. He took a glancing blow to the side of the head before he had time to regroup.

It didn't take long for a crowd to gather, and the four boys were soon surrounded by close to one hundred braying students who were all screaming for blood. Jimmy Squires was still on the floor, and one of his associates was limping and sporting a bloody nose. Leipfold, for his part, had a cut just above his eyebrow and his right knuckles had already started to swell. The three teens came together again and then went down on the floor in a heap of fists and heads.

"What the *hell* is going on here?"

Mr. Owen, the science teacher, barged his way through the crowd with his broad Celtic shoulders. His voice alone was enough to cause panic, and his appearance made sure that they scattered just as quickly as they'd gathered until it was just the teacher and the four boys.

Leipfold fell back against the wall of the building, panting and slouching with his hands on his knees. The two boys who were still standing looked as though they were thinking about continuing the melee, but they held back. Squires was still curled up on the floor like a human comma.

"Want to tell me what this is all about?" the teacher asked.

"It was Leipfold, sir," Squires whimpered. "He attacked us."

"Is this true, boy?" Owen asked, turning to look at Leipfold while keeping the other boys to one side where he could see them.

"They deserved it, sir," Leipfold said. "Squires and his friends tried to steal my lunch money."

"So you decided to dish out some vigilante justice?"

"It was three against one," Leipfold said, reproachfully.

"Hmm," the teacher said. He paused for a moment, looking from Leipfold to the other boys and back again. "Well, Squires here needs to see a doctor. You boys, follow me back to my office. We'll get someone to check Squires, and then I'll call for reinforcements. This is above and beyond my pay grade."

*   *   *

P. C. Jack Cholmondeley looked surprised to see James Leipfold again, especially in the grim surroundings of Mr. Owen's office. Owen was a typical science teacher, so the place was covered with books, stacks of paper, empty beakers and bottles and obscure-looking equipment. There were no photographs of his family. But after the first initial moment of confusion had passed across the policeman's face, it was back to business as usual and he acted as though everyone in the room was a stranger to him.

By the time that the cop arrived, Jimmy Squires had already been ferried off to the hospital and Leipfold and the other two boys were sitting quietly on plastic chairs in different corners of the crowded office.

"Cup of tea, inspector?" Mr. Owen asked glibly, affecting an air of nonchalance as though he had policemen in his office all the time. Perhaps he did.

"No, thank you," Cholmondeley replied. "I'd prefer to get down to business. Why exactly did you call us here?"

"These boys have been fighting," the teacher said.

"Boys fight. That's what they do. It's hardly a police matter."

"Normally, I'd agree with you," Mr. Owen said. "But normally my boys don't have to go to hospital. And normally it's because someone got smart and took a punch for insulting someone's mother. This time, there are accusations of theft."

"I see," Cholmondeley said. "Well, I'll speak to each of the boys individually and take some statements and then we can decide if any further action is necessary."

Leipfold was the last one to be spoken to. The policeman led him out of the science teacher's office and into an empty classroom just opposite. The room was covered in dust and the chairs were stacked on top of the desks. The blackboard still had some notes about *Hamlet* scrawled across it in faded yellow chalk, and a cool breeze blew in from a broken window.

For a moment, the two of them looked at each other in a wary silence. Then Cholmondeley said, "Well?"

"Well, what?" Leipfold replied. "Squires deserved what he got. Son of a bitch kept stealing my lunch money. My father doesn't give me shit. I have to work for it."

"So you sent him to the hospital?"

"He started it," Leipfold said. "Besides, I've got something for you."

"It had better be good," Cholmondeley replied. "You're costing me a hell of a lot of paperwork."

"And I'm about to cost you some more," Leipfold said. "The kid with the broken wrist is Jimmy Squires. The other two are the brothers, Mark and Donnie. They're who sprayed graffiti on your car."

"How do you know?"

"They hit the front of my house," Leipfold said. "It's the same paint and the same handwriting. Plus, I know Jimmy Squires, and I know his handwriting. He's a dickhead."

"I'll need some proof."

"Of course," Leipfold said. "And I'll help you."

"You'll be at school," Cholmondeley replied.

"Not when Mr. Owens is done with me," Leipfold pointed out. "I'll be suspended for at least a week. And I've got to spend my time doing something."

"I'll think about it," Cholmondeley said. "It depends."

"On what?"

"On whether Jimmy Squires decides to press charges because of his broken wrist," Cholmondeley explained. "Go on, kid. Speak to your teacher and tell him I'd like a word with him afterwards."

*   *   *

Everything went as expected, and Leipfold was suspended from school for ten days pending a further disciplinary hearing to decide his fate. Cholmondeley was waiting for him outside the school gates, and he gave the young man a lift home. Leipfold asked him to drop him off round the corner so his father wouldn't see.

They started their surveillance that evening. On the third day, their patience paid off. Leipfold watched from a distance as Cholmondeley and one of his colleagues parked their car outside the Squires's dilapidated council house and knocked on the door. The two men entered the house—after some to-ing and fro-ing with James Squires Sr.—and re-emerged ten minutes later with the kid in tow.

He wasn't cuffed, but he might as well have been. His wrist was in a cast and his face was screwed up in pain from the heavy handling. He was followed shortly afterwards by his father, whose face was already starting to swell and who was spitting blood from between a new gap in his front teeth. Squires Sr. was screaming bloody murder and fighting against the terrified-looking young cop who was shepherding him towards the waiting car. With the two Squires men safely locked behind the mesh in the back of the vehicle, the two cops climbed into the front and drove away into the evening.

Leipfold had a hunch that Jimmy wouldn't take long to crack, so he hopped on his bicycle and headed over to the Fox and Hound. The place was a quintessential English pub, not one of the quiet country pubs where farmers stopped off for a quiet pint after a hard day in the fields but a bustling spit and sawdust boozer that watered down the spirits and trained its staff on how to keep the peace with the baseball bat beneath the counter. Leipfold had been in there a couple of times to bring his old man home. While there was something undeniably magical about the stench of spilled beer and stale cigarette smoke, he wouldn't have wanted to live there, like the Flowers family.

Leipfold's hunch was proved correct when, just over an hour after his arrival, Cholmondeley and his colleague pulled up outside the pub. He watched the chaos that ensued after they walked in. Coppers weren't welcome in a place like that, and half the locals had a good reason to run at the sight of a badge or a uniform. When the two men entered, the hustle and bustle stopped abruptly, to be replaced—after a few moments of hostile silence—with an angry susurrus. Leipfold smirked as he spotted a dozen undesirables making their way out of the pub by a side entrance. Then he wandered over to the front of the building and lit a cigarette while he waited for something to happen.

He could see the backs of the officers through the window, and he watched as Cholmondeley's hand inched imperceptibly towards his baton. The barman, a middle-aged man with the faintest hint of fiery stubble around his chiselled jaw, was mouthing angrily. While Leipfold couldn't make out the words, he got the gist of it.

Then the barman reached for the baseball bat. He tried to raise it up into a batter's stance, but Cholmondeley reacted faster, swiping down with his truncheon and breaking the man's arm with a single sweep. Leipfold winced as he registered its unnatural angle and the way it hung off the man's body like a broken twig. He couldn't hear the sound that it made and he was glad of it, but he heard the bartender's guttural wail and was almost bowled over by the mass exodus of the remaining punters.

Cholmondeley's partner cuffed the man, dragging the broken arm roughly into place, and then the two men escorted him out of the pub on shaking legs and into the back of the police car. He spotted Leipfold leaning against the wall and nodded at him.

"He started it," Cholmondeley said. He shrugged. "And we finished it."

"Fucking cops," the barman was babbling. "I'll have you for this."

"No you won't, Sonny Jim," Cholmondeley replied. "Assault on a police officer in front of witnesses? They'll throw away the key."

Leipfold lit another cigarette and smoked it down to the filter, then flicked it aside and waited for Cholmondeley and his partner to re-emerge from the pub, which they did shortly afterwards. Donnie Flowers had cuffs around his wrist, but Mark didn't.

There was a scuffle, and for a moment or two, Donnie Flowers was free of his police escort while his brother grappled with Cholmondeley's partner. Leipfold cursed and tensed himself, then he started running half a second before Donnie Flowers did. Cholmondeley and his partner were busy taking care of Mark, with both men kneeling on his back as Cholmondeley secured him with cuffs. Cholmondeley turned to look just as Leipfold connected with Donnie's legs and dragged him to the ground in a rugby tackle. They hit the asphalt hard, with Donnie taking the brunt of it, and then Leipfold rolled over on top of him and held him there.

"Cheers, kid," Cholmondeley grunted. "Appreciate the help. We'd better get these boys in for questioning."

"What about their counsel?" his partner asked. "We need a legal guardian to ask them anything."

"We'll find someone," Cholmondeley replied. By this point, he'd finished shepherding Mark Flowers into the back of the waiting patrol car and was approaching Leipfold and Donnie. "They must have a mother or a father."

Leipfold started laughing, quietly at first until he'd built up enough steam for the two policemen to hear him. They turned to look at him expectantly.

"You just arrested him," Leipfold said. "He was the man with the baseball bat."

"You don't say," Cholmondeley said, thoughtfully. "Hmm. Better pay him a little extra attention."

His partner grinned. "You can never be too careful, Jack," he said.

"Go on, get in the car," Cholmondeley said. "I'll be with you in a minute."

His partner did as he was told, and Constable Jack Cholmondeley watched him as he retreated to the relative warmth and comfort of the police car. One of the support vehicles had already left for the station, and the driver of the other one gunned the ignition and set off after it. Leipfold and Cholmondeley were alone again.

"Thanks for your help, kid," Cholmondeley said.

"Don't mention it."

"You know, we could use a lad like you. How old are you, anyway?"

"Sixteen," Leipfold lied. He could tell from the cop's reaction that it hadn't worked, but Cholmondeley let it pass without comment.

"Want my advice?" Cholmondeley asked. Leipfold didn't, but he didn't have much choice. "Stay in school. Work hard and get good grades, then come and see me when you're ready. There'll be a job waiting."

"A job?"

"Yeah," Cholmondeley said. "In the police force. We're always on the lookout for new recruits, especially when they're as perceptive as you are."

But Leipfold shook his head. "Mister," he said, "I'm many things, but I'm no copper. Never will be."

Cholmondeley smiled and laid a hand on his shoulder. "Perhaps you'll change your mind," he said.

"I won't."

Cholmondeley smiled again. "Well," he said, "if you do change your mind, you know where to find me. You seem like a decent kid. Make sure you stay that way."

"I'll do my best," Leipfold said. Then they shook hands and Cholmondeley returned to his partner. He climbed into the passenger seat and they made their way back to the station.

He's a nice guy, Leipfold reflected, staring thoughtfully into the distance. *Shame he's a copper.*

But he knew he'd remember Cholmondeley's name, and not just because he found it difficult to forget things. It never hurt to make contacts, even if they were policemen.

You never know, Leipfold mused. *He might even turn out to be useful.*

Then he remembered his father's words of wisdom. "There are two types of copper," he used to say. "Bent cops and dead cops."

But Constable Jack Cholmondeley was different. Perhaps he was the exception that proved the rule.

The Murdered Truth

AT NIGHT, when the dry winds blew across the Kuwaiti sand, Leipfold thought he could hear the ghosts of the dead. They cried for lost love, knocked at the doors and walls with a rattatat-tat like machine gun fire or breathed warm air on his neck when he was sweating in his bunk surrounded by the smell of men and determination.

He was nineteen years old, young and gullible, and determined to serve his country. Not because he was patriotic, although he was, but because there was precious little else for him to do. And besides, women loved a man in uniform, even those who claimed to be against the war. Leipfold had never been much of a hit with the ladies, thanks to his floppy tuft of ginger hair, his height—which had almost ruled him out of joining the army—and his terse mannerisms and perpetual attitude.

The ghosts of the dead were getting louder. But Leipfold barely noticed.

Instead, he was lying back in his bunk, struggling to read through his letters in the half-light. They used to arrive twice a week, but that had slowed to once a fortnight. Rebecca, his fiancée, had begged him not to join the forces, but she'd eventually relented when he used the last of his savings to buy her a cheap ring from a pawn shop. He'd told her that the only way to pay for the ceremony was if he got a proper job, and the army was the only choice for a man like him. Rebecca had given him her begrudging approval on a Tuesday night, and Leipfold had volunteered the following morning.

Now, on a military cot in a foreign country, that other Leipfold seemed a lifetime away. The army had changed him from a boy into a man, with a man's stubble and a man's appetite to go with it. He smiled and turned the pages of one of the letters.

From a couple of bunks down, Corporal Hodges had received a parcel of his own. He was munching on some homemade cookies that his mother had sent, the same cookies that she always sent and which he always refused to share, although Leipfold couldn't blame him. He was reading the letter that had accompanied it and chuckling to himself.

"Anything good?" Leipfold asked.

"Letter from my fiancée," Hodges replied. "Janine. She's pregnant with our first at the moment. This is my last tour. Look, she sent a couple of photos."

Hodges shook the letter until a couple of Polaroids fell out. He picked one up and went to hand it to Leipfold, then saw what it depicted and hastily put it back inside the letter with a "whoops" before handing the other one over. It showed a strikingly beautiful young woman in a red dress and was clearly taken at some sort of high-class event, perhaps a wedding or an awards ceremony. She was wearing lipstick and winged eyeliner, but it was the smile that leapt out of the frame and into the hot Kuwaiti atmosphere.

Leipfold took one look at the photograph and said, "You're punching way above your weight."

"I know," Hodges replied. "I love her, James. She's everything to me. Do you believe in love at first sight?"

"No."

"Me neither," Hodges said. "But it wasn't far off. She's beautiful, yeah, but she's got great taste in movies and she's the only woman I've ever met who can beat my time in a 10k. If I'm yin, she's yang. We complement each other. Once this tour's over, we're going to settle down. Start building a family."

"Rather you than me, kid."

Leipfold returned the Polaroids and strolled back over to his bunk, then lowered himself into the cot and tried to get comfortable. He wasn't a big guy, but they weren't big beds. He'd just picked up his letter again when he heard a panicked shout, the kind of inarticulate "wuargh" noise that signalled trouble. Then there was the sound of an impact, followed by an explosion that rattled the walls and sent shivers of plaster cascading down from the roof in a fine snow, settling on Leipfold's shoulders like flakes of dandruff. That was followed by a second, smaller explosion, and then the rattle of automatic gunfire.

Not again, Leipfold thought. He'd been hoping to pen a response to Rebecca—he had decent paper and everything—but that was no longer looking likely.

Then a klaxon sounded, and mean-spirited Sergeant Grundy barged into the room, using his voice like a trumpet to rally the few troops who, like Leipfold, had made their way back from the mess hall to enjoy a little downtime. But in the army—at least in Leipfold's regiment—nothing was ever quite that simple.

"Come on then, ladies," Grundy bellowed. "Pull those hands out of your trousers, get off your arses and get your shit together. I want you kitted out and battle ready in five minutes."

Leipfold sighed and stashed the fragrant letters beneath his pillow, then stood speedily to attention, snapping off a quick salute before checking his kit bag and rummaging around for his lucky St. Christopher. He never went into action without it.

From a couple of bunks down, Private Williams—the only Welshman in the dorm—asked, "What the hell's going on, sir?"

"Damned if I know," Grundy replied. "All I know is someone sounded the red alert, and now it's all hands on deck."

Precisely three minutes and eight seconds later, Leipfold was lining up with the rest of the regiment. He checked his weapon and then checked it again while Sergeant Grundy relayed orders and grouped his men into teams.

At last, he reached Private Leipfold, Private Williams and Corporal Hodges, who'd arrived in the middle of the pack but somehow found themselves at the end of the line.

"You boys," he said. "You're coming with me. We're on patrol duty. Let's catch these arseholes before they break through the perimeter."

"Yes, sir," they chorused.

Secretly, Private Leipfold questioned the decision to leave the base in the middle of the night. Sure, they had technology on their side, but the insurgents had a huge advantage. They knew the lay of the land, and a little knowledge could be a dangerous thing in the wrong hands. But he also knew that an order was an order and that it was his job to obey it whether he liked it or not.

And so the four men piled into an army-issue off-roader. Leipfold had been in the back of one before, but that had been with Corporal Hodges at the wheel. Hodges signed up after being given an ultimatum. He had to either join the army or get kicked out of the family home. In the forces, Hodges had been able to apply the skills of his misspent youth in a number of legitimate ways, but it was his skill behind the wheel which had set him apart the most. He'd learned to drive in a succession of boosted cars, mostly old shitheaps with no alarms.

"The boy can drive," Sergeant Grundy had said. "Who cares how he learned to do it?"

That night, though, Corporal Hodges was relegated to the passenger seat. Grundy grabbed him by the arm and pulled him out of the way as they hopped on, saying, "I'll drive tonight."

Leipfold didn't know why, and he didn't care. His job was to keep a lookout, to use his eagle eyes and his observation skills to identify any threats before they became a problem. It was a role that he took pride in, knowing that he helped to protect the rest of the squaddies, and it was also a role that he was good at. He had sharp eyes and a sharp mind, and he'd once successfully saved his men from an ambush after picking up on a suspicious lack of birdsong and the faintest reek of cordite.

That night, their vision was obscured by a low rolling dust cloud, sand and grime and muck whipped together by a strong wind. A gunshot echoed out, a little too close for comfort, and was answered by the rattle of a coalition semi-automatic.

Leipfold held on tight and dug himself into his seat, his eyes still scanning the road ahead and the streets on either side of them. From the passenger seat, Corporal Hodges shouted out directions while Sergeant Grundy twisted the wheel and imposed his will on the ATV.

Their first patrol was uneventful, though there was tension in the air and the distant smell of burning gasoline.

From the seat beside Leipfold, where he sat with one hand resting on the open window and the other on his gun, Private Williams muttered under his breath. "It's too quiet," he said. "I don't like it. Let's wrap this up."

Sergeant Grundy nodded and said, "Son, let's make one last loop and then get the hell out of here."

There was movement on either side of the road ahead. Then the moonlight shone through a break in the clouds and illuminated a thin, metal wire across the road ahead. Leipfold saw nails and broken glass on the other side of it, but even in that moment of terror, his mind worked quickly to calculate the stopping distance. There simply wasn't enough time.

"Hostiles," he shouted, simultaneously adopting the brace position. He'd heard that it was useless at saving lives, adopted instead by airlines to save teeth so corpses could be identified by their dental records. But it was all he had. "Floor it."

But Grundy didn't floor it. He hit the brakes instead.

The ATV skidded and hit the tripwire at an angle. Metal crashed against metal and the wire snapped, but not before ripping through the bonnet and most of the engine. The vehicle slowed to a stop, its tyres deflated by the detritus of the road.

Then there was a flash of light, which the soldiers heard a split second before they were hit by the shockwave. It came from the road in front of them and buffeted the vehicle with sheets of glass and metal, caving in the windscreen and flipping the ATV on to its side. Sergeant Grundy was jabbed in the guts by the steering column at the same time as an eighteen-inch piece of steel shrapnel embedded itself through his eye. It poked out from the back of his skull and pinned him to the headrest. From beside him in the passenger seat, Private Williams howled in pain and tried to apply pressure to his shoulder.

Leipfold had shrapnel in his arm and had bashed his head against the roof of the vehicle, and Corporal Hodges was bleeding from the forehead and wearing a glazed expression. Hodges slumped forward in his seat. His head banged against the headrest, and then he spewed bile and stomach acid on to his chin. He shivered for a moment and then suddenly sat bolt upright.

"Are you hurt?" Leipfold asked.

Hodges didn't say anything, but his eyes seemed to focus a little and he looked at Leipfold and shook his head. As the smoke and dust settled, Leipfold choked on a lungful of sand, which burned his throat as he swallowed it, and ordered Hodges to call for backup.

But Hodges barely heard him, and Leipfold was hardly surprised. His ears were still ringing from the blast and he could barely hear himself. But there was something in the man's eyes that signalled danger. The man was berserk. Leipfold had seen it happen before. When a soldier lost their mind like that, they forgot everything, all of their training, and they could even overcome injuries or find sudden reserves of energy that they could never have imagined they had within them.

Hodges hopped out of the vehicle and crouched behind it before unslinging his rifle and returning fire. Leipfold swore and followed Hodges by crawling along the seat and rolling out onto the ground.

With Hodges covering him, shooting at moving targets that he couldn't even see, Leipfold crawled across to the passenger door. He opened it and picked his head up, noting as he moved that Private Williams had failed, as usual, to secure himself with a seatbelt. Leipfold took a couple of seconds to check the man over before dragging him from the car and onto the ground.

The air was thick with bullets, a mixed bag of calibres from handguns to submachine guns that pierced the air like the whine of a thousand angry hornets. When they'd been briefed on the militants, the soldiers' COs had shared a report from intel that listed some of the known weapons that they had access to, and it read like the results of a raid on a gun-smuggling jamboree. At the bottom of the list were six RPG launchers and enough grenades to take down the Houses of Parliament.

Leipfold heard the telltale whistle of one of the big guns and instinctively threw himself to the ground. Then the world erupted with a bang and a whimper and clods of sand flew through the air, turned into half-glass from the heat and the momentum and as deadly as the shrapnel it took with it. Leipfold took a glancing blow on the side of the head from something that looked horrifically like the severed limb of his former commanding officer, the last act of Sergeant Grundy as the blast tore his body apart.

Then everything went quiet and dark.

When Leipfold woke up, he was in the hospital. He'd visited a couple of times to see buddies who'd been hit by an IED or a stray bullet from a firefight, but he never thought he'd find himself inside for the long haul.

The ward was almost empty, which he supposed was a good sign. So far, they hadn't sustained heavy casualties, but there had been plenty of injuries as the insurgents fought the army's advance at every step of the way. As well as Leipfold, there were two other soldiers on the ward, both asleep and with the unhealthy, sallow skin of injured men who hadn't seen the sunlight for too many days and nights. One of them was missing his arm at the elbow and the other was bandaged across most of the top half of his body. But despite the extent of their injuries, Leipfold thought it was good news. They were the survivors, the people who were going to make it and who had been moved out of intensive care to somewhere a little more comfortable. Somewhere they could recover.

He looked down at his arms and his legs and found that they were still there. Then he flexed his muscles and tried to move a little. Everything seemed to be in order. He ached like he'd been through a dozen rounds, but he could move enough to sit up in bed and press the button to call for some attention.

The summons was answered by a field nurse with a flat face and a dour expression. He had a three-day stubble that was clearly visible on the other side of his face mask.

"What happened?" Leipfold asked.

"Insurgent attack," the nurse replied. "You took a hit to the head."

"Is anything broken?"

The nurse shook his head. "You were lucky," he replied. "Lacerations across your torso and some burns on your leg, plus a bad concussion. Overall, I'd say it's a miracle you're still with us. The fact that you survived without sustaining serious injuries is even more of a surprise. You're lucky to be here, Private."

Leipfold groaned and lay back in his bed. "What happened to the others?" he asked.

The medic shook his head again. "You should rest," he said.

"Rest?" Leipfold repeated. He sat up again, though it clearly cost him an effort. The nurse walked over to him in an attempt to placate him, but Leipfold grabbed his arm and twisted it uncomfortably. "Tell me what happened," he said.

"I'm sorry," the nurse said. Leipfold loosened his grip a little. "You were the only survivor from your unit," he said. "Sergeant Grundy and Corporal Hodges were dead by the time that backup arrived. They had to identify Grundy by his tattoos and his dog tags. There wasn't much of him left. Private Williams was wounded and brought back here, but we couldn't save him. He died last night."

"Died?" Leipfold repeated, his voice flat and his heart numb. Then he looked up again. "Last night? How long was I out?"

"You've been in here for three days," the nurse said. "I need you to calm down and get some rest. You're lucky to be alive."

"But I've been resting for three days," Leipfold replied. "I need to get back out there. I need to find out what happened."

"Forget about what happened," the nurse said. "Please. Get some rest."

Leipfold acquiesced and let go of the nurse's arm. The man beat a hasty retreat, mumbling something about patients and patience.

Leipfold watched the man go and lay back in the bed again. He meant to just *pretend* to be asleep, but he quickly found exhaustion was taking over. He fought it, because he knew that sleeping with a concussion was a bad idea, the kind of amateur idea that could get someone killed in a warzone. But at the same time, it was a difficult fight. Too difficult of a fight to win, and Leipfold knew when he was beat. Exhaustion won over and closed his eyes for him. He caved and let his body and his brain get some rest, no matter how severe the risks might be.

But the following day was a different matter entirely. Leipfold waited for the staff to change and simply checked himself out without telling anyone. He told himself that he had no time for resting and that he could better serve his fellow soldiers if he was up and on his feet.

He had to find the bastards who'd killed his friends.

Getting out of the hospital was the easy part. Getting hold of a set of civilian clothes and an SA80 proved to be more difficult, but Leipfold was a man of means. He knew a man called Larry who worked in munitions and who owed him a favour or two. His first favour was the short-term loan of an SA80 and a stash of ammunition. His second favour was the man's silence.

"All right, Leipfold," Larry had said. His voice was muffled because he was chewing on a toothpick, which poked out of the bristles of his moustache like a nail in a wire brush. "I can give you forty-eight hours. After that, if you haven't returned it, I'll have to report it missing. If you get caught, this didn't come from me. I hope you know what you're doing."

"So do I," Leipfold replied.

He was exhausted, but he refused to show it. He spent seven hours dipping in and out of the local watering holes, the places that the natives talked about in hushed voices when they provided intelligence in exchange for protection. They weren't safe places for a soldier to be in, but Leipfold didn't care. He was out of uniform, which helped, but he also had his firearm to fall back on if the shit hit the fan.

He was looking for names and information. He was looking for a lead on the vicious motherfuckers who'd attacked his unit. And eventually, after parting with enough money and talking to enough of the locals, Leipfold had the name of an abandoned farm on the outside of town. He coaxed it out of a contact, a man called Awni el-Halim who'd befriended a couple of the army boys when they'd carried out recon along the advance. Leipfold had been one of the squaddies that had been assigned to the recon team, picked purely because he knew a couple of languages.

El-Halim gave him a name and a set of coordinates. It wasn't much, but it was enough.

By then, it was night-time, which made it easier for Leipfold to head towards the farm without running the risk of being spotted, either by the militants or by soldiers from his own side. Even a civilian could be bad news if he didn't handle it correctly. But it was quiet, almost too quiet, and he wasn't weighed down by a kit bag on his back, nor slowed by the need to maintain a formation.

Even so, dawn was threatening to break and the first rays of sunlight were filtering over the horizon. Leipfold was tired, of course, but his training had taken over. His body ached, but the pain kept him alert. He wished he had a couple of shots of vodka, or maybe just a cigarette. But he had neither. He had only his wits and his determination, but that was all he needed.

The militant farm was near Mosudariya, a hamlet that wasn't on the maps. Leipfold had to follow his nose, allowing the stench of burning gasoline to guide him through the darkness. Later, as the sun rose to its full glory and Leipfold's skin broke out in a clammy sweat to cool itself, he could track the fire on the horizon by the plumes of smoke that disturbed the desert and clotted up the dry, fetid air.

Leipfold inched slowly closer, dropping to his hands and knees for the final approach before slowing to a stop in a natural ditch where a gully had once meandered millennia ago. He poked his head over the top.

On the other side of the ditch, maybe thirty yards away, there was a single man beside a bonfire. While Leipfold watched, the man threw a tyre on top of it, scattering ashes to the four winds.

Leipfold stood up slowly and drew his weapon. He aimed towards the man and shouted a short string of Arabic, then gestured with the barrel of his weapon for him to drop to the ground. He did so, slumping unceremoniously beside the fire, and Leipfold approached him. It was difficult to see him with his face and head covered and his loose clothing draped over his body. But then the man looked up at him, and Leipfold recognised his eyes even if he didn't recognise anything else.

"El-Halim," Leipfold said. "Fancy seeing you here."

"Hello, sir," the man replied. His English was about as good as Leipfold's Arabic, but he always said that he needed the practice and so English was their lingua franca. They switched to Arabic if they ever hit a stumbling block.

"What are you doing here?" Leipfold asked.

"I came to warn you, sir," el-Halim replied.

"Warn me? What about? And why didn't you warn me back in town?"

"The walls have ears," el-Halim said. "Eyes, too. I sent you here to get you out of the way."

"Out of the way of what?" Leipfold asked. "Is it the militants? What are they planning?"

El-Halim shook his head. "No, sir," he said. "Not the militants. The Americans."

"What have they done now?"

El-Halim shuffled uncomfortably on the ground, and Leipfold gestured for the man to get to his feet. Leipfold suggested finding someplace quieter, out in the empty dunes and away from the infernal smoke signal. El-Halim was all too happy to agree.

Leipfold found somewhere to his satisfaction, a small hollow amongst the dunes that kept them down and out of sight while offering a wide field of view if they needed it. It was quiet out there. The only sound was the howling of the wind and the sand as it formed mini hurricanes. They'd be able to hear people coming, but it also meant that their own voices were carried on the wind. Leipfold gestured for el-Halim to continue.

"Well, sir," el-Halim said, "it's like this. I heard about the attack on your unit."

"Three men died," Leipfold said. "I was almost the fourth."

"I'm sorry to hear that," el-Halim said. Leipfold knew that he was telling the truth. The war had torn el-Halim's life apart. It had taken his only son. But he wasn't anti-British or anti-American. He wasn't anti-Kuwaiti, either. He was on the side of humanity, which was why he dealt with the army in the first place. He wanted to minimise losses on either side. Leipfold thought it admirable.

"What can you tell me about the attack?" Leipfold asked.

"Just that it wasn't insurgents," el-Halim replied. "Well, it was, but it wasn't really. They weren't militants. They were mercenaries, working for the highest bidder. In this case, the highest bidder

29

was your friends, the Americans."

"You're not making any sense."

"The whole thing was set up by the Americans," el-Halim said. "They orchestrated it and arranged for it to happen."

"Why?" Leipfold asked.

"To cause outrage," el-Halim said. He shrugged. "To justify a revenge attack, perhaps. To justify their presence here in the first place. Who knows?"

Leipfold frowned, and his hands subconsciously drifted to the trigger of his SA80. He tensed his finger for a moment, then relaxed.

"Sounds sketchy to me," Leipfold said. "The army can afford to lose men. It can't risk a major international incident. If the British government found out that the United States had orchestrated an attack on its soldiers—"

"Hey, guy," el-Halim replied, holding his hands up defensively in front of him. "I'm just telling you what I've heard. These are rumours. That's what I deal in."

"Can you prove it?" Leipfold asked.

El-Halim shook his head. "Sorry, sir," he said. "But you can trust me."

"Trust you?" Leipfold repeated. "I hardly know you."

"Have I ever been wrong?"

"No," Leipfold admitted. "But shit, this is bad business. Okay. Let's assume for a second that you're right. Where did you get the information?"

"I know a man who knows a man," el-Halim said. "And that man knows a man in the mercenary group. There's a lot of them around. Trust me, sir, my contacts are never wrong. Especially not *these* ones."

"I need evidence," Leipfold said. "I can't go back to my superiors on the word of a local."

El-Halim shrugged. "It makes no difference to me, sir," he said.

"But please, listen to me. Take your men and get out of here. There's been too much bloodshed."

"We march in a few days," Leipfold replied.

"You must march now," el-Halim urged. "Believe me, sir. If you stay, lives will be lost."

Leipfold frowned. "I'll think about it," he said. "Where can I find these mercenaries?"

"You can't," el-Halim said. "You just need to hope that they don't find you."

A shout went up in the distance, followed by coarse laughter and Arabic chatter that Leipfold couldn't quite understand, although he got the gist of it. El-Halim glanced fearfully over the top of the dune.

"Someone's coming, sir," he said. "Quick. We must get out of here. No one can see us together."

"Yeah," Leipfold agreed. "That would be bad for both of us. You go. I'll keep my eyes peeled and head off in a different direction."

"Will you tell your superiors what I told you?"

Leipfold hesitated. Then he held out his hand and said, "I'll tell them."

El-Halim shook it and then disappeared into the dirt and dust.

Leipfold stayed put for as long as he could, but the Kuwaitis were getting closer and he had no way of knowing whether they were friendlies or hostiles. When they were close enough for a lucky shot to take someone out, he broke cover and burst through the dunes, heading south-southwest and back towards base. At any moment, he expected to hear a cry or the rat-a-tat-tat of automatic gunfire. He'd always made a rule of never looking back, but he chanced it this time and the sight he saw turned his heart into a block of ice in the middle of the hot sands.

They'd seen him.

The first he knew about it was when a distant shout went up, followed by the whine of an AK-47. They were far enough away that he wasn't in any real danger, but they were also too close for comfort. He started strafing, running across the sands in zigzags. As he ran, he realised that his planned route back to base was no longer viable. The militants had vehicles and he didn't. They could cut him off if he tried to head straight back. He'd have to take a diversion.

There was a whoosh as a rocket-propelled grenade pierced the air and flew into the sand. It was a good twenty yards away from Leipfold, but it still sent sand flying through the air at velocity and he had to throw himself to the ground to avoid it clogging up his lungs and clawing at his eyes.

As soon as he thought it was safe enough, he sprang to his feet again and raced away towards a rocky patch in the desert. In the distance, the militants revved up their engines and took chase, but Leipfold had a head start. Once he reached the rocks, they'd have to disembark and follow him on foot. It wasn't quite mountainous, but it was uneven and filled with hazards, including jagged boulders and quicksand which would play havoc with tyres and tracks alike.

Another rocket flew past Leipfold and smashed into the sand, a good sixty or seventy yards ahead of him, and there was another volley of machinegun fire. They were closer, and he could hear individual voices between the gunshots shouting "Allāhu akbar!" But he was closing in on the desert. While the militants were still hot on his heels, there were no more RPGs for him to worry about. He just had to run the gauntlet against the AKs and hope that he wasn't ripped apart by a lucky shot.

And then he was on the rocks and scrambling as quickly as he could down the side of a steep bank into a valley. He slipped when he was halfway down and ended up tumbling the rest of the way like a human cannonball. By the time he reached the bottom, the foliage had clawed at his eyes and his flesh and he was suffering from a couple dozen cuts and bruises, but he was alive and well enough to run. And not a moment too soon.

As he raced along the valley to the south east, he was reminded of one of his favourite movies, where the Dread Pirate Roberts escorted the Princess Buttercup into the Fire Swamp as Prince Humperdinck and the six-fingered man tried to ride them down on horseback. But they didn't have to deal with half-crazed zealots with automatic weaponry.

He was also going the wrong way, but that didn't matter. The more pressing issue was that of losing the enemy, but they were disorganised and in a group, and they took time to mobilise themselves. By the time that they'd descended into the valley, Leipfold had left them behind, although he didn't let that slow him. He had no choice but to keep on going, taking the long way back to camp through the valley and the rocky desert beyond it, taking a big loop around until he was heading due west.

For the first couple of hours, he maintained a steady pace somewhere between a jog and a run. He was weighed down by his kit and wanted to conserve energy, because he'd budgeted enough food and water for thirty-six hours and the route he was taking would mean being gone for at least twice that, if not longer. Worse, he didn't dare stop for a rest because if he did, he might not have been able to get back up again. And out there in the desert, where the elements were almost as deadly as the militants, sleep meant death.

It was a long, lonely walk back to base, and Leipfold was left largely undisturbed as he navigated the dunes with his compass. His weapon was concealed again, but he knew he could draw and fire within a second and a half if it came to it. But the Kuwaiti sands were quiet and empty, which was probably a good thing. Leipfold's nerves were shot, and he would've welcomed the reprieve of a little action.

He walked for three days and three nights. By the time that he saw the familiar haze of light pollution that marked the perimeter of the Anglo-American basecamp, he was barely conscious and prone to the occasional hallucination. As if that wasn't bad enough, he almost took a bullet as he approached the camp's perimeter. It winged out through the darkness and bounced off a metal sign somewhere behind him. Leipfold raised his hands.

"Halt," a voice shouted as a beam of light shone through the night and hit Leipfold in the eyes, dazzling him and knocking him slightly sideways. The beam remained on him as he dropped down onto his knees, as per protocol.

"It's me," Leipfold shouted. "Private James Leipfold."

"Private Leipfold?" The voice, which was distorted by a powerful megaphone but which still sounded familiar, went silent for a moment. Leipfold suspected that he was consulting a superior.

Leipfold saluted with one hand but said nothing.

"Come inside," the sentry shouted. His voice sounded doubtful, concerned even. "What's your status? We had you down as missing."

"I'm all right," Leipfold said. "It's a long story."

"The chief's going to want to see you."

"Who's on duty?"

"Does it matter?" the sentry asked. "I hope you've got a good explanation of where you've been. We've had people out looking for you."

"I ran into a little trouble. Look, are you going to let me in or not?"

"Fine," the sentry said. "But if this comes back and bites me in the ass, I'll find you."

Leipfold was met inside by an armed guard of a dozen men. They were led by a dour-faced sergeant that Leipfold had never seen before. They cuffed him and led him away to an interrogation room.

Leipfold found himself sitting on a crate on the other side of an Irish field sergeant's makeshift desk. He was so tired he could barely hold his head up, and the uncomfortable bed at the hospital felt like a dream he'd had half a lifetime ago.

"You're in trouble now, boyo," the sergeant said. He was chewing on a hunk of tobacco and it made his accent even murkier. Even with all of his skill with foreign languages, Leipfold found it difficult to understand what the man was saying. "You'd better have a bloody good reason for disappearing, Private."

"About that," Leipfold said. He told the sergeant about his recovery and his attempt to track down the perpetrators. He told him he'd borrowed a set of civvies and trekked into the local villages and that he'd found the burning tyres near Mosudariya. He told him about el-Halim and the message that he'd delivered, and about the rumour he'd heard of American involvement in the attack that had killed his colleagues. The only thing he held back was the SA80 and the name of the man he'd borrowed it from.

"That's all you've got for me, is it?"

"That's all you should need," Leipfold replied. His fatigue was beginning to show. He channelled his fury into striking his fist off the table.

"I need proof, Private," the sergeant said.

"You'll find your proof if you look for it," Leipfold replied.

It was the wrong answer. The sergeant sent him to the cells pending additional investigation, and Leipfold slipped into a deep, psychedelic sleep.

The following days passed by in a slow haze. Leipfold was questioned again and again and again, always by the same people. He asked to see a superior officer but was refused. He was given medical attention, but it took place in his cell and the doctor refused to speak to him. His wounds were healing nicely, despite the strain he'd put his body under, but his mind was still in turmoil and he wanted out again. He wanted answers.

Sometime during the second week, there was movement around the camp outside the bars of his window and Leipfold was cuffed, taken from his cell and stuffed into the back of an armoured van beside two armed guards. The Irish sergeant, who only ever identified himself with his number, completed the foursome in the back of the van.

"What's happening?" Leipfold asked.

The sergeant chuckled and said, "We're moving out, fella. Pressing further on. It's not a good idea to stick around after what we just pulled."

"What happened?"

"Revenge attack," the sergeant said. "Against the insurgents. Heavy casualties."

"On our side?"

The sergeant shook his head. "Just theirs," he replied.

"You idiots," Leipfold murmured. "You murdered the truth."

"Perhaps," the sergeant said. "I'd keep your mouth shut if I were you. If you're not careful, it'll get you into trouble."

"How much more trouble can I get into?"

"Not much," the sergeant said. "You're already looking at a court martial. Maybe jail time."

"What for?" Leipfold asked. He felt numb all over, as though the IED had exploded all over again.He felt the first, ghostly flashes of PTSD, waiting to detonate.

"That story of yours," the sergeant said. "Perhaps there was some truth in it after all."

Leipfold looked sharply up at him. "What do you mean?" he asked.

"Think about it," the sergeant said. "Why else do you think the army is cutting ties with you?"

"What do you mean?"

"Could be a cover up," the sergeant said.

Leipfold thought about it.

"Perhaps you're right," he said.

He stopped fighting. He stopped caring. He let the sergeant take full control of him, passing through cells and jails and finally into a military tribunal. They found him guilty quickly, but he dodged jail time thanks to a deal he signed. They wouldn't take the case further as long as he promised not to talk to the press.

But talking to the press was the last thing on Leipfold's mind. He hated journalists on principle, and he only ever read the paper when he knew there was a crossword in it. Besides, he had something else to occupy his thoughts. He was being shipped home to his fiancée. He was being shipped home to Rebecca.

* * *

Leipfold hadn't made any promises, but he felt like he had a promise to keep. Fate had played her game, and there was an injustice or two left to solve. His discharge from the army would have to wait for another day.

All he had to go on was the name Janine. Well, that and that she'd been engaged to Corporal Hodges, who came from Swindon. And that had been enough.

One gloomy, overcast day a couple of weeks after his final hearing, when all the dust had settled and he was a civilian again, he hopped on the train at Paddington Station and rode it non-stop to Swindon, where the rain had really started to pour. He hailed a cab outside the station and asked to be taken to the city library, where a tired-looking young woman had shown him to the archive room and taught him to use the equipment. He was the only one in there and she seemed hesitant to leave him, but then the ring of a bell from the front desk forced her to excuse herself.

Leipfold barely noticed. His interest lay in the archives and the thankless task that lay before him. He knew where to look but not *when*. It was like looking for a needle in a haystack but with an extra dimension. Before he knew it, the best part of half an hour had passed and the librarian had checked on him four times, her suspicion growing deeper as the day wore on.

But Leipfold still had his head down. He was looking through the announcement pages, starting with the most recent and slowly working back through them until finally, after almost an hour had ticked by on the cheap plastic clock above the door, he found it. The engagement notice for Caleb Hodges and Janine Taylor of Canterbury Road.

When the young librarian came in again, Leipfold asked her to show him to a telephone directory, and within ten minutes he had an address to go with his name. Then he ventured back out into the rain and flagged down another taxi.

Canterbury Road was a long, residential street that stretched out from the outskirts of town towards the suburbs. The monotony was broken every now and then with a bus stop or a convenience store, but the drive was uneventful except for the inevitable awkward chitchat.

Leipfold knocked on the door of 137B Canterbury Road and recognised the woman as soon as she opened the door, even though he'd last seen her in a photograph on a different continent. He had his memory to thank for that.

"Do I know you?" she asked.

"I'm, uh...," he stammered. For a moment, he pictured himself as she saw him, a rain-soaked young man with scruffy ginger hair and a five-day stubble in a mackintosh that was two sizes too big for him. He was surprised that she'd opened the door in the first place.

"You want to start that again?"

"My name's James Leipfold," he said, finding his voice at last. Once he started talking, it was like ripping off a plaster. The wound was crying out to be aired. "I knew Hodges. Corporal Hodges. Your fiancée."

The colour drained from the woman's face, although Leipfold guessed that at some level, she'd been expecting it. He knew what he looked like, he had army written all over him. It wouldn't have taken much for the woman to put two and two together.

"Do you want to come in?" she asked.

Leipfold shook his head. "Better not," he said. "This is hard for me too, but it's the right thing to do. I have a message."

"A message?"

"From Corporal Hodges," he said. "Caleb. I served with him. Just before we went out on patrol, before it happened, he said something."

"What?"

Leipfold licked his lips nervously and delivered the message. "I told him he was punching above his weight and he said he knew. He said that he loved you and that you were everything to him. He said that he didn't believe in love at first sight, but that it wasn't far off. He said that you were beautiful, that you had great taste in movies and that you were the only woman he'd ever met who could beat his time in a 10k. He said you were the yin to his yang and that once the tour was over, you were going to settle down and start building a family."

The woman had held back the tears while Leipfold was talking, but they burst out of her as soon as he'd finished and without warning, she threw her arms around him and pulled him close in an embrace. He returned the hug until she broke it.

"Thank you," she said. "How can I repay you?"

"You already have," Leipfold said, thinking about the nightmares he'd been having and how he'd be able to sleep a little more soundly at night. "I'm sorry I couldn't do more."

"You've done enough," she said. "Are you sure you won't come in?"

But Leipfold just shook his head, shook her hand and walked away into the night. He'd done what he could, but his heart still weighed heavy beneath the weight of the murdered truth. It was a weight that he'd continue to carry.

A Wild Goose Chase

LEIPFOLD HAD A HANGOVER.

It was a banging hangover, the kind that took his legs from beneath him and left him with a gritty, bloody taste in his mouth. He hadn't showered for several days, he'd been drinking for about as long, and he couldn't remember when he'd last had something to eat. He had a vague recollection of dry-roasted peanuts, but he couldn't place it. From a bar the night before, perhaps.

He groaned and raised his head. It throbbed like he'd been kicked in the skull by an angry mule. The world was spinning in front of him. He dropped his head, which thudded off something solid. The pain blinded him all over again and he blacked out.

He'd been drinking like this for a while. Rebecca, his fiancée, had called it quits after his dishonourable discharge, and he'd been using the booze to fill the hole she'd left behind her. That had been a little over a year ago.

He'd loved her, in his way. He'd loved her almost as much as his old pal Corporal Hodges had loved his fiancée until he'd been killed in action. But Leipfold was haunted by things, things that he couldn't share even with his shrink, and his nightmares were getting worse. Meanwhile, Rebecca's friends were pouring poison into her ear, and he was doing nothing to disabuse her of the word on the street, which was that he was a good-for-nothing bum. She was an easy target. She was already pissed off that they'd had to postpone the wedding until Leipfold found some other way to support them.

But Leipfold also had something in his heart that held him back from giving someone his everything. Sometimes he wondered if he even had the capacity to love, at least in the same way that other people did. He felt like a robot, running through a simulation. Perhaps it was for the best that she'd left him. She'd just gathered up her clothes in the middle of the night, shoved them in the back of her car and then driven the thing off into the night. He guessed she was back with her parents in the Home Counties. But it didn't really matter.

Leipfold woke up for the second time several minutes later. He sighed and massaged his temples, then forced himself to stand up and to look around. He was at home in the bedsit he'd moved into after his dishonourable discharge from the army. He hated the place, but it was all he could afford. And without a fixed job, he didn't think much of his chances of getting out of there.

He brushed his teeth and made himself a strong cup of coffee, then whipped together a bowl of instant noodles. He smothered it with soy sauce to give it some flavour, then scooped the noodles lazily into his mouth with a plastic fork. It tasted like shit in a sandwich, but it was all he could afford. According to his calculations, it offered the most calories for the lowest price. The soy sauce was his only luxury.

Leipfold didn't have a phone, so he started every day by taking a trip down the stairs to the front door, where his mail was thrown on the floor in an ugly bundle by the building's lazy postman. He sorted through it, dropping his neighbours' mail into the relevant slots and keeping hold of a couple of pieces that were addressed to him. But his mail could wait. He could already tell that they were bills, and there was no point opening them until he knew he had the money to pay them.

He tottered outside and breathed deeply as the cool, spring air hit his nostrils. The fresh air helped. The hangover slipped to the back of his mind, at least for a moment. He wondered if he was safe to drive, then figured that even if he was, he wouldn't be for much longer. So he decided to walk to the Rose & Crown instead.

The old pub wasn't the most inspiring of places, but it was good enough for Leipfold as a base of operations. Cedric, the landlord, was a happy-go-lucky kind of guy who didn't ask too many questions of his customers. And he owed Leipfold a favour—a big one—from back when he'd been too young to even drink in the establishment. Leipfold took it as an excuse to use the pub's telephone, making a dozen or more calls a day to potential employers. He needed work.

He ordered a pint from the bar and carried it over to his usual table in the corner. Cedric had already stacked up the day's papers with *The Tribune* on top, so Leipfold settled into his routine by skimming through the paper until he reached the crossword. Then he removed a stub of pencil from behind his ear and got stuck into the first clue.

When he'd finished the crossword, he ordered another pint and then flipped back through the paper until he reached the jobs section and the personal ads. They were always the same, or close enough for it to make no difference. Since his discharge from the army, he'd worked a number of dull, dead-end jobs which had helped to pay the bills but which had left him feeling worn and exhausted, his spirits crushed. And most had only kept him on for a couple of days—a week at the most—before letting him go.

The door opened and a man walked in, but Leipfold was in a world of his own. His hands were absentmindedly circling possible opportunities while his mind wandered off by itself. Then someone sat a glass down on the table in front of him and startled him so much that he knocked the papers to the floor.

Leipfold looked up at the man and found himself facing another surprise. The man wasn't just a man. He was a policeman in full uniform, a sight that he didn't often see in the Rose & Crown. The officer smiled, and Leipfold looked at him—*really* looked at him. There was something in his eyes or his chiselled brow that reminded him of—

"James Leipfold," the policeman said. "Long time no see."

"It's you," Leipfold replied. "I remember you. Jack Cholmondeley."

"That's me," the cop said. He smiled. "Good to see you again."

"I suppose it's good to see you, too," Leipfold replied. "How have you been?"

"Not bad," Cholmondeley said. "Not bad at all."

They paused. Leipfold took a swig from his drink and looked at the policeman, who smiled and slid another pint across to him.

"I can't drink on duty, James," Cholmondeley said. "But that doesn't mean you can't have a drink on me. I heard about what happened to you."

"Nothing happened to me."

"That's not what I heard," Cholmondeley said. "But perhaps it's for the best. You were always too good for the army."

"People died," Leipfold murmured.

"That's what people do."

Another silence descended on the two men. Leipfold stared moodily at his pint while Cholmondeley's radio crackled.

"How are you making your money, James?" Cholmondeley asked. Leipfold glanced across at him, but he could detect no malice in the policeman's eyes. For what it was worth, it seemed like a genuine question.

"I'm not," Leipfold said. "Not really."

"I thought as much." It went silent again. Leipfold left Cholmondeley with the stack of papers while he nipped to the little boys' room. When he came back, the policeman was still there. He'd even ordered Leipfold another drink.

"Two drinks?" Leipfold said. He raised an eyebrow, the hint of a smile in the corner of his mouth. It was the early afternoon and Cholmondeley had just lined up pints number four and five, which meant Leipfold was already a little merry and well on the way to the blissful stage where anything seems possible, the best stage to be in when trying to land a little work. "Anyone would think you're trying to corrupt me."

"Something like that," Cholmondeley said. "Listen, I have a favour to ask."

"You have a favour to ask?"

"That's what I said."

Leipfold laughed. "You haven't seen me for years. How did you even find me?"

"I have my ways," Cholmondeley said.

Leipfold chuckled. "You think I'm yours for two pints?" he asked. He thought it over. "What the hell. What's the favour?"

"Well," Cholmondeley said. "That's just it. I wanted to pick your brain about something. Something off the record."

"Why me?" Leipfold asked. "Why not ask one of your copper friends?"

Cholmondeley shook his head. "I don't want any of them to know. But I *do* need help. I think you can help me, and I also think you can keep a secret. Better still, you don't know anyone that I know. I can talk to you in confidence."

"You hardly know me."

"That's rather the point," Cholmondeley said. He looked around the room and felt satisfied by what he saw. Then he reached into an inside pocket and pulled out a plain-looking envelope. He tossed it over to Leipfold, who held it suspiciously in front of his eyes before slitting the seal with a fingernail and opening it up. He tipped it upside down and a half dozen rigid sheets of paper slid out and onto the beer-stained table in front of him.

"They used glue and old newspapers," the policeman explained. "Looks like a kid's art project."

"What the hell is this?" Leipfold asked.

"See for yourself," Cholmondeley replied.

So Leipfold did. He picked up the first of the notes by the corner, then held it up to the light to examine it. Someone had made the note by cutting different letters out of a newspaper and sticking them to the page in a haphazard jumble of different colours and fonts. The first note read, "FOllOw thE CLUeS, MR. P0LicEMaN." It was followed by another note, and then another, both of which read like the riddles from the adventure books that Leipfold used to read as a boy. It was all, "I'm tall when I'm young and short when I'm old."

Leipfold gasped as he continued to work his way through the letters. Cholmondeley asked him what he made of it.

"Hard to tell," Leipfold said. "But whoever sent them was well-educated. At least, they were well-educated enough to use correct grammar, spelling and punctuation."

"But what do they want?"

"It's a treasure hunt," Leipfold said. "Looks like you need to follow the clues."

"No shit," Cholmondeley replied. "I figured that out already."

"How did you get the notes?"

"The first one was delivered to the station," Cholmondeley said. "Addressed to me in a plain white envelope."

"Does anyone else know about it?"

Cholmondeley shook his head. "Not yet," he admitted. "It felt... personal, somehow. I didn't want to share it."

"But you shared it with me," Leipfold reminded him.

"Well, that's just it," Cholmondeley said. "I need help. I tracked down the first four clues without a hitch. Each one pointed to a location, and each location had another clue for me. But now I'm stuck on this one."

Cholmondeley sorted through the sheets of paper until he found the one that he wanted, then slid it across to Leipfold over the table. Leipfold reached over to grab it, nudging his forgotten pint aside as he did so. He read the message out loud.

"I'm a place of worship, but I live atop the river," he intoned. "I'm the final little secret for the city to deliver."

"Weird, right?"

"Not at all," Leipfold said. "That's Vauxhall Bridge."

Cholmondeley looked across at him, stunned. "It is?"

45

Leipfold nodded. "There's a sculpture of St. Paul's on it. It's down the side, but you can't miss it if you look for it."

"And you just happened to look for it?"

"I just know things," Leipfold said. He grinned. "Have you wondered what this is all about? What these things mean and why they were sent to you in the first place?"

"Of course," Cholmondeley replied. "Who wouldn't? In fact, that's the question that I want an answer to. And it's why I'm trying to solve the bloody thing in the first place."

"You must have some idea."

"I have several," Cholmondeley said. "But if I follow the clues to the end then I won't have to speculate. I'll know."

"Spoken like a true copper," Leipfold muttered.

"What was that?" Cholmondeley asked.

But Leipfold refused to repeat it, so Cholmondeley shook his hand and left him to scouring the paper for vacancies while cradling the remnants of his free pint of lager.

*   *   *

Cholmondeley headed back to the station and cracked on with his work, ploughing through case notes like there was no tomorrow until clocking off time, when he packed it all neatly away and headed out of the building. His meagre salary wouldn't stretch to a vehicle, but he was more than happy to take the tube around or, when he was on duty, to hop behind the wheel of a police car.

It was getting late by the time that he left the office, but the treasure hunt felt like a stone around his neck. He knew that if he didn't visit the bridge, he wouldn't sleep. So he hopped on the Victoria line and raced over to Vauxhall Bridge, arriving in the south of the city just as the sun was setting.

Cholmondeley walked up and down the bridge with his usual policeman's swagger, trying to get a feel for the place before he bit the bullet and looked for what he was looking for. He found it on the upstream side of the bridge, a sculpture of a beautiful woman who held a pair of calipers in her right hand and the cathedral in her left. She was tall—taller than any woman Cholmondeley had ever met—and she was imposing. The policeman had no idea how he was going to get down to her.

And then he saw the message, and he laughed and laughed and laughed. It was written in waterproof chalk on the pavement and read "for a good time, call…" It was followed by an eleven-digit phone number. Cholmondeley wrote the number down in his notebook and made his way to the nearest phone box, then entered a few coins and punched a few digits. There was a click and then somewhere a phone began to ring.

It rang, and then it rang some more. Then it clicked through to an answering machine and a familiar voice transmitted itself through the airways.

"Hello, Jack," Leipfold said. "It's me."

"Son of a bitch," Cholmondeley growled.

"Listen, there's a point to all of this," Leipfold continued. "You're probably asking what this is all about and why I put you through your paces to get you this far."

"You're damn right."

"Do you remember the Squires kid? Well, he's not a kid anymore. Word on the street is that he did something. He did something bad. Now, I'm willing to help you to take him down, but I needed a little assurance. If I help you out, you have to promise that you'll take him down. If this comes back on me, he'll have me killed."

"It was a test," Cholmondeley murmured.

"I need you to keep going on this one," Leipfold said. "Bear with me, Jack. This one's a tough one. I want you to find me the garden where sovereigns grow. Then find the place where the fish swim and jump into it. You'll find the woman you're looking for with her feet in the silt."

"And why should I do that?" Cholmondeley asked, although he knew he was talking to a recording. But Leipfold didn't answer, and there was a click on the other end of the line as Leipfold's cassette recorder kicked in. Cholmondeley slammed the phone back onto the hook and scowled at it, then headed underground again to retrace his steps.

Leipfold was still in the Rose & Crown when Cholmondeley got back there, although his voice was significantly more slurred and his eyes were like two pricks of light at the end of two tunnels. Cholmondeley wondered how many more drinks he'd had and whether he'd had any success with his job hunt.

When the policeman entered, a morose silence descended amongst the punters. Even out of uniform, he had the look of someone official, and the evening drinkers at the Rose & Crown were the kind of people who didn't like to be overheard by strangers. Cholmondeley ordered a pint—*what the hell?* he thought—and went to sit down next to Leipfold. The younger man didn't even look up from his newspaper.

"How can I help you, Jack?" he asked.

"You bastard," Cholmondeley replied. "What's the deal? I should charge you for wasting police time."

"You listened to the message, then," Leipfold observed. "I know you, Jack. I know your kind. I'm willing to bet that you played it by the book. You wouldn't have wasted police time. That's why you're here right now in your civvies and not your uniform. You're off-duty."

"You still wasted *my* time," Cholmondeley said. "Why test me in this way?"

"A guy's got to have a hobby."

Cholmondeley growled and pushed himself back on his seat. Then he stood upright and motioned for Leipfold to do the same.

"You want to fight me?" Leipfold asked. He sounded wry, almost amused. The other punters had drawn back in a semicircle around them. For them, this was the night's entertainment. They wouldn't be happy until fists were flying.

But Leipfold refused to get up, and Cholmondeley's anger dissipated as quickly as it came when he felt the eyes of the drinkers upon him. Leipfold eyed him warily and gestured to the seat opposite him. Cholmondeley took it and stared right back.

"Listen," Leipfold said. He looked around the room, daring the drinkers to meet his eyes. He couldn't risk being overheard, not with such a sensitive subject, and definitely not in the middle of the Rose & Crown. "Don't cause a scene, okay? This is private business. That's why I started the damn treasure hunt in the first place. I wanted to make sure you were up to the job. If Squires finds out about this..."

"He won't," Cholmondeley said.

"Follow the clues, Jack," Leipfold insisted. "You won't regret it."

"Why do you care so much about Squires, anyway?"

"The son of a bitch used to steal my lunch money," Leipfold replied. He felt Cholmondeley's eyes on his face and knew exactly what the cop was doing. "I'm not joking. If I wanted food, I needed money. If I wanted money, I had to take it from my father's wallet while he was passed out drunk. If I got caught taking it, he'd beat me with his belt. And if I didn't have anything to give to Squires, he'd do the job for him."

"So this is about revenge?" Cholmondeley asked.

"No," Leipfold replied. "It's about playing the game."

Cholmondeley wanted to ask for further details, but Leipfold held up his hand and excused himself to go to the little boy's room. Then he climbed out of the window and headed off into the night.

*　　*　　*

It was the following afternoon, and Cholmondeley was still following the clues on the sly. He'd roped in a little help from the diving team, a man called Wilko who looked a little like the fish he swam with. Wilko was an unpopular man, but that worked in Cholmondeley's favour. He didn't have many friends at the station, but Jack Cholmondeley was one of the popular cops who seemed somehow destined for greatness. So when Cholmondeley asked him for a favour—"strictly off the record, of course"—the man felt almost contractually obliged to help him.

And so Wilko suited up while Cholmondeley drove the car, and they parked outside the Rose & Crown before cutting across the back and along the riverbank. The water was muddy there and visibility was slim, and Cholmondeley didn't even know what he was looking for. Wilko went under for ten minutes or so, then surfaced again to get his bearings. He waved at Cholmondeley and removed his mouthpiece, then shouted, "I found something!"

"What is it?" Cholmondeley asked.

But Wilko just shook his head, reattached the mouthpiece and dived back under. He resurfaced a couple of minutes later with a leather case in his hands, which he hauled to the side of the river and dumped onto the bank. Cholmondeley couldn't wait for the diver to resurface and disengage himself from his equipment, so he worked his hand at the straps and tugged the case open. The water had rusted the buckles and the leather had lost some of its colour, but it held together until Cholmondeley managed to get one of the straps unhooked.

Then a mini waterfall spilled out on the pavement as the leather folded in on itself and the bag collapsed. The water was the colour of urine and smelled just as bad, and the bag itself had the smell of death all over it. Cholmondeley had smelled it just once before as the first responder to a grizzly suicide, and he knew that it would clog up his nostrils for the days and weeks to come.

Inside the bag, he found a severed arm, half a leg and a clump of scalp with the hair still attached. The stench was unbelievable. It took everything Cholmondeley had to hold his lunch in. Wilko, meanwhile, was spared the smell by his breather, which he was wisely still wearing. He looked quizzically at Jack Cholmondeley, who returned his gaze with a baleful frown.

"We'd better call this in," Cholmondeley said.

The diver nodded at him and backed away from the bag, then took his mask off and switched back to the natural air that the planet had to offer. "I'll see you back at the station," he said. "If anyone asks, I wasn't here."

"I won't involve you unless I have to," Cholmondeley said. It wasn't quite a promise, but it was good enough for Wilko, who left the scene and put the call in while Cholmondeley waited for backup to arrive.

Back at the station, they took a closer look at the bag and its unpleasant contents. But Cholmondeley had seen enough, so he left it to the boffins to do their work and told them to have a report on his desk as quickly as possible. Cholmondeley wasn't even in charge of the case. That dubious honour had been passed onto one of his superiors, a man called Bilstone who scared the bejeezus out of everyone he worked with.

So Cholmondeley found a quiet room with a telephone line and put a call in to the Rose & Crown. Cedric, the landlord, answered on the second ring. He sounded like he'd been drinking on the job, and Cholmondeley figured he probably had. It was that kind of pub.

"Get me James Leipfold," Cholmondeley said.

"Never heard of him," the man replied.

"Funny looking chap," Cholmondeley explained. "Red hair. Drinks like a thirsty cat. Sits in your pub while trying to find work."

"Oh, *him*," Cedric said. "I know the one you mean. Hang on. I'll go and get him."

Cholmondeley waited impatiently for Leipfold to pick up the receiver. He could hear a dull chattering of voices in the background, the sure sign of a British pub in the inner city. Then

Leipfold grabbed hold of the phone and said hello. He was breathing heavily, like a smoker who'd just placed last in a marathon.

"Leipfold," Cholmondeley growled, "you could have warned me."

"Warned you about what?"

"The body parts, goddamn it," Cholmondeley said. "How did you know they were there?

"I didn't," Leipfold replied. "It was just a good guess. Let's just say it was the word on the street."

"I could bust you as an accessory after the fact."

"You could," Leipfold admitted. His voice was slurry but still legible, a little soft around the edges but still clearly the voice of a man who was in possession of all of his faculties. "I hoped that the little treasure hunt would impose upon you the seriousness of the help that I gave you. If word gets out, I'll be skinned alive. I'm trusting you to keep it to yourself."

"You made me prove myself," Cholmondeley said.

"I had to," Leipfold replied.

Cholmondeley laughed. It was a bitter laugh, but it had its undertones of geniality, like a department store Father Christmas being made redundant.

"Well, I proved myself, all right," Cholmondeley said. "And now there's a Jane Doe in the morgue. At least, we think she's a Jane Doe. We don't have enough of her to be sure, but that's the hypothesis. Her fingers had nail varnish on and the hair on the scalp looks... well, expensive. Long, blonde and professionally done. I don't suppose you know what happened to her."

"Blunt force trauma," Leipfold replied. "At least, that's what I heard."

"Well, we'll see if that's true."

From the other end of the phone line, Cholmondeley could hear Cedric kicking up a fuss and trying to get Leipfold to hang up. The policeman guessed that another of his punters—probably one who paid better—wanted to make a call.

"Who is she?"

"I don't know," Leipfold said.

"Bullshit," Cholmondeley replied. "You know all this, but you don't know who she is?"

Leipfold paused for a moment, trying to figure out just how much he could trust the policeman. It went against everything he'd been raised to believe in, but there was something about Jack Cholmondeley that Leipfold couldn't help trusting. Besides, he'd passed his test. He'd proved himself worthy.

"Okay," Leipfold said. "What I'm about to tell you has to remain confidential. This is between the two of us."

"I can't promise that."

"You'll understand why I'm asking when I tell you what I have to stay," Leipfold said. "The dead woman is called Janine Taylor. I knew her."

"Intimately?"

Leipfold shook his head. "Not like that," he said. "She was engaged to a lad from my unit. I think she was killed because she learned something."

Cholmondeley stared at him for a moment, then reached into his pocket to pull out his pencil and his notebook. "Go on," he said.

And so Leipfold told Jack Cholmondeley about his time in the army and his subsequent dismissal, along with the meeting with Awni el-Halim, his flight from the insurgents and the subsequent revenge attack. But Cholmondeley seemed unimpressed.

"What does this have to do with the woman?" he asked.

"When I saw him, el-Halim said something about a conspiracy," Leipfold replied. "I hadn't even thought about the man since I came back to Blighty."

That was a lie, but there was no need for Cholmondeley to know that. Leipfold thought about Awni el-Halim and his cryptic words every night before falling asleep.

"You're giving me about as much to go on as you did for your little treasure hunt," Cholmondeley said with distaste.

"I haven't finished," Leipfold said. "El-Halim is here, in London. I spotted him in Croydon a couple of months ago, and I've been tailing him on and off ever since. He met a man at a Muslim-owned dry cleaners. I couldn't get close enough to hear what they talked about, but I followed the guy he met back to the Ledbury. He's a big hitter. Government, maybe."

"Still sounds like a conspiracy theory to me," Cholmondeley said. "And where does Jimmy Squires come in?"

"I'm getting to that," Leipfold replied. "I kept tailing the government guy and followed him to Jimmy's council house. And then I followed him again, all the way through London to Swindon, to a little house at 137B Canterbury Road, where Janine Taylor lived."

"Swindon isn't part of my jurisdiction," Cholmondeley said.

"I know," Leipfold said. "But she died in London, which is. I think she was coming here to meet someone. I think she was coming to spill the beans."

"About what?"

"About the truth," Leipfold said. "The murdered truth. The real reason why her fiancée died."

"Which is?"

"I don't know," Leipfold answered. "But I intend to find out and I want you to help me."

Cholmondeley sucked thoughtfully at his teeth. "I see why the need for secrecy," he said. "If what you're saying is true, this goes all the way up to the top. I'll have to go through the official motions with Jimmy Squires and investigate on my own time. And if anyone finds out what I'm up to, there'll be hell to pay."

"You mean you're going to take it on?"

"Doesn't look like I have much choice," Cholmondeley replied. "I'm a sucker for the truth as much as you are. I'm not amused by your antics, but I'd be lying if I told you that you don't have a certain style. Are you sure you won't reconsider joining the force?"

"I'm sure of it," Leipfold said. "Jack, I really need to go. I have some investigations of my own to make."

"You have a talent, James," Cholmondeley replied. "A rare talent. If you won't join me, perhaps you should work against me. Form a detective agency. Start putting those skills of yours to good use instead of wasting my time."

Cholmondeley waited for a response that never came, but he did think he heard something in that final half a second as he pulled the receiver away from his ear and slammed it back into the cradle.

It sounded like laughter.

But Jack Cholmondeley wasn't in the mood for laughter. He had half a body in the morgue and a whole heap of unanswered questions. He thought about Jimmy Squires, now grown older and uglier. And he wondered whether he was sleeping well that night.

Whether he had anything on his conscience.

The Worst Hangover

LEIPFOLD HAD A HANGOVER AGAIN.

But this wasn't just any old hangover. It was ferocious and had a kick to it, like snorting a line of horseradish and following it up with a shot of tequila to the eye. When he stood up, it almost knocked him right back over, and the throbbing in his head felt like a major artery was about to burst and send his brain leaking from his ears like the filling of a pasty when it's been bitten into.

He groaned and rolled over, then hit his head on something. He focused a bleary eye on the obstruction and realised it was a paperweight, which could only mean one thing. He was at his desk again.

Leipfold rubbed the sleep and the scum from his eyes and sat up, then immediately wished he hadn't. Everything hurt—his head in particular—and all the aspirin in the world couldn't help him. Not that it stopped him from trying. He poured himself a glass of tepid water from the kitchen tap and then drained it in one while double dosing. His stomach rumbled cautiously, but he managed to hold it down...just about.

Back at the desk, he checked the calendar to see what day it was. Realising it was a Thursday, he opened up his notebook to see what the day had in store for him. When he reached the right section, he gasped in surprise. A couple of pages had been ripped from his diary, and his messed-up memory could surface nothing to explain what had happened.

He thought back to the night before and found a blur of shapes and colours, faces and places. He remembered being inside the

Rose & Crown while Dodgy Dave told a story about a girl he met on a dating site. The next thing Leipfold remembered was buying a kebab from a van, followed by some night club that seemed both strange and familiar at the same time. He thought that the name had a bird in it. *The Pink Flamingo? The Red Duck? The Purple Ostrich?* Leipfold just couldn't remember.

But even with the hangover, something ticked inside him and made him need answers. Something had made him tear out the pages of his notebook, and he wanted to know what and why.

He started by calling Sandra, the woman in his life. He'd been seeing her off and on since Rebecca left after his dishonourable discharge from the army. They'd first met a couple of years ago, but it had never become serious. Well, not *too* serious. Leipfold liked his alone time, and while he had no intentions of cheating on her, he also didn't want her to fall in love with him.

Leipfold had hoped that she might have some answers, but the call wouldn't connect and he surmised that either the line was down or she had the phone off the receiver.

Not a good sign, he thought. But he didn't let that put him off, so he climbed into the driver's seat of his second-hand Ford and set off for the heart of the city. Sandra worked at an international bank whose name Leipfold had never been able to pronounce, but he knew where the offices were and that was enough.

He parked the car a couple of streets away, wondering whether he was still over the limit, and then walked slowly along the pavement. Sandra's office was inside a converted church, and Leipfold was in luck. Their security guard was off on a cigarette break, and their receptionist was powerless to stop him as he ran past her and up the stairs to the marketing floor. Leipfold had never been inside the place, and its labyrinthine interior confused the hell out of him, especially with his hangover.

"Sandra!" Leipfold shouted as he barged on to the floor amongst the confused stares of a dozen milling executives. "Where is she?"

"Sir, you can't be in here," one of the men said, although he looked uncertain and not a little afraid, despite being half a foot taller than the intruder. Someone else shouted for security.

"Just tell me where I can find her," Leipfold said. "Please. It's important."

"She's not here," the man said. "She said she was going to her mother's."

"Can you give me the address?"

The man looked at Leipfold as though he was a piece of shit on the bottom of his shoe. "Even if I could," the man said, "I wouldn't. Now please leave."

Leipfold thought about trying his luck and decided against it, then thought about decking the guy anyway just for being a dickhead. He decided against that, too.

Luckily, he thought he had a solution. *The dinner*, Leipfold thought. *The family dinner.*

Leipfold cast his mind back to an invitation he'd received many moons ago. Sandra's parents were throwing one of their family dinners, and they'd sent him a letter to invite him to it. After having a panic attack and pretending to have an important job on at a building site in the morning, he'd managed to get out of it. He'd thought nothing more of it ever since. Now, all it took was a little wandering through his mental labyrinth and his memory threw up the address. He walked the couple streets to his car and climbed back into the driver's seat. Then he gunned the engine and headed for Hammersmith.

It was a bad neighbourhood and a long way to drive through the inner-city traffic. Leipfold's hands were shaking a little and the car was low on petrol, so he drove it back to the office and parked up before heading straight to the tube station. Another memory reared its ugly head, this time of a bottle of whiskey in the back of a cab. The sharp taste of bile rose up in his throat and he swallowed it back down again. The soot and the smog were even worse underground, and Leipfold wiped cold sweat from his face as he hung from the straps in the carriage.

He alighted in Hammersmith and walked the rest of the way to Sandra's mum's address. He'd never been there before, but he knew the area well enough and it didn't take him long to find it. It was helped by the fact that it had a bright red door on a street of dead, grey houses, and the fact that the woman was standing outside, pruning the bushes of her urban front garden. She looked like Sandra after a couple of nights without sleep. Leipfold could tell from a distance that she was the woman he was looking for.

"Hi," he said. She lowered her secateurs and looked across at him, then scuttled towards her front door. Leipfold had to run to stop her from slamming it in his face, although he didn't step into the building. He just allowed her to smash the door against the side of his foot. "I'm too hungover for this."

"What do you want?" the woman asked.

"Just to talk," Leipfold said.

"I know who you are," she replied. "My daughter told me to look out for you. Let me ask you again. What do you want?"

"To speak to her."

"Tough," she said. "She isn't here."

"Can you tell me where she is?" Leipfold asked.

"I can," she said. "But I'm not going to. She doesn't want to talk to you."

"Why not?"

"You know why not."

"What did I do?"

"You know what you did," the woman said. "My daughter's too good for you, James. Why don't you just piss off back to the Rose & Crown?"

He tried to get her to talk, but she wouldn't budge. So he followed her suggestion and headed back to Cedric.

*   *   *

The pub was quiet when Leipfold arrived, unusually so considering that the construction workers were at the end of their shift and the electricians were knocking off for the day. The Rose & Crown was the kind of working-class English pub that showed replays of the horse racing in the off season and installed dodgy fruit machines that stole people's money and shut down in the middle of a game. Leipfold had a tab there and usually just sat at his table and waited for the landlord to bring his drinks over. But that day was a little different. The missing pages from his notebook were still conspicuous, and he wondered what they could possibly have contained. He couldn't shake the feeling that they were somehow important.

So he sidled up to the bar and nodded at Cedric, the bearded barman who was somehow more popular than the pub was. Cedric winked back at him and started pouring out a pint before Leipfold even asked him.

"Not today, Ced," Leipfold said. "I need a favour."

"You want an ambulance?" Cedric asked. "I've never known you to turn a drink down. This one's on me, if you'd like."

"Ah, what the hell?" Leipfold said. "Go on then."

Cedric poured Leipfold a lager and slid it across the bar. Leipfold caught it and drank a third of the pint in a couple of long gulps, then set the glass back down and smacked his lips.

"Is there something else?" Cedric asked.

"Ah," Leipfold said, sheepishly. He took another swig from his drink and then tried and failed to meet Cedric's eyes. "I was wondering whether I came in here last night."

"You don't remember?"

Leipfold winced. He remembered something all right, but he wasn't quite sure what it was.

"What happened?" Leipfold asked.

"You don't remember the fight, then?"

Ah, Leipfold thought. *That's it. That's definitely what I remember.* Out loud, he said, "Remind me."

"You were at the pool table, you silly sod," Cedric said. "Hustling for booze and cash. You know, a regular night to begin with. But then things got a little out of hand."

"How so?"

"You started a fight," Cedric said. "And then you finished it. Don't you remember?"

"I did?"

Cedric nodded. "You invited them out back. That's the last I saw of you."

"I see," Leipfold said. "Mind if I take a look?"

"Go for it," Cedric said. He nodded at Leipfold and then shimmied along to the other end of the bar, where a stony-faced old man was signalling for aid and ale. Leipfold drained the rest of his pint in one and set it down on the bar, then walked through the back of the pub and into the smoking area.

It was dark outside, mostly because the bulb had blown in the security light, and it was a couple of hours too early for the drinkers to have started to gather. Leipfold had a vague memory of being out there the night before, but it felt more like a dream than anything solid. He remembered the faces of the two men, but it was as though time had stood still for him and for no one else. The memory broke around him like wind against the bonnet of a car.

Leipfold looked at the cars. He wondered whether there might be some sort of clue there, something that might spark his memory. He prided himself on his ability to handle his drink. While he liked to get smashed on a near daily basis, he didn't like to forget things. He didn't drink to forget. He drank to numb himself.

None of the vehicles in the car park looked familiar, but that was hardly surprising. Leipfold didn't smoke—at least, he didn't smoke *much*—and the back of the pub was as alien to him as the women's toilets. At first, it looked like nothing more and nothing less than a regular car park. But there was something out of place, something subtle that he couldn't put his finger on. Then he got it.

"Someone skidded out here," Leipfold murmured, dropping to his knees to take a closer look at the ground. It was stained with burned rubber in a couple of twisted rainbows. He gauged their width and made a good guess at the distance between them, then mentally compared them with his own car. It was a match, but it was a match for plenty of other cars, too. The treads were more revealing, especially when they sank into a pothole after rolling through a patch of mud. While Leipfold wasn't exactly an expert, he had a good eye for patterns and, hungover or not, his vivid memory wasn't letting him down. The tracks were smudged and incomplete, but they were also a match to his own.

If it was *me,* Leipfold thought, *I must have been in one hell of a hurry. What happened?*

He went back inside and ordered another beer to steady his hands and to buy him some thinking time while he planned his next move. If he'd been in the country, perhaps he could have tried to track the vehicle. Here, in the city, there was no such luck, although he had a good guess as to where he might have headed.

Leipfold retraced his usual steps, following the path he always took after a night on the town. It led him back home, but it led him back the long way, past another handful of pubs with unusual names down the city's side streets. He called in at each one of them, stopping for a couple more drinks along the way, but none of the staff remembered him. That could only be a good thing.

It was starting to get late, and Leipfold shivered and tugged his jacket a little closer. He was tipsy, but not drunk enough for the booze to keep him warm as he wandered through the city. He tried to avoid the eyes of the passers-by as he beat the streets, but he had to look up when he saw the uniformed legs of a policeman blocking the path in front of him. Leipfold slowed to a stop and looked around.

The policeman was standing by a crossing in the road where a dozen bundles of flowers had been attached to the metal railings with plastic clips. Leipfold stared solemnly at the flowers and made awkward eye contact with the policeman, who stared straight back at him. He looked both bored and resigned. Leipfold guessed he was at the start of his shift.

The policeman caught his eye and said, "Can I help you?"

"What happened here?" Leipfold asked.

"There was an accident," the policeman said. "A bad one." He shifted slightly, and Leipfold looked over at the flowers again.

"Did someone die?"

The policeman shook his head. "Not quite," he said. "But she's in intensive care. A little girl."

"What's her name?"

"Can't tell you that."

"Fair enough," Leipfold said. Instead, as the policeman watched, he checked out the names on the tributes that had been left at the accident site and came up with an ID: Jane Bison."

"What happened?" Leipfold asked.

"You ask a lot of questions," the policeman replied. "What are you, one of the hacks from *The Tribune*?"

Leipfold laughed at that, thinking of the crosswords he liked to solve, and said, "Just a concerned member of the public. So come on. What happened?"

"Drunk driver," the policeman said. "Same as always. Some tanked-up idiot who thought his own life was worth more than a little kid's. Scum."

"Indeed," Leipfold said. He lowered his head a little and looked across at the flowers again. He had a horrible feeling in the pit of his stomach, a sickness in his throat and a cold ice flow taking over his bloodstream. He thanked the policeman and continued on his way.

Pieces of the night before were starting to fall into place, and Leipfold didn't like it. He remembered the Rose & Crown in a little more detail, and he remembered the fight outside and how it had ended, with Leipfold holding his knuckles and the two men running from the scene. Then he'd climbed behind the wheel of his car, and…that was all he could remember.

He shook his head and brought himself back to the present.

Leipfold got home when the night was still young, but he'd picked up a couple of bottles on the way and spent the night in contemplation with a glass beside him. It always seemed half-full or half-empty because he always topped it up before it reached the bottom. He whiled away the evening by thinking, drinking and staring into the abyss while trying to find a way out to the other side.

He barely slept. When he woke up in the morning, he found it hard to tell whether he was drunk or sober. Everything hurt. He took a shower while he waited for the newsagents to open, then nipped to the shops to buy the papers and a bottle of vodka, just in case.

Leipfold read the paper in a backstreet café while gulping down black coffee. He automatically flicked through to the job ads to begin with, before backtracking to the first few pages for news on the accident. He found an article on the fourth page that seemed to cover it, although it was sparse on details. Leipfold read it with mounting concern. It said that the driver was still at large and that the injured child had been taken to St. Martin's Hospital.

So that was where Leipfold went.

It was still early in the morning, and the streets were thronged with tourists and commuters. Leipfold loved the city, but he hated its people and he was in no mood for the cramped conditions on the tube, not with his hangover. So he set out on foot, working up a sweat to blow the hangover away as he meandered from street to street like an unemployed prostitute.

The hospital was a couple of miles away, but Leipfold made good time and he was starting to feel a little better by the time that he got there. He had a smile on his face when he reached the reception.

The desk was being staffed by a young man and two women. When Leipfold arrived, one of the women was just finishing a conversation with the only other patient at the desk. As the conversation drew to a close, all three of them turned to help him.

"I'm looking for my niece," he lied. "Jane Bison."

"Ward Nine," the young man said without looking up. "Second door on your left."

The hospital was like a labyrinth, of course, but Leipfold's memory helped him to map it without a problem. He spotted the kid—it *had* to be her—as soon as he entered the ward through a pair of double doors. She was lying on top of a hospital bed with her face smashed in and half her body wrapped in plaster. Leipfold tried to go in to see her, but the door was locked with a passcode. He got the feeling that if he caused a scene, he'd find himself in a prison cell. And besides, if his suspicions turned out to be grounded then he'd done enough damage already. The girl deserved to recover in peace, if she was able to recover at all.

So he turned his mind to another problem. *Where in the hell is my car?* Leipfold thought.

Finding it seemed like an impossible task, but he'd done it before after big benders. This was different, and he'd felt it from the start. He already knew that the vehicle wouldn't be easy to find. But there *was* one clue, and he wondered why it hadn't occurred to him before. When he'd first woken up without his memory, he'd spotted an anomaly. Mud, lots of it, caked all over his shoes and trampled into the carpet.

At the time, he'd thought nothing of it. But now that he considered it, he knew exactly what it meant as well as where it was from. There was only one place it could possibly be, and it was less than a mile away.

Leipfold's destination was a small tunnel beside the river. It was one of his favourite places, or it had been as a child, and he liked to go there when he needed to think. He used to sit there with the newspaper in one hand and a pen in the other, filling out the crossword as the world passed by. People rarely went down there, which was why Leipfold liked it.

This time, something was different, and it didn't take him long to figure out what it was. There were fresh tyre tracks in the mud, tracks that looked suspiciously like the ones in the car park of the Rose & Crown. And there was something there inside them, something squashed into the mud beneath the treads. Leipfold bent down to take a closer look and came up with a leather key ring with the letter L on it. It was attached to Leipfold's car key.

His memory came back in a flash with all the force of a boot to the face. He remembered where he'd been that night. He remembered what he'd been doing. And he remembered what he'd done.

He remembered the impact and how it had set off his airbags. He remembered screeching to a halt at the side of the road. He remembered the look the mother had given him as she knelt beside her daughter. He remembered how even in the darkness and through the alcoholic haze, he'd seen the girl's blood on the road beneath the streetlights.

Then he remembered the long walk home.

Leipfold's blood ran cold. He remembered it in all of its gory detail, and he cursed his memory and his own curiosity for hunting down the missing hours in the first place. Then another memory surfaced.

Sandra. He'd talked to her. He'd called her up from a payphone, still flooded with adrenaline, and told her what had happened. *That* was why she'd disappeared.

Jesus Christ, Leipfold thought. *This can't be happening.*

But it *was* happening, and it was too late to change it.

Leipfold stayed beneath the bridge for a couple of hours, staring moodily at the water. With his right hand, he absentmindedly picked up pebbles and skimmed them across the water. He was thinking about his future. It had never been particularly bright, but it was starting to look more like a black, empty void, a bottomless pit that he was skirting around and about to fall into.

Eventually, he pushed himself up and set off again. He took the same route home that he'd taken the night before. Now he could remember it, and the streets seemed to take on a dull, grey glow around him. They felt like a prison. Even with the sun still rising in the sky to the side of him, he felt like he was walking through the darkness. He stopped at an off-license, barely aware of what he was doing, and was dragged rudely back to reality when the proprietor spoke to him.

"Back so soon?" he asked.

Leipfold stared at him. "What's it to you?" he asked.

"Nothing," the man replied. "No offence meant. It's just that you were in a state last night. I thought you might have woken up with a headache."

"Something like that," Leipfold said. "I've got to go."

Leipfold rushed out of the shop without collecting his change, oblivious to the shopkeeper's voice as it followed him out of the store and into the street. He rushed home as fast as his little legs could carry him, the carrier bag banging against them.

That night, he got as drunk as he possibly could. He wanted to black it all out again, the whole of the last three days. He wanted to drink so much that it would cancel out his very existence. He wanted to be back in the womb so he could start everything all over again.

But life had never been kind to James Leipfold, and it wasn't about to break a habit. He woke up in the morning with a thumping three-day hangover and the kind of dry mouth that only rolls around once a lifetime. But somehow, despite the haze of alcohol that had half-blinded him, he saw more clearly on that morning than he had for months. Maybe even years.

He hopped in the back of a taxi and told the cabbie where to go. He gave him a £20 note and told him to keep the change. He wouldn't need it where he was going.

Leipfold walked into the police station and approached the man who was working the desk.

"Hello," he said. "My name's James Leipfold. I'd like to confess to a crime. Tell Jack Cholmondeley to get out here."

Jailed

READING JAIL WAS A MISERABLE PLACE.

Leipfold had already spent a couple of months there, and he was glad that there was talk of the facility shutting down, even if that meant he'd be transferred to someplace with a more imposing reputation.

Life behind bars was a life of routine, which suited Leipfold just fine. The prisoners woke with the rising of the sun, showered and dressed themselves and then made their way down to the canteen for breakfast. After they ate, the guards watched as they headed out into the yard for some exercise before being cooped back up in the cells for the rest of the day. On Sundays, the monotony was disrupted by the weekly church service. Leipfold wasn't religious, but he went along anyway. He'd even befriended the priest who led the service and promised to look him up after his release.

Leipfold had earned a little respect from his fellow inmates. It helped that they didn't know what he'd done to get himself locked up, but he'd also served his country. That counted a lot in certain circles, and he hadn't found it hard to make friends. Well, maybe not friends, but there were people who'd have his back if a fight broke out.

Seven weeks in, Leipfold had already earned himself a nickname. They called him The Fixer because he fixed things. He helped when they needed help, he knew things that the other inmates could never have dreamed of, and he knew how to talk to the guards and the warden. Nobody really *knew* him, but everyone knew *of* him.

But Leipfold's adjustment from disgraced ex-soldier to popular prisoner wasn't easy. It didn't take long but, like a quick trip to the dentist, that wasn't much consolation. He'd cemented his reputation as someone who shouldn't be messed with by punching a con called Bear, the biggest guy he laid eyes on, the first time he was let out into the yard. For that, he'd earned himself a sprained wrist and a trip to lockdown.

On Leipfold's next trip out, he was jumped by five guys from Bear's posse, but he redeemed himself by swinging his fists like a champion boxer and fighting toe to toe with the meanest guys in the unit. The brawl had landed Leipfold in lockdown again, but only after his discharge from the hospital wing. When he was finally allowed back out, he was on his final warning. But there was no more trouble after that, and Bear and his crew adopted Leipfold as one of their own after witnessing him in action.

Politics in prison, Leipfold reflected, *aren't much different to the politics in Whitehall.*

The other inmates thought he was fearless, but that wasn't true. Leipfold was full of fear and racked with remorse to boot. He just didn't care what happened to him. If he was destined to wake up one night with a shank in his back, then…well, he probably deserved it.

He couldn't undo what he'd done.

During his second week in the facility, he'd spotted a familiar face. Jimmy Squires, the no-good hoodlum who used to live on his estate, had grown older and uglier. He was in a different wing to Leipfold, but they'd been escorted past each other one time when Leipfold was on his way back from the medical unit. He'd looked at Squires and almost immediately tried to turn away, but it was too late. Squires saw him.

"Hey, dickface," Squires shouted. He was being marched down the corridor by two burly prison officers, with his hands cuffed behind his back and chains around his legs. For most prisoners, it would be overkill. Leipfold wondered what he'd done to earn such special treatment. The guards were hurrying him along, not at all keen to facilitate a conversation between two of their charges, but Leipfold had just enough time to laugh and to shout a reply.

"I see Jack Cholmondeley got his hands on you, Jimmy," Leipfold said. "It couldn't have happened to a nicer guy."

"You just wait until I get *my* hands on *you*."

"Yeah, whatever."

Their conversation was cut short at that. Jimmy's warden had cuffed him in the back of the head—not hard enough to knock him out, but hard enough to be a violation of the penal code—and the two men had been dragged along the corridor away from each other.

That had been a couple of weeks ago, and Leipfold hadn't seen him since, much to his relief. He hoped that the two of them wouldn't cross paths again, either in the corridors or out in the rec yard.

But as dangerous as life in the jail was, it also made Leipfold feel alive, and he hadn't allowed it to stop him from the pursuit of knowledge, the only thing that had kept him going throughout his tumultuous life. It had all started after the second fight, when the warden had summoned Leipfold into his office.

"Ah, Leipfold," the warden said. He was an older man called Simon Mogford, a dour-faced, unshaven chap whose only concession to his personality was a single photo of his son that sat in an old iron frame on his desktop. "The last person I expected to see in here. What's the problem?"

"What do you mean, sir?" Leipfold replied, politely. His voice was muffled slightly by his swollen face, but he could still see through one of his eyes and he could tell from the warden's expression that the state of his face had made an impression.

"You're a former soldier, Leipfold," the man said. "And an educated man to boot."

"I went to Walthamstow Comprehensive."

"You know what I mean," the warden snapped. "I'm saying that you're not like the rest of the cons. You could have done something with your life. You could have been someone. Why fritter your life away?"

Leipfold shrugged.

"You want my advice?"

"No," Leipfold said.

"Tough," the governor replied. "You're about to get it anyway. Find something to keep your mind busy. Don't give up. And for goodness' sake, don't cause any more trouble."

Leipfold paused for a moment and thought about it. He shuffled uncomfortably from foot to foot.

"What is it?"

"Icoulduseabook," Leipfold mumbled.

"What was that?"

"I could use a book," Leipfold repeated, more slowly this time.

"Oh," the warden said. "Is that it? What do you read? I'll get some books sent over."

So Leipfold recited a long list of books from memory. There were a few specific ones, the ones from his youth that had some personal meaning, and the rest of the titles formed a weird mixture of Greek classics, self-help books and detective novels.

When all was said and done, Leipfold had given the warden a list of seventy-three books, and some of them were rare or out of print. The warden stared across his desk at the prisoner, his sunken eyes like big black holes in the void of space. He whistled.

"That's a lot of books," he said. "I can't do that. I can get someone to bring you a couple of Stephen King paperbacks from the prison library. I can't order anything in."

"Have you got *The Brothers Karamazov*?" Leipfold asked.

"I'll have someone take a look."

Leipfold grunted. "That's a start," he said.

The warden nodded. He stroked his chin theatrically and stared morosely into the distance.

"All right," he said. "Here's what I'll do. I'll get you what I can from the prison library. If you want more, we can request them. But first, you'll need to do something for me."

"Here we go," Leipfold murmured.

"Can I trust you?"

"It depends what for."

"Hmm." The warden looked thoughtfully at Leipfold and stroked his beard again. "Well, what the hell? I need your help. I've heard rumours about an escape attempt. I need you to find out if there's any substance there."

"Who's planning it?" Leipfold asked.

"I don't know."

"I see," Leipfold said. "Well, what's the plan? When's it going to happen? What are they going to do?"

"I don't know that, either."

"That's not much to go on."

The warden shrugged. "Take it or leave it," he said. "If you get me some information, I'll get you your books. Otherwise, you'll have to take what you can find in the library."

"No offence, guv, but the library is full of Barbara Cartland," Leipfold said. "And let's just say I have more refined tastes, especially when it comes to non-fiction."

"You mean you're picky."

"Something like that," he replied. "Can I have a notebook and some pens to record my findings?"

"I'll see to it," the warden said. Then he leaned closer and spoke again, in a lower, deeper voice. "Don't make me regret this."

Leipfold accepted the challenge, albeit reluctantly, and his investigation started immediately. He didn't know what he was looking for, but he had the kind of nose that could track information like a police dog tailing a criminal. But Leipfold didn't want to start asking around. That sort of thing could get a man killed.

Over the days and then the weeks that followed, he kept his

ear to the rumour mill. He also kept his eyes peeled for Jimmy Squires during the church services. The two men knew better than to start any trouble in the house of God, especially with so many wardens watching them, but that didn't stop Squires from pulling up a pew behind Leipfold and carrying out a muted—and often interrupted—conversation during the hymns.

"You're dead, Leipfold," Jimmy said.

"If you can get your hands on me, Jimmy," Leipfold replied. "I heard they got you for murder. What happened?"

Jimmy looked around to see whether anyone could overhear them, but their fellow cons were too focussed on the first verse of "Nearer My God to Thee." The nearest guard was a good fifteen feet away.

"Yeah, I killed her," Jimmy said, matter-of-factly. His face was pressed up close to Leipfold's ear, almost like a mother whispering a goodnight story to a sleeping child. "And I picked up a pay cheque for it, too. A government man and everything. Said it was a case of national security. So yeah, I'm in here for murder for hire. But for you, dickface, I'll do the job for free."

"What happened to the child?" Leipfold asked.

"What child?" Jimmy replied, an ugly leer creeping its way across his face. "Oh, didn't you hear? Looks like my intelligence is better than yours is. She never had the baby. She had a miscarriage instead. Grief is a terrible thing."

Leipfold cursed and said, "What do you want, Jimmy?"

"I want to kill you."

"Big words," Leipfold said, his mind whirring. "And how are you going to get your hands on me for long enough to kill me?"

"Who says I won't do it here?"

"You've got no chance," Leipfold said. "I'd be expecting it, and I'm ex-military. I can hold my own. No, you'd want the element of surprise, and you can't get that on the inside. Perhaps you're waiting until we get out."

"*If* we get out," Squires growled. "Or at least, if *you* get out. I've got my ticket out of here."

"A ticket that involves a jailbreak?"

Leipfold couldn't see Squires because he had his back to him, but he could tell from the man's silence that he was off the mark. It was a confused silence, and not the silence of a guilty man. Besides, Leipfold knew Squires. If he was involved with the jailbreak, he would have had a response prepared.

"I have no idea what you're talking about," Squires said. "But make no mistake of it, I *will* get out of here. And when I get out of here, I'm going to finish the job I was paid to do and kill the Kuwaiti, too. Then I'll wait for you to serve your time and one day, when you least expect it, I'll be there for you. Sleep well, pal."

Squires had good timing. The rest of the cons had just finished singing the last hymn and the guards were getting ready to take them back to the cells.

*   *   *

Leipfold didn't see Squires again that week, and he also made no further progress on the case. So he thought about the problem in his own special way and approached it from a different angle. He sat back and asked himself, "How would *I* do it?" The trick was to first solve that problem and then to work his way back from the solution.

The next couple of weeks passed slowly and unremarkably, and Leipfold made little progress. Still, he took mental notes on everything he could, and he also kept an ear out for gossip amongst the inmates. It wasn't an easy task because they kept themselves to themselves. Gossip wasn't traded freely. It was traded between cellmates or purchased from the guards in exchange for cigarettes.

By the start of the third week, Leipfold had finished *The Brothers Karamazov* for the fourth time and had no new books and barely any notes to show for it. The grapevine was suspiciously short of gossip. The most interesting thing he'd learned was that Oscar Wilde had been an inmate at the jail almost a hundred years earlier, and that was hardly news. His theoretical approach had worked a little better and he'd been able to identify a couple of weak spots in the facility's defence, but he didn't know what to do with the information.

The first weakness was the changing of the guards. Paradoxically, though there were more people to keep the cons in check, the exchange of information was at its weakest and the guards were less focused on the job at hand. The Sunday morning church service was another one. Security was lax, and the cons could take a hostage by subduing the priest. But that was as far as Leipfold got, and he couldn't take it seriously as a viable option. If anything, it would lead to the convicts forming a smaller prison within the prison, stuck inside the chapel in a siege situation until one of the sides caved and surrendered.

The weekly sermons started to take on more and more importance to Leipfold as he carried out his investigation. His gut told him that there was something there, even while his brain protested. But he'd trained himself to follow his instincts, so he started to pay more attention to the services, as well as to the people who attended them. There were three people in particular who stood out, three bruisers from the white supremacist group who were all swastika tattoos and shaved heads. They might have found religion, Leipfold supposed, but they didn't look like the type. Besides, they hadn't been there for Leipfold's earlier visits, and there was talk on the yard that they were up to something.

After three weeks on the case, that was all Leipfold had. Unfortunately for him, the warden was pressing for answers, and Leipfold was called up to his office a couple of times a week to provide an update. The day after the Sunday service, he found himself back in the warden's office, breaking the unwritten rules of the prisoner's code by snitching on another con. But it was a small price to pay for a stack of books.

The warden asked Leipfold whether he had any proof, and Leipfold was honest when he said that he hadn't. "Just a hunch," Leipfold said, "but I usually trust them."

"A hunch," the warden repeated. "Well, a hunch is better than nothing. I'll pull their chapel privileges and get my guards to keep extra tabs on them."

"Fine," Leipfold said. "Can I have my books?"

The warden laughed. "Not yet," he said. "Let me follow up on the information. If it turns out to be good, you'll get your books."

Leipfold was dismissed shortly afterwards, but the issue of the books still weighed heavily on his mind. He felt sure that there was something more to the story. So he resolved to do a little more digging.

If the warden can have his little spies, Leipfold thought, *then I can have mine.*

He ended up paying Bear and his friends in cigarettes in exchange for services rendered. They didn't know why Leipfold wanted them to spy for him, and they didn't care. They just cared about the cigarettes.

The reports started to filter in. Big Jim overheard one of the men boasting that he'd be getting out within a month or two, and Bear himself beat another rumour out of one of the racists that the three men liked to hang around with. Spitting blood and teeth to the floor, cornered in the back of one of the rec rooms and out of sight of the guards, the man had shouted, "They have a man outside. I swear to God. And one time, I heard them asking if something was strong enough, but I didn't catch what they were talking about. That's all I know, I swear. Please don't hurt me."

Bear was a violent man, but he was also a man of honour, so he allowed the battered man to pick himself up and get out of there.

Leipfold handed out a couple more packets of cigarettes for the information and then returned to his cell to mull it over. There wasn't much to go on, but he needed to think and act fast if he wanted to stop them. The warden needed to know, but it was dangerous for Leipfold to *ask* to see him. The cons might get suspicious. So instead, he followed his meagre clues through to their logical conclusion, charting his progress in the pages of his notebook.

When the warden finally called Leipfold into his office, he was ready to deliver his results. He was more than ready; he was hopping from foot to foot. His sources—or rather, Bear's sources—said that the escape attempt was going to take place that night.

"What have you got for me?" the warden asked.

"Nothing more than a theory," Leipfold replied. "But you're going to want to look into this. I'm right, I know I am."

"Right about what?"

"The escape happens tonight," Leipfold said. "That much I know. You understand that I can't disclose my sources."

"Of course," the warden said. "I assume you can trust this source of information?"

Leipfold thought about Bear and his big, battered fists.

"Yes sir," Leipfold said. "I believe we can. But understand that the rest is pure conjecture. We can trust that today is the day. But as for the plan…well, all I've got is how *I* would do it."

"That might have to be enough," the warden said. "Perhaps you'll earn those books after all. Tell me. What do you think the plan is?"

Leipfold held out his notebook and the warden gratefully accepted it.

"I'll talk you through it," Leipfold said. "Let's start with the riot."

"The riot?"

"The riot," Leipfold confirmed. "Remember the white supremacists? The ones that you banned from church?"

The warden nodded.

"Well," Leipfold said, "they're planning on starting a riot. Soon, if I'm not mistaken. They're going to use their gang as a front to distract you while they make their escape. When are the guards changing over?"

"Any minute now," the governor said. "It's probably already in progress. Why?"

Leipfold shook his head. "We may be too late," he said. "That's when it's supposed to—"

The conversation was interrupted midsentence as a loud klaxon pierced the air. The warden looked at Leipfold and then picked up his phone. He placed a call and had a short conversation, then angrily slammed the receiver back into its cradle. He looked over at Leipfold.

"Sounds like your prediction is coming true," the warden said. "They're going to need me out there on the floor, so I want you to tell me everything you can. But you'd better make it quick."

"I'll do my best, sir," Leipfold said. He cleared his throat. "The riot's just the first step, a distraction. The next bit is a little... well, there's no finesse there. It's a brute force attack. They've got someone on the outside."

"Who?"

"It's impossible to tell," Leipfold said. "But whoever it is, they'll need a large vehicle. A lorry perhaps, or maybe a fire truck." He paused for a moment. "Yes," he added, "I think they'll use a fire truck. They can use the hose as a weapon or get the ladder out. They'll have to steal it first, of course."

"Hang on," the warden said. "I won't be a moment."

Leipfold watched as the warden rushed over to his desk again. He placed two more calls in quick succession, babbling into the receiver so quickly that it was hard to understand what he was saying. He sounded like an auctioneer on speed.

When he put the phone back down, he rushed over to Leipfold and said, "A fire truck has gone missing. Word is that they were carjacked by masked gunmen."

"It's happening," Leipfold said. "You need to set up a roadblock. Call in the army if you need to. Put everything you've got on it. They're going to smash and grab."

"Where?"

"How should I know?"

"Well, what would you do in their place?"

Leipfold rubbed his chin thoughtfully. "And if I'm right, I get the books?"

"Damn it, Leipfold," the warden said, slamming his fist against his desk. "If you're right, you can have all the books you'll ever need. Tell me."

Leipfold rubbed his chin again. He took his time to answer.

"I'd grapple the bars of the cells, hook it up—"

There was an almighty bang, a huge, oppressive sound that was like a bomb going off. The walls shook and plaster snowed down from the ceiling, settling like dandruff in Leipfold's ginger hair. The aftermath of the explosion—or whatever it was—still shook the building's foundations. The floor started to buckle beneath them.

"What was that?" the warden shouted. He doubled up in a coughing fit as his lungs filled up with plaster, dust and detritus.

"We're too late," Leipfold said.

"Wait here."

"What about my books?" Leipfold shouted, but the warden had his back to him and just kept on scuttling away towards the cellblocks.

And so Leipfold was left alone in the warden's office as the building continued to shake. The siren had stopped blaring and been replaced by an unearthly rumbling sound. Leipfold wondered what was happening and whether the three men had made good on their escape. He hoped not.

The warden had left his door open, and Leipfold walked out into the reception area and then found himself on the other side of another door and out in a hallway. There was a fire exit at the end of it, barred shut but presumably still useable. A ticket to the outside world.

Leipfold sighed and stared at the door for a few moments. Then he doubled back on himself and headed into the warden's office. He closed the door when he entered and settled back to wait for the warden to return.

He watched the escape attempt unfold from his perch on the window. He could see the ladder, and he could see the bodies crawling across it. Even from a distance, he could tell who the figure at the front was.

Jimmy Squires, Leipfold thought. *You jammy little bastard. Now, there's something I wasn't expecting. I was wrong.*

Squires was halfway across the extended ladder when Leipfold saw the next man, one of the skinheads from the Sunday services. He was a bulky guy, twice the weight of Leipfold, and his weight was making the ladder wobble. Squires glanced backwards and sped up, scuttling along two rungs at a time.

Then the shaking increased, and Leipfold guessed that another man had climbed on to the end of the ladder. A siren rang out on the horizon somewhere. Squires had reached the end and climbed onto the roof of the fire engine. Another man was already there to help him down. Back on the ladder, the first of the skinheads was two-thirds of the way along it.

And then the ladder slipped.

Somebody screamed and Leipfold could hear it even from his perch inside Warden Mogford's office. He could also hear the horrific screech of tortured metal as the ladder shuddered and scraped down the side of the prison's wall. The skinhead at the front lost his grip and went tumbling to the ground, and Leipfold winced as he pictured the moment of impact. It wasn't the kind of drop that was impossible to survive, but it wasn't far off.

The fire engine went into reverse and scraped against the wall, but the sound of the siren was even closer. Before the truck could build up momentum, they were ahead of it, blocking off the street. The driver gunned the engine and there was another big crash as it ran into the cop cars and their makeshift barricade. The cars moved, but the barricade held.

Leipfold couldn't see what happened next, but he could hear it all right. There was a lot of shouting and a lot of movement. There was some sort of commotion, and then there was relative silence again. He climbed onto his tiptoes and tried to peer out of the window, but the angle wasn't right and he couldn't see anything.

So instead, he went to sit back down on his chair in front of the warden's desk. He hummed a little tune to himself while he waited for the warden to return and send him back to his cell.

He slept soundly that night. His books arrived the following morning.

Heroin

LEIPFOLD WAS READING *The Brothers Karamazov* again. It was the thirteenth time he'd read it, and it was up there in his top five books of all time. It was a long book that took a lot of commitment, but he was in jail and he had nothing but time. Besides, he'd already worked his way through all the new books that the warden had stocked the library with after he'd performed his little favour.

There was a noise from outside his cell and the door unlocked. Leipfold looked at it suspiciously, then smiled when he saw that it was Simmonds, one of the younger guards who'd struck up a rapport with Leipfold over a shared love of puzzles and trivia. Simmonds had a habit of remembering brainteasers and then asking Leipfold for the answers, but it didn't look like that was what he wanted this time.

"Leipfold," Simmonds said, "the guvnor wants to see you."

"Me?" Leipfold replied. "Uh-oh. You'd better take me there."

Simmonds cuffed Leipfold and led him through the labyrinth towards the warden's office. The jail was in the shape of a cross with three tiers, and Leipfold was on the top floor. He had to pass through half the prison to get to the administration block where the warden's office was, but he liked the walk. In prison, it was the closest he got to a holiday. Simmonds ushered him to the warden's door, knocked on it and then handed him over before turning on his heel and walking away. Leipfold barely heard him leave.

"Ah, Leipfold," the warden said, grabbing him by the arm and leading him into the office. "Thanks for coming."

"It's not like I had a choice," Leipfold murmured.

"What was that?"

"Nothing."

"Good." The warden paused for a moment. He stared at Leipfold with his shrewd, appraising eyes. They were bright and disconcerting. "Leipfold," he said, "I need another favour."

"Oh no," Leipfold said. "What is it this time?"

"I just thought that after the success of your last operation—"

"That was a fluke!" Leipfold insisted.

"Whatever it was, you got results. I want you to do it again."

"Why would I do that? I've got my books."

"And I can take them away again if I want to," the warden said. "If you help me out with this one, I'll get you more books."

"I don't need any more books."

"I don't care," the warden said. "Take it or leave it. But if you leave it, I'll send you to the hole."

"Eurgh," Leipfold said. "What do you need?"

"That's more like it," the warden said. "Here's the problem. Someone's bringing drugs in. Heroin, to be precise. I've had word that people are smoking the stuff inside the prison. That won't do. Not on my watch."

"And you want me to find out who's taking the stuff?"

The warden shook his head. "I already know who's taking it. You might want to talk to that Bear of yours."

"Bear's on smack?"

"Afraid so," the warden said. "He won't be a bear for long. I've seen what that stuff does to people."

"But if you already know who's responsible, what do you need me for?"

"You think Bear is the only one?" the warden asked. "No, he's just a symptom of the disease. We need to cut off the head and go straight to the supplier. I need you to find out how it's getting in."

"Why me?" Leipfold asked.

"I don't have anyone else that can get the job done," the warden said. "And besides, I know you can do it."

"And if I don't, you'll take my library privileges away?"

"Correct."

"Well then," Leipfold said, "it looks like I don't have much choice."

"That's the spirit."

Leipfold started the investigation immediately. Ever since he'd investigated the jailbreak, the warden had allowed him to keep his pens and his notebook as a token of gratitude. He was about to get some more use out of them.

After the failed escape attempt, which had resulted in the prisoners' transport to a new facility, Leipfold had been on edge. The skinheads were being held up as heroes, and their escape attempt was already sure to go down in prison history. If the rest of the cons ever found out that Leipfold had a hand in stopping them…well, he'd rather not think about it.

The idea of snooping for drugs didn't sit well with him. And as for Bear, he was Leipfold's protector, the closest thing he had to a friend there. Leipfold had no desire to start poking around and upsetting the only backup he had.

Still, there were plenty of other convicts. Leipfold spent the next couple of days putting some feelers out and finding out what he could. The junkies were easy to intimidate, but Leipfold couldn't get them to talk. Either they didn't know anything or they didn't want to risk cutting off their supply. Then he started to tail them and learned to recognise the faces of the dealers as they handed the goods over in the shower block or took even bigger risks by throwing them from cell to cell in what the prisoners called "kites."

Leipfold thought he was even making a little progress. Then the warden took the war to the next level with a formal announcement in front of the inmate populace.

"Right, you lot," he said, marching up and down the middle

gantry with his chest puffed out like a hot air balloon. "Listen up. Someone is bringing drugs into my facility. I don't know who it is, but I do know who's been taking them. I can assure you that the long arm of the law has got its boxing glove on. I hope you sleep well tonight."

He paused for a moment. Leipfold knew that the eyes of a hundred or more convicts were bearing down on the man. Even to an ex-army man from a rough estate, the idea of it was unsettling. But Leipfold liked the guy too, and he almost felt a little sorry for him.

"Now," the warden continued, "as none of you have been forthcoming with your information, I'm going to escalate the situation. Here's what we're going to do. We'll start by cancelling all visitations until further notice."

A grumble of outrage surfaced from the inmates, but the warden held his hand up and the rabble died down. "I hadn't finished," he said. "While we're at it, we're also going to suspend your telephone and mail privileges until further notice. We're going to put your cells on lockdown as well."

This time, the grumble of outrage was more like an outright roar. The din from the prisoners reminded Leipfold of waves crashing against rocks in a thunderstorm, but he wasn't at the epicentre. He wasn't the guvnor, looking up at them all. He was a convict, looking down at him. It must have been awful down there.

"Hey!" the warden shouted. But his voice was swallowed up by the space and the sound between them all. He reached down to unhook his truncheon from his belt and then banged it against the gantry's metal railing. The sharp, metallic sound carried well and echoed throughout the complex. The din died down, not completely but enough for his voice to be heard, and the warden spoke again. "If I can't find out who's bringing the drugs in, this sorry state of affairs is going to continue. I'd advise you to think about that when you're spending those long days alone, wondering how your family are and whether they're missing you. Some of you have little children. Well, you won't be seeing them for a while. Not until I have some information."

The warden waited for his words to sink in and basked in the uproar. He gave it a few moments and then held up a hand again. This time, there was still some muttering, but the warden allowed it to continue. He simply raised his voice to shout over it.

"Of course," he bellowed, "if someone was to provide me with some information, perhaps I could lift the ban. Just something to think about." The warden turned on his heel and left them to it.

Leipfold sank gloomily back onto his bed. The cancelled visitations weren't a problem for him—after all, no one came to visit him—but it would change the status quo amongst the convicts. He wasn't looking forward to the inevitable power struggle.

Bear wanted to know what Leipfold made of it. Leipfold shrugged.

"Doesn't affect me," Leipfold said. "Although..."

"Although?"

"If people are bringing stuff in, why didn't anybody tell me?" Leipfold said. "I could murder a bottle of brandy."

"Brandy, huh?" Bear was a man of few words, and this was the most that Leipfold had heard him talk for weeks. "I can get you that."

"Don't worry about it," Leipfold said.

"I won't worry," Bear said. "But I will get you some brandy. I know what it's like to need something."

Leipfold thought about it. He'd been dry since he'd handed himself over to the police, but he still felt the same old urge.

"What the hell?" he said. "Let's do it."

*   *   *

The warden's ban stayed in place, but it did little to stop the flow of contraband. Bear delivered Leipfold's brandy a couple of days after they struck their deal, and Leipfold quickly placed a second order and then a third. Each order was delivered within 48 hours, and each order got him no closer to unravelling the mystery and left him that little bit poorer. He was almost running out of the cigarettes that the inmates traded instead of money.

And then everything changed a couple of weeks later, when Leipfold witnessed a hushed conversation between Bear and one of the prison guards. Even from a distance, Leipfold recognised Simmonds. And he could spot a package changing hands.

That evening, alone in his cell with the latest bottle of brandy, Leipfold thought back over the events of the day. He opened up the bottle and took a sniff from it. It smelled angelic, like a taste of home. He sniffed it again. Then he sighed and put the cap back on the bottle.

"Not tonight, old boy," he murmured. He slid the bottle beneath his pillow and fell asleep.

The following day, the warden called Leipfold back into his office. Leipfold had spent so much time there since his incarceration that it was starting to feel like a second home. He was cuffed and ushered inside. Then the guards were dismissed and the warden gestured for Leipfold to sit down in the chair on the other side of his desk.

"I've got something for you," Leipfold said. "Have someone check my cell and look beneath my pillow."

"Why?" the warden asked.

"I managed to get something smuggled in," Leipfold replied. "A little bottle of brandy. Cheap stuff, I'm afraid, but you're welcome to it."

"Interesting. How did you manage it?"

"Well," Leipfold said, "that's the whole story, isn't it?"

The warden placed a call to get one of his men to check Leipfold's cell and then he leaned in close to hear what the man had to say.

"I'm not going to tell you who I got it from," Leipfold said. "But if you really want to know, I'm sure you can figure it out. What I can tell you is how they did it."

"Go ahead."

"You're not going to believe this," Leipfold said. "But it's the truth. I saw it with my own eyes."

"Damn it, Leipfold," the warden said. "Just tell me how they did it."

"They made a bloody blimp," Leipfold said. "Rigged it all up using a couple of balloons and a paper basket. Then they just floated it over the wall."

"Bullshit."

"I swear," Leipfold said. "I saw it. Once it cleared the walls, someone brought it down with an air gun."

"From inside the walls?"

Leipfold shook his head. "No," he said. "From the outside. Although if they keep this up, there could be guns on the inside any day now. I'm surprised none have made their way in already. That brandy wasn't exactly lightweight, not like a couple of baggies and a lighter."

"Point taken," the warden said. "I don't know, Leipfold. It seems a bit far-fetched. Are you sure?"

"Positive," he said.

"How do they get rid of the evidence?"

"Simple," Leipfold said. "The gas disappears, and the balloons and the paper get flushed."

"Hmm," the warden said. He thought it over for a minute. "I don't know. But it's better to be safe than sorry. I'll order a search of the cells and sweep away any contraband. And I'll get a man on the roof to keep watch. See if we can't catch these bastards in the act."

Leipfold laughed, slowly at first before descending into a cacophony of wheezes and giggles.

"What?" the warden asked. "What's so funny?"

"It's nothing," Leipfold said, pulling himself together between breaths. "Well, almost nothing."

"Go on."

Leipfold cleared his throat. "I wouldn't bother if I was you," he said. "Especially if you were planning on asking Simmonds."

"Simmonds is a good man," the warden said.

"Yeah," Leipfold said. "I guess he is, if you've got the money."

"What are you talking about?"

"He's taking bribes," Leipfold said. "Bringing stuff in for the cons. You want to know how drugs are coming in? You'd better have a little chat with Mr. Simmonds."

"Simmonds?" the warden murmured. "I don't believe it."

"Take it or leave it," Leipfold said. "It's either that or the hot air balloons."

"You mean the balloons didn't happen?"

"Of course they didn't happen," Leipfold said. "Jesus, if you believe that then you give these idiots way more credit than they deserve. It was Simmonds. Who do you think brought me my brandy?"

"Have you got any proof?"

"Pah!" Leipfold said. "What do you think? I saw him talking to my contact and passing over contraband. That's enough for me and it'll have to be enough for you. Besides, have you seen Simmonds's watch?"

"Of course," the warden replied. "What about it?"

"It's a Rolex," Leipfold said. "One of the best. You think he paid for that on his prison salary?"

"Perhaps it was a gift."

"Some gift," Leipfold said.

The warden thought about it for a moment. "Hmm," he said. "I'll look into it."

Leipfold waited expectantly for the guvnor to reward him, perhaps with more books or with a better cell. Maybe he'd even knock some time off the sentence. But no, there was none of that. Leipfold heard nothing from the warden, and he never saw Mr. Simmonds again. He didn't even get to drink his brandy.

A Little Justice

LEIPFOLD WAS MINDING HIS OWN BUSINESS when the guards came in. He was alone in his cell, lying back on his bunk and staring absentmindedly at the ceiling. Even up there, the paint and the plaster were covered with the rambling graffiti of a dozen different prisoners. Sometimes, when he was bored, he'd allow his eyes to wander over it again, just in case he saw something he'd missed. But that was unlikely, not with his memory. Like an elephant, he never forgot.

The screws ordered him to stand with his back against the wall, and he quickly obeyed them. He knew what happened if you tried civil disobedience and he didn't feel like being taken to the hole. So instead, he stood back and allowed them to cuff him and to drag him unceremoniously out of his cell, along the gantry, down the steps and through the administrative building towards the warden's office.

"What's this about?" Leipfold asked.

But the guards just shook their heads and continued to lead him on in silence. When they arrived at the warden's office, the guards were quickly dismissed and Leipfold was shown to his usual seat in front of the mahogany desk.

"Ah," the warden said, "Leipfold."

"Good morning, sir," Leipfold said. "To what do I owe this pleasure?"

"Yes," he replied. "About that. Thing is, Leipfold, your name has been brought to my attention in connection with an assault."

"An assault?"

"An assault," the warden repeated. "An assault on your good friend Bear to be more precise."

"When did this happen?"

"Best guess, a couple of hours ago," the warden said. "You didn't happen to leave your cell, did you?"

Leipfold shook his head.

"Can anyone corroborate that?"

"Like who?" Leipfold said. "My invisible cellmate? What's this all about, anyway?"

"Yes," the warden said. "Well, about that. You see, my network of…uh…informants says that you're responsible. I don't need to remind you, of course, that this is a serious matter. Bear is in the hospital wing."

"Is he okay?"

"He'll live," the warden said. "But he's livid. If he hears these rumours, he's going to want to ask you a couple of questions of his own. The attack left him blind in one eye, for God's sake. It doesn't look like there's any neural damage, but it's not always easy to tell."

"But it wasn't me," Leipfold protested. "Bear should know that. Have you talked to him?"

"Of course," the warden said. "He doesn't remember a thing."

"Let's hope he gets his memory back," Leipfold said. "What happened to him?"

"I was hoping you might be able to tell me," the warden said. "It looks like he was attacked by some sort of heavy weight inside a sock. It must have been personal. They did their best to try to kill the guy."

"That's awful," Leipfold said. "I'll send him some grapes."

"I don't think you're taking this seriously," the warden replied. "Do I need to remind you that you're up for parole?"

"No," Leipfold said. "I'm aware of that."

"This could seriously compromise your chances."

"I didn't do anything," Leipfold protested.

"Would you tell me if you did?"

"No," he admitted. "But that doesn't mean a thing."

"You may be right," the warden said. "But I have to do something. I'm giving you a week. Find out who did it and report back to me. If you don't come up with the goods, I'm going to hold you on suspicion of assault."

"Listen," Leipfold said. "I'm not admitting anything and I can't condone anything that your mystery assailant did, but from what the other cons have been saying, he got what he deserved."

"What's the rumour?" the warden asked. He leaned towards Leipfold until their faces were barely a foot apart. "Tell me."

"I don't know if I should," Leipfold said. "I haven't decided whether I believe it."

"Goddamn it, Leipfold," the warden bellowed, smashing his fist into the table and upsetting a half-eaten plate of wilted salad. "Tell me what you know."

Leipfold sighed and leaned back in his chair to avoid the worst of the warden's spittle. It settled in Leipfold's ragged, ginger beard like little flecks of dandruff.

"There's a rumour," Leipfold said. "Just a rumour, mind you. They're saying Bear is up for appeal and that he might be getting out. The boys on the yard think there's someone who doesn't want him to ever see the outside. And there's more."

"More?"

"Bear's in for armed robbery, right?" Leipfold said. He didn't wait for the warden to reply. "Well, there are people who think he's paying karma's price for something else. They say he's a sex pest. That he's done a few things that he shouldn't have done, to put it mildly. And as you can imagine, that puts him pretty low on the prison's pecking order. You want me to find out who beat him up? It could have been anyone."

"I'll search his quarters and see what I can find," the warden said. "But you're going to have to work with me on this one."

"Will there be anything else?"

The warden shook his head and said that there wasn't.

Leipfold heard about the search a couple of days later. The warden didn't take the time to update him, so he had to hear it through the grapevine. A Scotsman named Rod—one of Bear's cronies and a strong contender for the hardest man in the prison—gave Leipfold an update in hushed tones in the rec room.

"They found some nasty shit in there," Rod said. "Photos beneath his bed. Photos you'd never want to see."

"Photos?" Leipfold repeated. "What of?"

"Kids," Rod said, but he left it at that.

The news had spread halfway across the jail by the evening, and it was the main topic of conversation in the morning. Leipfold had spent the night thinking, catching just an hour or two of sleep. When he woke up in the morning, he was ready.

He cornered Rod in the exercise yard—if you could call it that when the man could have ploughed Leipfold into the ground without breaking a sweat—and outlined his proposition while the sun was still climbing in the sky.

"I need a favour," Leipfold said.

"I'm listening," Rod replied, which was a good sign. Leipfold had expected the man to laugh in his face, so he steeled his nerves and told Rod what he wanted from him. "What's in it for me?"

Leipfold thought about it for a moment. "Well, for a start," he said, "you'd be helping me to get out of this dump."

"Not interested."

"Okay," Leipfold replied. "Perhaps there's something I can help you with. Something I can do in return."

Rod thought it over for a moment. He looked Leipfold up and down again, trying to figure out how much he could trust him. "Well," he said, eventually. "There is one thing. But I don't think you'll be able to do much."

"You'd be surprised," Leipfold said. "What is it?"

"I was in a gang," Rod explained. "Back in Glasgow. I was one of the Scallies, but I wasn't exactly spoiled for choice."

"I can imagine," Leipfold said.

"I'll cut to the chase," the man replied. "I hear you're a good thinker. Well, perhaps you can think on this. I've been offered a reduced sentence if I testify, and our Joan has a kid on the way. I want to talk. I want to get out of here."

"So what's the problem?"

"You don't understand," Rod replied. "If I talk, they'll kill her. They'll kill me, too. They'll kill everyone I care about."

"It could just be a threat."

But Rod shook his head, exposing the tattoos on his thick, bullish neck. They wormed their way across his veins like lines on a cartographer's work-in-progress.

"Okay," Leipfold said. "I can see how that might be a problem. And if I help you, you'll help me, right?"

"Right."

"Why don't you just go to the cops?"

"I ain't no snitch," Rod said. A vein popped on his forehead and he cracked his knuckles threateningly. Leipfold found himself taking an involuntary step backwards in case the man punched him, but there was no need to worry. He whirled around and punched the wire mesh around the exercise yard instead, earning himself a stern reprimand from one of the guards in the process.

"But you're talking to me," Leipfold said.

"Like I said, I ain't no snitch," Rod replied. "But if I tell you and then you snitch…well, that's not my problem. Besides, I just want my family to be safe. This gives me some extra protection."

Leipfold thought about it for a moment. Then he said, "What the hell? Let's do it. Can you give me any names?"

"Yeah," Rod said, and so he did, starting with the Scotsman at the top, a guy called Angus MacDonald. Leipfold jotted them dutifully down inside his notebook and promised that he'd do his best, a plan already forming inside the brain that hid beneath his thick crop of ginger hair. Leipfold nodded at Rod and then quickly walked away to spend some time alone to mull things over.

*   *   *

Leipfold and his fellow prisoners were allowed one call a week. They had to be placed from a dreary communal room with grey walls and no windows. He was separated from inmates on either side by a pair of thin metal wings and a half-length curtain that was designed to give prisoners privacy while still allowing the guards to see what—if anything—was going on.

But Leipfold had a good reason for not wanting to be overheard. He was calling the local police station, and he asked the receptionist if they could put him straight through to Jack Cholmondeley.

Cholmondeley didn't let him down.

"Leipfold," he said. "Calling from Reading Jail, no less. How's it treating you?"

"Ah, you know," Leipfold said. "Can't complain. The food could be better."

"Right."

There was an awkward pause, and Leipfold and Cholmondeley both fell back into detective mode, listening to the ambient noise that was filtering in from the other end of the line and trying to picture the other man's surroundings.

"Listen, Jack," Leipfold said eventually. "I need a favour."

Cholmondeley whistled softly through his teeth. "You've got a lot of guts, James," he said. "You're a convict, and I'm a policeman. By rights, I shouldn't even be talking to you. Why should I help?"

"Easy," Leipfold said. "Because if you help me, I'll help you to catch a criminal."

"Interesting. Tell me more."

"It's out of your jurisdiction," Leipfold said, "You'd need to work with the Scots. Get it right, though, and you'll be on the front page of the papers. This isn't just any crime. It's international."

"Have you got any proof of wrongdoing?"

"I'm working on it."

"If there's no proof, my hands are tied," Cholmondeley said. "Sorry."

"What if I get some?"

"Then perhaps I can help," Cholmondeley said.

"Great," Leipfold replied. "Listen, I can get you the proof you need. But I need you to make a call for me."

"Why can't you do it yourself?"

"I get one call per week," Leipfold said. "And I just used this week's call on you."

"So wait until next week," Cholmondeley replied.

"I can't," Leipfold said, and then he explained why. Cholmondeley listened with mounting interest as Leipfold told him about the attack on Bear, the deal with Rod and the parole that he was hoping—perhaps naively—to be awarded. Then he started listing names and accusations, and Cholmondeley jotted them down as quickly as he could, occasionally asking Leipfold to repeat himself.

"Why didn't this geezer try to cut a deal during his arrest?" Cholmondeley asked.

"Some bullshit about honour," Leipfold replied. "You know how it is with cons. He didn't want to be a snitch. And he doesn't want his family to get hurt."

"If we can catch a few of these bastards, we'll take care of him," Cholmondeley said. "We'll put him and his family on witness protection, if we have to. But we'll need to do a little digging first. Can you call me again?"

"Not for another week," Leipfold reminded him.

"Okay," Cholmondeley said. "Then I'll be waiting."

They finished just as Leipfold's call hit the limit. He was

automatically cut off just as Cholmondeley was repeating his instructions back to him.

* * *

Leipfold and Rod weren't idle as they waited for the week to pass for their next phone call. Rod had a lead of his own to follow up with.

"Ever heard of the Joyner twins?" he asked. It was late one evening, when most of the convicts were locked away in their cells, but Rod ran the block and so the guards—and the prisoners—gave him certain privileges. One of those was the right to talk to whoever he wanted to whenever he wanted, within reason, although it had been getting harder since Simmonds had left. The warden had been cracking down on corruption, and it was beginning to show.

Leipfold shook his head and Rod continued, "They were old cronies of Bear's, back in the day. Then they got involved in the underworld and started working for MacDonald. Now they're in here. Not on our wing, perhaps, but I can pull a few strings and get a meeting."

"To what end?"

"To put the frighteners on them," Rod said. "Maybe see if we can get them to testify."

Leipfold thought about it for a moment. "How?" he asked.

But Rod already had an answer. "Blackmail," he said. "What else? Word is, the guvnor has a soft spot for you. These two lads have more than enough reason to want to get back at Bear. They might not have carried it out, but they sure as shit had something to do with it. We'll tell them to testify against the Scallies or we'll have them up in front of the warden for the assault on Bear. They could be looking at attempted murder."

"I don't like it," Leipfold admitted. "But perhaps it's for the greater good."

"Yeah," Rod said. "Something like that."

It wasn't the best plan, but it was the only plan they had. Rod pulled a few strings and the meeting went ahead the following afternoon. He'd bought ten minutes alone in the rec room by paying one of the guards the equivalent of a week's wages. It had taken Rod two months to earn it, and he was one of the major players in the prison's black market.

Simon and Charlie Joyner were two big, bald dudes, and Leipfold knew they were trouble as soon as he set eyes on them. They were at least six feet tall and had to stoop to enter the rec room. They were also good looking in a way, with chiselled, stubbly faces, although Simon's nose had been broken in some fight or another and lay a little off centre. They shared the same dark hair and the same unforgiving eyes.

"Better make this quick, Rod," Simon said, while his brother leaned nonchalantly against the wall and picked at his teeth with a dirty fingernail. "We've got places to be."

"Who's this guy?" his brother asked.

"This is James Leipfold," Rod said. "But don't you worry about him. I've got a proposition to put to you. I want you to testify against the Scallies."

The two brothers looked at each other for a moment, a silent understanding passing between them. Then they burst out laughing.

"I'm serious," Rod said, while the laughter continued, raising his voice a little to make himself heard.

"Why would we want to do that?" Charlie asked. He stopped laughing as he said it, and his brother followed suit shortly afterwards. He cracked his knuckles. "You going to make us?"

"Not at all," Rod said. "I'm not asking you to do anything I wouldn't do. With your testimony and mine, the Scallies will be put away and we'll all get sweeter deals. Maybe they'll even knock a couple of years off your sentences."

"Bullshit," Simon said.

"I'm giving you a choice," Rod continued. "Either you testify against the Scallies and help me to put them away, or I tell the warden that you were behind the attack on Bear."

"He won't believe you."

"No," Rod admitted. "But he'll bloody well believe James Leipfold here."

The twins turned to look at Leipfold. It looked as though his reputation in the jail hadn't gone unnoticed because they didn't ask who he was. They already knew.

"So," Simon said. "It's blackmail, is it?"

"That's about the size of it."

Simon laughed. Then, without warning, he threw a fist at Rod and caught him with a solid right hook to the eye. Rod took the hit, but he reacted quickly and swung his head forward to give Simon a Glasgow kiss. Meanwhile, Charlie had moved on Leipfold, but Leipfold saw the guy's size as a weakness and used his speed to stay on top of him. By the time that Rod had climbed on top of the first brother and started pummelling his head against the concrete, Leipfold had the other one in a headlock. Charlie was trying to elbow him in the side to loosen his grip, so Leipfold applied a little more pressure, cutting off the man's oxygen.

"This isn't a fight you boys can win," Rod said. Simon Joyner was showing no signs of resistance. While he was still conscious, he'd have one hell of a concussion. His brother was a little better off, but not much. "Think about what we said here. Testify against the Scallies."

Neither of the Joyner twins was in much shape to reply to him, but they wouldn't have had the time either way. A couple of the wardens, two faces that Leipfold didn't recognise, hustled into the room and took in the scene.

"Jesus Christ," one of them said. "I thought you said you were just going to talk."

"I did," Rod said. "And then they jumped us. It's a good job Leipfold was here to help me."

"That's the story, is it?"

Rod smiled a twisted smile, his eye already beginning to swell from the punch he'd taken. "It's the truth," he said. "Check the tapes, if you have any. You'll see exactly what happened."

*   *   *

It was a couple of days later, and Leipfold was starting to worry. His usual fortitude had been replaced by a perpetual state of nail-biting nervousness. He spent most of his time sitting in his cell and working on his case, although he had no idea whether he'd ever get to argue it.

In the afternoon, Leipfold was called into the warden's office. He allowed himself to be manhandled along the gantry with unusual aplomb.

"Sit down, Leipfold," the warden said, but Leipfold was way ahead of him and had already lowered himself into his usual seat in front of the warden's desk.

"What's up?"

"I thought you'd like an update," the warden said. "I've just had your pal Jack Cholmondeley on the phone."

Leipfold tensed and leaned forwards in his chair. "What did he want?" he asked.

"Seems like you provided him with some information," the warden replied. "He wanted me to tell you that the Scottish police have made an arrest. He said, hang on…ah, here it is. He said, 'Tell him the boys did good. They caught the Scallies in action. Last I heard, they had three members of the Scally Gang in custody.' Oh, and he said to tell you that the birds are singing."

"Uh-huh," Leipfold said. "Well, that's good news."

"But what does it mean?"

"Just a little justice," Leipfold said. "Did he ask to speak to the Joyner twins, by any chance?"

"He's already been in to interview them," the warden said. He looked astonished, with one of his eyebrows trying to climb right off his face. "How did you know that?

"I have my ways," Leipfold said. "That means they've decided to talk. Good for them."

"What about Bear?" the warden asked. "Have you figured out what happened to him?"

"Not yet," Leipfold replied. "Is he awake?"

"He's conscious," the warden replied. "But he doesn't remember the attack."

"Tell him not to worry about it," Leipfold said. "I have a feeling that I'll have something for you any day now."

*   *   *

The next stage of the plan went without a hitch. Leipfold gave Rod the nod, and the two of them met up in the canteen, facing away from each other as they ate and talking in low voices so that they wouldn't be overheard.

"We got them," Leipfold said. "Your boys, the Scallies."

"Yeah?"

"Yeah," Leipfold said. "Three of them, but they matched the descriptions you gave me. You sure that'll be enough?"

"I hope so," Rod said. "We got the ringleaders."

"So you'll testify?"

"I might do," Rod said. "I'll think about it. These are powerful people. They'll make bail, and they'll be able to pay it. And even if not, their lawyers will get them off the hook."

"But you're going to help me," Leipfold said. It wasn't a question. "I held up my end of the bargain. Now it's time for you to hold up yours."

"How about I fight you for it?"

"I'd rather not."

"Another time," Rod said. "I don't know, Leipfold. What if I've changed my mind?"

"Perhaps you should think about your family," Leipfold said. "Remember, Jack Cholmondeley is an old pal of mine. If you don't come through for me, I won't come through for you."

"All right," Rod said. "I'll think about it."

*   *   *

The Scotsman disappeared the following day, and Leipfold later heard a rumour that he'd agreed to testify.

Good on him, Leipfold thought.

He was unsurprised that afternoon when the guards rattled his door and ordered him to follow them to the warden's office.

"How can I help?" Leipfold asked, once he was safely sitting down in his usual place in front of the mahogany desk.

"Ah, Leipfold," the warden said. "I have news for you. Looks like you're off the hook. I've received some new information on the attack on Bear."

"You have?"

"I have indeed." The warden paused for a moment, his lips twitching like the curtains on a suburban street. They broke into a smile. "I'm sorry for ever suspecting you, James."

"So who was behind it?"

"Oh," the warden said. "Just some Scottish chap. Rod, I think his name was. He came clean and told me all about it. Must have had a guilty conscience."

"Must have," Leipfold said. "So what happened to him?"

"I'm sure he'll get away with it," the warden said. "What with those photos we found, the guards will turn a blind eye to it. And besides. He testified against his old gang, and your pal Cholmondeley's lot locked them all up. Rod's getting out early and joining his family. They'll be given new identities, and we can all sleep easier knowing there's a little less scum on the streets."

"Fancy that," Leipfold murmured.

"Anyway," the warden said, clapping him on the shoulder. "That's good news for you, of course. I'll be giving you a clean bill when they put you up in front of the probationary board. I'll even recommend that they release you, as much as it pains me to do so. We've got a date, too. Six weeks. Think that'll be long enough for you to pack your stuff?"

"Only six weeks?" Leipfold replied. "Well damn, I'd better start getting ready."

* * *

That night, alone in his cell as the other convicts slept off another eventful day in the jailhouse, Leipfold was settling in for the night. He was lying on his bed and scoring a narrow gash in the wall with a fingernail, ticking the first day off in the tally chart that would count out the days until he was released. He was ready for it. He'd been rehabilitated.

When the graffiti was complete, he turned to the sock beneath his bed. It was just a plain, white, prison-issue gym sock, but with a few red stains on it that looked like little spots of rust. And it was heavy, bulky, like a foot was already in it. Leipfold held it up to the light.

He climbed out of bed and surveyed his cell, then spent a few cautious seconds listening at the door. When he was as sure as he could be that he wouldn't be disturbed, he upended the sock and scattered pebbles and grit across the floor.

He swept them beneath his bed with a bare foot, then spent the next two hours unpicking the sock and flushing the threads down the toilet. He whistled while he worked.

The Interviews

IT WAS AN EARLY AUTUMN EVENING, and Leipfold was sitting alone in the beer garden at the Rose & Crown, wondering how and why the last six years had happened.

Leipfold wasn't drinking, and his mind and his body both felt better for it. Not that he had much else to do with his time. No girlfriend, no friends, and two dead parents who'd left the world too early. He was living in a halfway house, a hostel that had agreed to take him in for thirty days while he sorted his life out. All he had were his meagre savings, and they wouldn't last for long.

So he did the only thing that he could think of. He hopped on his bike and cycled off towards the dole office. He needed to sign on.

The woman that he spoke to was a dowdy fifty-something in a shapeless frock from a charity shop. She had a husky voice from too many cigarettes and smelled faintly of stale alcohol. Leipfold couldn't stop thinking about it. The smell haunted him, and he had to constantly remind himself of the work he'd put in to get clean.

"What do you want?" she asked him. She sounded bored and angry at the same time.

Then again, he thought, *why would they care? They're doing me a favour, after all. I guess they don't get paid extra for human kindness.*

"I'd like to register as a jobseeker," Leipfold said. "I need some money. Give me what you've got."

"Uh-huh," the woman said. "And what kind of work are you looking for?"

"Anything where I can use my brain," Leipfold said. "I've always thought about becoming a private detective."

"A private detective?" She laughed. "I don't think so. The police force, maybe. But you've got a record, so that's gone. A bouncer, perhaps? But no, you're a little on the short side. Maybe we could get you some work in a warehouse."

"I don't want to work in a warehouse," Leipfold said.

The woman shrugged. "Sometimes we just have to take what we get given," she told him. "You don't have the luxury of being picky."

"Still," Leipfold said. "There must be something else."

"Okay, Mr. Leipfold, let me see what I can do. We've got a few potential matches. I'm going to get you all set up, and then I'll give you a call in the next few days once we've arranged an interview. Please can you double check your phone number?"

"I have an impeccable memory," Leipfold said. "That's the right number. And if it doesn't work, you can call my probation officer or the halfway house. Trust me, I'm not going anywhere."

The woman frowned at him and pursed her lips. Then she shook her head. "You're not very good at obeying authority figures," she said. "Are you, Mr. Leipfold?"

Leipfold just ignored her.

*   *   *

The first interview was scheduled for the following Tuesday. Leipfold had been told to go to a garage on the outskirts of town, and he dutifully turned up at the appointed hour. He found the place without too much trouble. There were a half dozen cars pulled up outside with prices in their windscreens. To the left of them, a single motorbike was propped up on its kickstand, its chromium gleaming in the sunlight. It was a beautiful machine. It seemed to sing. It seemed to sing to *him*.

Then the garage's owner came out, a weasel-faced guy who reeked of cigarette smoke. He was wearing bright yellow coveralls that were stained with oil and mud and gunk. Leipfold was wearing his only suit, and the man took exception to him immediately.

"Do you know what a mechanic does, boy?"

"Boy?" Leipfold repeated. "Who are you calling 'boy'? I'm not much younger than you are."

"That doesn't matter," the mechanic said. "When you're working for me, I'll call you whatever I want to."

Leipfold growled, but he bit his tongue and managed to stop himself from replying. He pointed over to the motorbike.

"How much for the bike?"

"You could never afford it."

"One day, she'll be mine," he said. He looked the man directly in the eye. The mechanic took a step backwards. There was a ferocity in that gaze, the kind of stare that could bubble up the paint on a wall.

"**I don't like you,**" the mechanic decided.

"You don't know me," Leipfold replied. "You only just met me."

"Still," he said. "I don't like you. I haven't liked you since I set eyes on you. But I believe in giving a man a chance where I can, so here's what I'm going to do. I want you to start right away and show me what you've got. We've got a bunch of odd jobs that need doing and no hands to do them. You can start on grease duty. Go and help the boys. They're refitting an engine in Bay C."

"In this suit?"

"You can change into overalls," the mechanic said. "We'll have some spares in your size. Get someone to check the lost and found."

"Great," Leipfold said. He shook hands with the boss and followed him through into a back room.

It was a tedious first day. Leipfold wasn't exactly a petrol-head, but he liked to think he knew cars. He certainly knew them well enough to identify a half-dozen inefficiencies by the time that they broke for a brew and a sneaky cigarette. But none of the men would listen to him. It was as though they didn't *want* to work more efficiently. As though they didn't *care* about their jobs. Well,

Leipfold didn't care for the job either, but that didn't stop him from suggesting improvements.

At the end of the day, when the final vehicle had rolled off the premises, Leipfold was left alone with the owner, who didn't look too happy to see him again.

"So how did I do?" Leipfold asked.

"About that," the mechanic said. "You did a good job. The boys were impressed with your work, and so was I for that matter. But there's something I just don't like about you. I'm sorry, young man."

"Don't call me young man."

"Hmph," the man replied. He held out a couple of bank notes. "Take these. It's your pay for today. But don't come back tomorrow."

Leipfold groaned. "Why not?" he asked.

"I don't like your attitude," the mechanic said. "You have thoughts above your station. I've no use for that. I need a man who can follow instructions. A cog in the machine. I don't need a man like you."

"I see," Leipfold said, and he did. The man felt threatened. He knew that Leipfold wouldn't stand for any shit, and he knew that his business was full of it.

It wasn't until he got home and started running a shower that Leipfold realised he was still wearing the garage's blue overalls.

And that meant that his best—and only—suit was still at the lot.

*　　*　　*

The second interview was at Tesco. Leipfold hadn't collected his suit, so he showed up wearing a smart blue cardigan and a pair of black jeans. They were complemented by plain trainers and a smart leather bag that hung from his shoulder. He was interviewed by an efficient young woman who could have passed for his little sister, but Leipfold wasn't bothered by her age. He had no problem with taking orders from people who were younger than him, as long as he agreed with the orders.

It was going surprisingly well. Leipfold had made no secret of his bigger ambitions, but the woman was sympathetic and Leipfold guessed that she had big plans of her own—plans that didn't involve working at a supermarket.

Leipfold had been shown around the warehouse and taught how to use the pricing machine. He was looking forward to trying his hand behind the counter. If there was one thing that he thought he was good at, it was talking to people. But he wasn't expecting them to station him behind the cigarette counter.

"It's not the cigarettes that are the problem," Leipfold explained. "It's the bottles of brandy and the whiskey. Even the vodka. I don't want to be around them."

"Why not?"

"I'd rather not say," Leipfold said. "Would you ask a vegetarian to work the meat counter?"

"If they wanted the job, I would," the woman replied. "We have no use for specialisms here. We're looking for people to work on rotation, covering staff that are on leave or otherwise absent. You don't get to pick and choose what you work on."

"Ah," Leipfold said. "That might be a problem."

"Why's that?"

Leipfold considered it for a moment and then mentally shrugged. *What the hell?* he thought. So he told the woman about his problems with the bottle.

"I see," she said when Leipfold had finished.

"So do I get the job?" Leipfold asked.

She looked him up and down as though she were trying to read his mind or guess his weight.

"Are you clean now?" she asked.

"I am," Leipfold said. "I haven't touched a drop since I got locked up. I go to meetings and everything. I'm a changed man."

The woman nodded. "Okay," she said. "Well, thanks for being honest with me. I'm going to have to think on it."

*   *   *

It was two weeks later, and Leipfold hadn't heard anything from the friendly woman at the supermarket. He assumed, correctly, that he hadn't got the job. It was a blow, but it was hardly a surprise. At least he wouldn't have to serve the other booze-hounds and handle his nemesis on a daily basis.

Leipfold's third interview was at McDonald's. He wore the same outfit he'd worn to the supermarket, already resigned to the fact that he'd come home reeking of chip fat and desperation. He was expecting another failure of an interview, but he was offered the job there and then and started the following Monday.

He was working with a familiar face. Donnie Flowers was all grown up, but he still had the same mischievous face that Leipfold remembered from his youth. Flowers remembered him too, if only vaguely, and they struck up an unlikely friendship as they worked together behind the counter. It turned out that Flowers had served time in the same facility as Leipfold, although he'd been released a couple of months before Leipfold had been shown inside. He'd been in the same unit as Jimmy Squires.

Neither of them liked their job, but it was the best they could hope for. The fast food chain, with its profits in the hundreds of millions of dollars, paid minimum wage, but Leipfold was still living in the halfway house and so the money went straight into his wallet. Better still, with no booze to bother him, he didn't have to spend it on the bottle. Not that it wasn't tempting.

Still, the job seemed to be going well, at least in the early days. Then, towards the end of his third week as he was finally making plans to move out of the hostel, disaster struck.

It all started with a troublesome customer who wouldn't take no for an answer. It was a kid in a shell suit, maybe fifteen years old at best with a wispy little moustache that made him look like a potato that had started to go off. He wanted some McNuggets.

"But, sir," Leipfold said, "we're all out. We've put a fresh batch on but they're not going to be ready for a while. You'll have to pick something else from the menu."

"Nah, mate," the customer said. "I'll have the McNuggets."

"We're all out," Leipfold repeated. "Are you deaf? What do you expect me to do? Pull them out of my arse?"

The kid's face flushed and made him look like he'd had a sudden allergic reaction. Leipfold imagined stabbing him in the eye with an epi-pen and suppressed a smile.

"Get me the manager," the kid said.

"I am the manager," Leipfold lied.

"Then get me head office."

Leipfold leaned in close to the kid and grabbed him by the collar. He dragged him across the counter towards him, not caring who was looking but wondering vaguely about the implications if his parole officer heard about it. He leaned in a little further until the kid's spotty nose took up half of his peripheral vision and said those three fatal words.

"Go fuck yourself," Leipfold said.

And that was the end of his career at McDonald's.

*   *   *

Leipfold was depressed.

He'd been turfed out of his lodgings and called a timewaster by the employment agency, who'd told him they'd give him a call if something came up. Leipfold suspected that it wouldn't.

So he'd fallen back into old habits and made his way to the Rose & Crown. Cedric was still the landlord, although he'd started to look his age. His hair had been clipped short on the top and sides, and it hung low in a little grey ponytail from the back. Still, his wizened face broke into a smile as his eyes alighted on Leipfold.

"It's you!" Cedric said.

"It's me!" Leipfold replied.

"How the devil are you?"

"I'm grand," Leipfold said. "It's been too long."

"It has," Cedric agreed. "What can I get for you?"

"Just a lemonade."

"A lemonade?"

"I'd rather not talk about it," Leipfold said, gloomily. "Just get me a lemonade."

"Sure thing," Cedric said. Leipfold waited for him to finish pouring it and then carried it over to his usual table, which was still in its usual place, though it looked a little faded by the weight of time. Cedric was even still ordering the papers, although one of them had gone defunct while Leipfold had been inside. He opened up *The Tribune* and browsed through the job ads.

Half an hour or so later, when he'd reached the bottom of his glass of lemonade, he walked back up to the bar and ordered a lager.

"Are you sure?" Cedric asked. "I thought you were dry."

"I was," Leipfold said. "I am. Or maybe I was. I don't know. Just go ahead and get me that lager."

"If you say so." The landlord stroked his beard thoughtfully and hesitated before he pulled the pump, but he did as Leipfold asked and poured out a tall glass of amber. He slid it across the bar to Leipfold, who thanked him and then took the drink back over to his table.

He spent twenty minutes examining it from different angles, smelling it, swilling it gently around the glass and watching the thin froth die down. He was barely aware of the thoughts that were running through his head, but even if he'd noticed them, he wouldn't have been able to explain them.

Leipfold held the glass up to his face and put it to his lips. Then he put it back down again as he spied a familiar face walking in through the doorway.

Rod was wearing a hat pulled low across his face and a heavy coat to ward off the weather, but it was unmistakably him. The time between their meetings had treated him kindly. He'd dyed his hair and grown a beard, but there was something in the way that the man held himself that oozed confidence. Leipfold caught his eye and nodded at him.

Rod bought a drink at the bar and then came to sit down beside Leipfold. He perched himself with his back to the rest of the pub and kept his voice low as though he didn't want to be overheard. That didn't surprise Leipfold. Last he'd heard, the man sitting in front of him was under witness protection, living under a changed name so that the Scottish Scally gang didn't hunt him down and cut him into pieces.

"Fancy seeing you here," Leipfold said. "What happened to witness protection?"

"Shhh," Rod said. "Keep your voice down. No one knows I'm here. Let's keep it that way."

"Fair enough," Leipfold replied. "So what do you want? I assume you're here to talk to me."

"You assume correct," Rod replied. "How did you guess?"

"It'd be a bit of a coincidence if the two of us just happened to bump into each other," Leipfold said. "Do you know the odds?"

"Nope."

"I do." Leipfold stared moodily at the full pint glass in front of him. "How can I help?"

"I've got a job for you," Rod said.

"I don't need a job."

"That's not what I heard." Rod grinned and took a swig from his drink, then lifted it up in a toast to Leipfold. "Nothing like being a free man, eh?"

"I guess."

Rod leaned in a little closer. "Look," he murmured. "I've got two grand with your name on it. It's an easy job, nothing illegal, and you're just the man to do it for me. I need you to tail a business associate of mine and report back on his movements."

Leipfold looked at him, cautiously. "You're not talking about one of your old Scally friends, right?"

"No, nothing like that."

"Hmm," Leipfold murmured. "Well, I guess I could use the excitement."

*   *   *

Rod and Leipfold used the next hour to hatch plans, and then Leipfold left the bar without touching his pint.

He woke up the next morning with a clear head and an investigation to embark upon. He spent the next couple of days following the man that Rod had told him about.

Leipfold hadn't been given the mark's name, but he didn't need it. Rod had also given him a handful of Polaroids in a plain brown envelope, and Leipfold had committed each one of them to memory so that he could follow his mark without having to constantly check his face against the photograph. The man had a plain face and the thinning thatch of hair that was the common uniform for men of a certain age. He had that going for him, at least. Luckily for Leipfold, he also had an unusual gait, and Leipfold could have pointed him out in a crowd from fifty paces just by looking at the way he walked.

But for the first couple of days at least, nothing unusual happened. Then came the third day, when the suspect broke his routine by cancelling an appointment and heading instead to a hotel. It was a grubby little place, a seedy dive that was quite clearly the domain of travelling students and shady businessmen. Leipfold's mark fit into the latter category.

He watched from a distance as the man walked inside, then he approached the hotel himself at a steady pace. He even tried to go inside, but the receptionist shooed him away when it became clear that he hadn't booked a room. So he did the next best thing, waiting nonchalantly outside the building and trying to look like part of the scenery. It didn't really work, but no one told him to move on, and so Leipfold just lurked there, fading away into the background as the tourists and the commuters worked their way around him.

Leipfold's mark came out an hour later, but this time he had a beautiful, dark-skinned young woman on his arm. He'd seen enough. Even from a distance, he knew it was the same woman he'd seen in some of Rod's photographs.

He tailed them along a couple of streets for as long as he dared and then lost them when they hopped into the back of a taxi cab.

* * *

That night, he met Rod in the Rose & Crown and gave him an update. The ex-con was in a good mood to begin with, but that soon changed when Leipfold gave him the news. When Leipfold told him about the rendezvous at the sleazy hotel, Rod dropped his head into his hands and cursed into his pint of lager.

"Goddamn it," he murmured. "That little bitch."

"She's a friend of yours?"

"Something like that," Rod said. "She's my lover."

"Aren't you married?"

"Yeah," Rod said. "So what?"

"Carry on, then."

"Yes, well," Rod said, taken aback somewhat and losing steam. "She's supposed to be mine. She's supposed to be waiting for me. But she's not, is she?"

"Apparently not," Leipfold said. "Who's the guy?"

"That's Steve," Rod said, waving a hand dismissively. "He's an... uh, an old business acquaintance."

"Is he a Scally?"

Rod hesitated for a moment and then slowly nodded his head.

"You bastard," Leipfold said. "You told me this wasn't dangerous. I was following a gangster?"

"Retired," Rod said. "But I get your point. Sorry, Leipfold, but you know how it is. He knows me. He would have recognised me. I needed help, and I figured you were the only person in the world that could give it."

"Well, I'm sorry to be the bearer of bad news," Leipfold replied. "You asked me to carry out surveillance, so I did. You can't complain about what I saw. That's not how it works."

"You're right," Rod admitted. "But I knew if I told you the full story, you wouldn't help me. That son of a bitch. I'm going to kill him."

"No," Leipfold said, shaking his head. "Don't do that. Beat him up if you need to, but no weapons. It's not worth it. You've got the chance to have a new life. Why risk it all to get even?"

Rod sighed. He looked down at the table and cracked his knuckles, picked up his drink and took a deep gulp from it and then set it back down on the table.

"You're right," he said. "Of course, you are. But he'll get what's coming to him."

"Do what you've got to do," Leipfold said. "But keep the woman out of it."

"You're too much of a gentleman," Rod said. "I'm glad you're not on the inside."

"Likewise."

"You're good at this." Rod grinned at Leipfold and then reached into his wallet. He withdrew a handful of notes—more notes than Leipfold had ever seen in a single place—and then threw them on the table in front of them, not even bothering to count them. "Maybe you should do it for a living."

Rod finished his drink and set the glass down, then shook

Leipfold's hand, stood up and walked out of the pub. Leipfold looked down at the table and started to gather the bank notes in his fist.

"Maybe I should," he murmured.

In Business

LEIPFOLD WAS IN BUSINESS.

Sure, he was sleeping on a friend's sofa and running the business from the Rose & Crown, but he'd made a start and that was the main thing. He'd registered the company with HMRC, opened up a speculative bank account and put a couple of adverts in the Yellow Pages. It wasn't much, but it was a start.

Besides, he was already bringing in a little business through word of mouth alone. He'd been surprised by how many people had heard of him, the people whose lives he'd touched when he was younger. They all bubbled up out of the woodwork. He was making so much money that he'd put a deposit down on an office, a cosy, empty little place on Balcombe Street, just round the corner from Marylebone Station. He hadn't moved in yet, but he was looking forward to picking up the keys and he'd already planned out the layout to the last square foot.

Against his better judgement, Leipfold had taken out a loan from one of Rod's mates from the underworld. The guy was a shark, but that was okay. Leipfold had found a way to manage him, and they'd struck up a deal where Leipfold did a little work for him in exchange for paying no interest, although he still needed to earn a couple of grand to finish paying him off and to square up. But it was worth it, especially now that he was turning over something resembling a profit, and it made up for the fact that no bank in the world would have lent a man like him any money.

Most of the work was boring and repetitive, research-based stuff that Leipfold could carry out from anywhere. His days followed a simple routine. Every morning, he'd head over to the library and do the crossword in one of their reading rooms before winding his way between the shelves to find the books that he needed for the day. He got most of his information from a combination of the local papers and obscure records from nearby parishes, but he also learned a lot from non-fiction books about fingerprinting and a new, up-and-coming field called forensics.

One of his main clients was *The Tribune*, the local paper. Leipfold had come across one of the adverts in their classifieds, replied to it, been invited in and eventually offered up a first assignment, which he passed with flying colours. His work consisted of tracking people down for the journalists, mostly people on the shadier side of society, the working-class hustlers looking for a quick buck in the big city by playing fast and loose with the law.

One morning, a couple of days before his move to Balcombe Street, Leipfold was summoned to *The Tribune*'s offices for a new brief. They handed him a file with the little information that they'd been able to gather, then sent him off to find a woman called Jessica Beard.

"Who is she?" Leipfold asked. "And why do you want me to find her?"

"She killed her husband and went on the run," Jan Evans, the paper's editor, said. As well as being Leipfold's boss, she was a skilled writer and an amateur cryptologist, so the two of them got on like brothers and sisters from other mothers and misters.

"Great," Leipfold said. "Thanks for telling me. Shouldn't we leave this to the police?"

"I don't need you to confront her," Evans replied. "You know us. We don't want trouble. We just want to sell papers. If you find her, we'll have to tell the cops, and I'm not sure that we want that attention. But if you can get us a statement—maybe even an interview—then we get the best of both worlds. What do you say?"

Leipfold frowned. "I'll do my best," he said. "Where do I start?"

"We've managed to track down a childhood friend of hers. We've also got rumours that the husband had a lover, a Miss Rita Long."

"Give me the information on Beard, I'll talk to her first," Leipfold said.

And so Evans gave him an address, and he followed the trail up north to the Midlands. The childhood friend of the murderess came from a small town called Nuneaton, a dull little place that seemed to be full of working-class grafters and OAPs. To Leipfold, it was the epitome of working-class Britain, a typical small town that was built on the sweat of coal miners and factory workers.

According to the brief he'd been given, Jessica Beard was suspected of shooting her husband. The police had released a statement to say she was a person of interest, and they'd warned the public to stay away. There was even a hotline for anyone with information. Meanwhile, friends and relatives were coming out of the woodwork now that the story was starting to break. One man, an ex-boyfriend of hers, had told *The Tribune* that she was in the habit of making death threats. He'd also shared his theory that she'd killed her husband for his money. He'd told the paper that "she's the type" and dropped a hint that her husband had been cheating on her. Leipfold didn't know how much to credit this guy, but intelligence was intelligence. He'd learned back in the army that sometimes you had to trust it until you could prove otherwise.

All of this information gave Leipfold a few ideas, but Evans had a few of her own. She'd ordered Leipfold to track down the childhood friend and to follow any leads from there. Leipfold was expecting resistance, but the friend had been paid off by the paper and was more than happy to answer his questions.

"I might not be much help, mind," she said. "We ain't that close."

"That's okay," Leipfold replied. "Can I come in?"

"Sure."

"What's your name again?" he asked.

The woman laughed and told Leipfold that she was a Pamela, a fact that he remembered just as soon as she mentioned it.

"Thanks, Pamela," Leipfold said. "Mind if I call you Pam?"

"You can call me Thomas if you like," she said. "Makes no difference to me. What do you want?"

"I'm trying to get hold of Jessica Beard."

"Of course," she said. They'd reached her living room. She gestured for Leipfold to sit down in one of her battered leather armchairs. He obliged, but she remained standing, looking down at him from a position of power. "You're just like the rest of them."

"The rest of who?"

"The rest of the bloody journalists who won't leave me alone," Pam said. "They're trying to dish up some dirt on Jess, and I want no part in it. For the record, I think she's innocent."

"Interesting," Leipfold said. "Why's that?"

"It's just not like her," Pam said. "She's a vegan for a start. She wouldn't hurt a fly."

Leipfold shrugged. "People change," he said.

"Not Jess," Pam said. "I've known her since we were kids."

"Perhaps you don't know her as well as you think you do."

"Perhaps." Pam sighed and unfolded her arms, then flopped down next to him on the sofa. Leipfold was slightly to her left, but the tension was already starting to dissipate and he almost felt welcome. He decided to chance it by asking for a cuppa, but Pam told him the milk was off and so he settled for a glass of water.

"Well," Leipfold said, "I love a good conspiracy. You say that you think your friend is innocent?"

"Yes."

"I can believe that," Leipfold replied. "I haven't seen anything that convinces me she's guilty. But then, I haven't seen anything to prove her innocence, either. Maybe I can help."

"You can?"

"I can try," Leipfold said. "But you're going to need me to help you to help her."

"Just tell me what you need me to do."

Leipfold grinned. "I need you to make an introduction," he said.

*   *   *

It took some time, but Leipfold managed to convince Pam that he was neither a cop nor a journalist. His best—and only—evidence was the brand new pack of business cards that he'd had delivered a couple of days earlier, but their effect was lessened somewhat because they were still wrapped in plastic. Still, the fledgling detective was a top-tier talker, and he managed to convince her of his integrity if not his abilities.

As a result, he soon found himself in a face-to-face meeting with the woman who he was never supposed to meet. They met up in a small café just off the high street. It was the kind of place that served greasy strips of bacon on chipped plates with little sachets of brown sauce as a side garnish. It was overflowing with builders, painters, decorators and plumbers, the kind of people who wore overalls to work and catcalled women as they walked past.

Jessica Beard was an attractive young woman with blonde hair and a pleasant smile. She carried herself well and exuded confidence, as Leipfold quickly discovered.

"So how can I help?" she asked.

"It's more a case of how I can help you," Leipfold replied. "But you'll need to tell me what happened."

"I assume you're referring to my husband."

"Correct," Leipfold said. "You're a wanted woman. You're on the run from the police, for God's sake. You're not going to last long, innocent or not. They'll find you."

"But that's not fair," Jessica replied.

"Life isn't fair. Sorry to be the bearer of bad news."

There was a lull in the conversation, which Leipfold punctuated by slapping his fist against the table, splattering a fly and smearing

122

its insides across one of the menus. Jessica flinched and leant away from him.

Hey, Leipfold thought. *She really wouldn't hurt a fly. That friend of hers was right.*

He also thought that if she reacted like that to the death of a fly, there was no way she'd kill a human being. Leipfold knew from experience that it took more than a swat to do the job.

"My client will want to speak to you," Leipfold said. "Would you be willing to talk to the newspapers?"

"Hell no," Jessica replied. "They think I'm guilty. And besides, all they want is a story. They don't want me to tell them what actually happened."

"And what did happen?"

"I have no idea," she said. "I left for work as normal, headed to a few meetings, grabbed some lunch. You know, the usual. I stopped to call the office before I headed back in, and one of my colleagues told me that the police had been over."

She paused for a moment and stifled a sob. Leipfold reached into his shirt pocket and pulled out a handkerchief. He offered it to her, and she took it gratefully. She wiped her eyes on it and then blew her nose. When she handed it back to Leipfold, he took it gingerly and stowed it away in the back pocket of his jeans.

"Do you need a moment?" he asked.

Jessica took a half dozen deep, heaving breaths in an attempt to centre herself. Leipfold read her lips as she counted from zero to twenty. Then she shook her head from side to side like a cat trying to dislodge a drop of moisture.

"I'll be okay," she said. "Where was I?"

"Your colleague told you that the police had been over."

"That's right," Jessica said. "She said they thought I'd killed my husband, so it seemed like a good idea for me to keep my head down. I didn't do it, you understand. I don't want to go to jail for something that I didn't do. It was a set up."

"Perhaps it was," Leipfold said. "I wonder. They must have had their reasons for it. Something doesn't add up here, I wonder—"

"Excuse me, sir?"

Leipfold looked up and took in the newcomer, a man in a chef's outfit who had raggedy black hair that was pulled back behind his head in a net. It didn't take a genius to figure out that he was the chef—or the cook, perhaps, if "chef". was too grand a title for a man who shovelled greasy strips of bacon around on a blackened grill.

"Are you James Leipfold?" the chef asked.

"I might be," Leipfold replied, suspiciously. "It depends who's asking, and why."

"There's a call for you," the man said. "If you could come with me to my office, please."

Leipfold flashed an apologetic glance towards his companion and followed the chef into the inner workings of the restaurant. He tried to ask further questions, but the man was in a rush and brushed him off hurriedly, leaving him alone in the office. The phone lay off its cradle, on the desk. He picked it up.

"This is Leipfold," he said. "What is it?"

"James!" The caller was clearly excited, but Leipfold knew exactly who it was. It was his client, Jan Evans from *The Tribune*, and he had no idea how she'd tracked him down. "Have you met the woman yet?"

"Yeah, I'm with her now," Leipfold replied. "How did you know where to find me?"

"I didn't," Evans said. "I figured you'd be in a pub or a café, so I rang around until someone recognised your description."

"I don't appreciate you looking in on me."

"That doesn't matter," Evans said. "As long as you're working on a job for me, you're an employee. And as long as you're an employee, I can check in on you. Now listen to me."

"I'm listening," Leipfold replied. "But try to make it quick. I've got Jessica Beard waiting for me to go back to the table."

"But that's just it, James," Evans said. "She's dangerous. You need to get out of there."

"I don't think she did it."

"*You* might not," Evans said. "But I do. I've had a tip off from one of my sources. A leak from the police department. They've had the results back on the husband and the cause of death was a single gunshot wound to the head. It was a handgun, James, and guess who's the registered owner of a gun that could fit the bill."

"Jessica Beard?"

"Got it in one," the editor said.

"She doesn't seem the part," Leipfold said. "Listen, I've got to go. She's waiting for me."

"James? Don't you dare—"

But he didn't hear the rest of what she said because he'd already put the phone back in its cradle.

He checked his watch and found that he'd only been away for five minutes or so, but he was worried that Jessica Beard would have been spooked by his disappearance and that he'd go back to an empty table. He'd be able to track her down again if he had to, but he had better things to be doing with his time. He needn't have worried. She was still happily sitting where he'd left her.

"Sorry about that," Leipfold said sheepishly, sitting back down at the table. She looked across at him, shrewdly.

"Important call?" she asked.

"Something like that," Leipfold said. "Listen, I have to ask you something." He leaned a little closer, speaking quietly so that his voice wouldn't carry. "I need you to tell me about the gun."

"What about it?"

"You admit that you're the registered owner of a firearm?" Leipfold asked. Jessica Beard was smiling at him, and Leipfold felt a little unnerved by it. He didn't know many people who had a firearms license, and those who did were generally bad news.

"Why shouldn't I?" she asked. "It's all perfectly legal and above board."

"So are a lot of things," Leipfold said. "That doesn't make them a good idea. Why do you own a gun?"

"For protection."

"From what?"

"From my husband," she said.

Leipfold looked at her. "Did you shoot him?"

"No!" she exclaimed, banging her fist against the chequered tablecloth. A couple of people turned to look at them, and the two of them tried to act inconspicuous until the attention slowly filtered away like water off a duck's back. "I swear to you, Mr. Leipfold. I didn't do it."

"I believe you," Leipfold said, reluctantly. "Do you still have this gun?"

"Of course," she said. "Although for obvious reasons, I don't have it on me right now."

"Right," Leipfold said. "You got it to protect you from your husband, and now your husband's dead."

"That's not quite what I meant."

They trod carefully when they approached Jessica's house, where she'd lived with her husband before his untimely demise. They were both worried that there might be a police presence, and perhaps even a panda car waiting to arrest her as soon as she dared to show her face. But to their surprise, they made it to her front door unmolested, and she was soon offering him a glass of wine from a healthy-sized kitchen cupboard.

"I don't drink," Leipfold said. "Not anymore."

Beard let his response pass without comment, silently pouring a glass of her own before sitting on one of the stools at the kitchen counter and taking a long, deep sip from the wine glass.

"The gun, Jessica," Leipfold said. "Show me the gun."

"Of course," she replied, taking another sip from the glass

before lowering herself gingerly to the floor. "Follow me."

She led the way upstairs, past a small bathroom that was painted a garish lilac, and into the master bedroom. She made a beeline for one of the bedside tables and opened up the drawer. Then she gasped.

"It's not here!" she said. "The fucking thing's not here!"

And then there was a loud knock at the front door, followed by a deep, booming voice that shouted, "Open up, this is the police. We have a warrant."

*　　*　　*

That evening, Jan Evans from *The Tribune* called Leipfold at his hotel. She wasn't happy with his lack of progress. She'd asked him to invoice her for the time so far and to cancel the rest of the investigation, which Leipfold had agreed to do. But he'd already committed himself, and not just by making the journey up north from the capital. Something just didn't seem right.

He met up with Jessica Beard again the following morning. After Leipfold had accompanied her to the police station, she'd been asked a bunch of questions and then released without charge. They didn't have enough to keep her in, not yet at least, and they'd been interested to hear about the missing firearm.

They'd arranged to meet in the hotel's lobby, and she led the way from there to a nearby coffee shop. It was a quiet place, which meant that the two of them could talk without being overheard.

"What the hell am I going to do, Mr. Leipfold?" she asked.

"You need to get a good lawyer," he said. "Tell your side of the story and force them to prove otherwise. But you should talk to the press, too. They can be a powerful ally."

"They've already made up their mind," she said. "But I didn't do it."

"We just need to come up with a different narrative," Leipfold said. "We need to present an alternative set of events to explain what happened here. For example, perhaps your husband committed suicide and set you up to take the fall. Or perhaps it was a hired hit. Did your husband have any enemies?"

"Not that I know of," she said. "But I'm starting to find out that I didn't know my husband as well as I thought I did. That is, if the press can be believed, which they can't."

"If you don't trust the press, you'll have to trust the police," Leipfold said. "You can't do this alone. You need help."

"I thought *you* were going to help me."

"I'm trying to," Leipfold told her. "I'm giving you advice. Tell them your side of the story. If you really are innocent, and I believe you are, then they're looking at you while there's someone still out there."

"You're saying that if I don't turn myself in, they'll kill again?"

"They might do," Leipfold said.

"And what about you?" she asked. "What are *you* going to do?"

"Don't you worry about me," Leipfold said. "I'm going to figure out what happened to that gun."

*   *   *

Leipfold left Nuneaton that evening. All thoughts of Jessica Beard were pushed from his mind the following morning when he moved into his shiny new office. In fact, the next two weeks were so busy that he didn't think of her once. As far as the press was concerned, the story was over. He hadn't heard so much as a rumour.

But that all changed one day when Jack Cholmondeley stopped by. He'd recently been promoted to the rank of sergeant, and he wore it like a badge of honour. It had changed the way he held himself, the way he talked. He was clearly proud of who he was and where he'd come from. Leipfold could relate to that. The new office was doing wonders for his self-esteem, reminding him that he was so much more than just an ex-con who used to have a drinking problem. He was a functional member of society, and no one could take that away from him.

The office was still just a skeleton. Leipfold didn't have the budget to kit it out properly, so it consisted of a second-hand desk from a charity shop and five plastic chairs that he'd salvaged from a skip. He also had a couple of books in the inbuilt bookcases, as well as a cheap plastic kettle in the kitchen area. It didn't look like a serious place of business, but some serious business was already taking place in there.

"Come on in," Leipfold said. "I'll give you the tour."

The tour didn't take long, and the two men were soon sitting side by side on the plastic chairs, drinking coffee and talking about the good old days. For Leipfold, it was just a chit chat, until Jack Cholmondeley mentioned Jessica Beard.

"She's in custody," Cholmondeley explained. "I had my reservations, but the orders came down from above. West Midlands Police took her in and brought her down to us. Then we charged her."

"What with?"

"Murder," Cholmondeley said. "Although she told us a different story. We know that you talked to her, for example. I wondered if you could tell me what happened."

"You know I can't talk about a case, Jack," Leipfold said. "You're asking me to share research that I carried out on someone else's time, and without their permission to boot."

Cholmondeley chuckled. "What else is new?" he asked. "Come on, James. For old times' sake."

"Are you going to make it worth my while?"

"You wouldn't be asking a police officer for a bribe, now, would you, James?" Cholmondeley asked. "I could bust you for that."

Leipfold looked at him and then the two men started laughing.

"Point taken," Leipfold said, and then he launched into the story of his journey up north and Jessica Beard's insistence that she was innocent. Leipfold had no proof, of course, other than the woman's word, but that was all he'd needed.

"As far as my boys are concerned," Cholmondeley said, "it's case closed and Jessica Beard is a murderess. But something just doesn't sit right with me."

"Perhaps there's another option," Leipfold murmured.

"What do you mean?"

"I mean that I think we should look into it," Leipfold said. "What do you say, old friend? Will you help me to uncover the truth?"

* * *

The two men met up later that day after Cholmondeley finished his shift. They knew that the dead man had a lover. Better still, they had a name and address. She was called Rita Long, and she lived on a council estate in Hammersmith. Cholmondeley drove them there in his brand new black BMW, which he'd bought for himself as a treat when he was awarded his promotion. He regretted driving it when he realised where he'd have to park, but he comforted himself with the knowledge that if someone tried to damage or steal her, he'd do his damnedest to come down on them with the full weight of the law.

Rita Long was living with a housemate and a large dog that looked like it had been hit in the face with a shovel. To Leipfold's surprise, they were invited into the living room and granted an audience.

"What can I do for you gentlemen?" Rita asked.

"Good question," Leipfold replied. "We're here to talk about your ex-boyfriend."

"You mean Anders?"

"Is that his name?"

"Yep," Cholmondeley murmured.

"He's not my ex-boyfriend," she said. "It was just sex. Strictly no strings attached."

"And now he's dead," Leipfold said. "Doesn't that bother you?"

She shrugged. "Not really," she said. "I mean, I didn't know him too well. It's sad that he died, but you know. Life moves on."

"Not for Anders," Cholmondeley said.

"We were wondering whether there's anything you could tell us about his death," Leipfold said. "I understand that the police never came over to talk to you, so I thought we'd make up for it."

"What do you want to know?" she asked.

"Do you think it's possible that he committed suicide?" Cholmondeley asked.

"Who can say?" she replied. "But he didn't seem the type."

"What type was he?"

She shrugged. "Like I said, it was just sex."

"Interesting," Leipfold said, even though it wasn't.

The rest of the interview followed a similar pattern—Leipfold and Cholmondeley asked the questions and Rita Long gave them answers that didn't really answer them. Their suspicions were awakened, although neither man really knew why. It was a joint hunch, but it was enough for them to act upon.

Rita and her housemate allowed them to search the house, but they didn't find anything unusual. Both women refused them access to their cars, which set off a warning bell in Leipfold's head. He took a closer look at them when he left, peering in through the glass to see if he could spot anything untoward, and he found something. It wasn't much, but it was something—just a single drop of crimson on the driver-side mat. Probably blood, but possibly not.

Later that evening, Leipfold and Cholmondeley discussed the new developments over soft drinks in the Rose & Crown. They'd independently arrived at the same theory, although a theory was all it was.

"Perhaps there was a murder after all," Leipfold said. "And perhaps we just met our murderer."

"Perhaps," Cholmondeley agreed. "Maybe it was an accident and when she realised what she'd done, she tried to shift the blame."

"We need to prove it," Leipfold said.

"Leave it to me," Cholmondeley replied. "I'll see if I can get a warrant for an official search. You can bet my boys will be more thorough."

"Hmm," Leipfold said. "I wonder."

*   *   *

The days passed slowly, and Leipfold had almost lost interest in the case by the time that Cholmondeley stopped by to provide an update. He met Leipfold at his office again, which was starting to look a little more lived in. He'd even got hold of a couple of potted plants, although they were already starting to look worse for wear. It wasn't really Leipfold's fault. The office didn't get much sunlight.

"So what's the latest?" Leipfold asked.

"We got a hit on the blood in Rita Long's car," Cholmondeley said. "The boffins at the station used this new technology called DNA profiling and were able to match it to Anders Beard. So we brought Long in for questioning. And guess what."

"She changed her story," Leipfold said.

"Got it in one," Cholmondeley replied. "The blood was a smear, not a drop. We put it to her that the only way it could have got there would be if she tracked it in herself after being present at the scene."

"Is that true?"

"No," Cholmondeley replied. "But she didn't need to know that. The upshot is that she changed her story. She told us that she discovered the body but didn't want to call it in because she didn't want his wife to find out about her."

"Hmm," Leipfold said. "So she's saying it was a suicide?"

"That's about the size of it."

"But that doesn't work," Leipfold replied, shaking his head. "We know it wasn't a suicide."

"We do?"

"Of course," Leipfold replied. "If it was a suicide, then where in the hell is the gun?"

*   *   *

After that, the case stalled, at least for a couple of weeks. Without any further evidence and with no new witnesses, the crown had pulled together its strongest circumstantial case against Jessica Beard and started formal legal proceedings. It wasn't a strong case, and Leipfold suspected that the chances of an acquittal were at least even, but it was all they had.

And then that all changed one morning when a jogger came across a group of teenagers waving a firearm around. At first, he thought he was about to be robbed, and indeed he'd started to turn around when the kids caught sight of him and shouted, "Hey, mister."

Fearing the worst and hoping for the best, at least according to the report that he later made to Jack Cholmondeley, the jogger had frozen in his tracks and asked them what they'd wanted.

"We found this in the bushes," one of the kids said, offering him up the gun by handing it over butt first. "Do you think it's real?"

"Hell if I know," the jogger replied. "You shouldn't be touching that thing. We need to call the police."

The kids had tossed the gun on to the grass and scattered, and the jogger had called the police from a payphone shortly afterwards. The gun had been collected by a crime scene team and the bush had been cordoned off. And then the gun had made its way to the laboratory and, eventually, to ballistics.

Leipfold had learned all this when Cholmondeley had made an impromptu visit to his office while he was still settling in. The cop had talked to Leipfold with a frenetic energy and paced in circles around the room. Leipfold had listened intently, perched on one of the plastic garden chairs that he was still using in lieu of furniture.

"The gun was the missing firearm that was registered to Jessica Beard," Cholmondeley explained. "And we got a match from ballistics on the bullet that killed her husband. That was the weapon that killed him. But here's the thing. We found some prints, and they weren't a match. They weren't a match to her husband either, which seems to rule out suicide."

"So someone tossed the weapon," Leipfold said.

"That's about the size of it," Cholmondeley said. "He could still have killed himself, of course, but if he did then someone else tossed the weapon. And why toss the weapon if it was a suicide?"

"There's always the other alternative," Leipfold replied. "That it's not a suicide. He was killed and then the murderer tossed the weapon."

"But who?" Cholmondeley asked. "We ran the prints but didn't find a match."

"Have you talked to Rita Long?"

"Of course," Cholmondeley said. "But we didn't get her prints. And now the warrant is no longer valid."

"Do you still have her vehicle?"

"She's due to collect it any minute."

"Then what are you waiting for?" Leipfold said. "Get on the damn phone and tell someone to scrape the steering wheel for her prints before she gets there."

*   *   *

Leipfold didn't hear back from Cholmondeley that day, but he wasn't expecting to. In fact, the detective had simply filed the final report for his client and then moved on to another case. He'd been hired to track down a missing pet, the proverbial dog that didn't bark in the night-time, a job he was unwilling to take until he'd heard how valuable the animal was. That put an entirely different spin on things.

Besides, Leipfold's mind was on something else. He had a lot of work on, but his cash flow was close to zero. He wasn't paying anything into his pension. He didn't have a penny to spare. That left him working overtime in the hope that some invoice or other would clear well within the twenty-eight days that were specified in his standard terms and conditions.

That meant that when he finally received an update on the case, he'd all but given up on it, although he hadn't forgotten. He couldn't, not with his memory. That was what the booze had been for, and even then it was far from perfect. He didn't miss it.

It was a couple of weeks later, and Leipfold was in a good mood. He finished off the crossword and then turned back to the front-page story in *The Tribune*.

The headline read: *Cops Make New Arrest in Beard Murder Case.* Staring out at him from beneath the headline was a black and white mugshot of Rita Long. Leipfold smiled and threw the paper across the room and into the trash.

Corruption

"I'M WORRIED, JAMES," Cholmondeley said.

"Aren't we all?" Leipfold replied.

They were sitting in a private room at the police station. Since his promotion, Jack Cholmondeley had been awarded the luxury of his own office, but he didn't take Leipfold there. There were too many interruptions.

Cholmondeley pinched the bridge of his nose and sighed. He'd been doing that a lot lately, Leipfold had noticed, and he wondered whether it was from the stress of the job or whether something was happening at home.

"There have been some accusations," Cholmondeley said. "Corruption in the ranks, that sort of thing. They call them the Boys in Blue."

"Like the Men in Black?"

"Exactly," Cholmondeley said. "Unfortunately for me, I'm the poor sod who has to look into it. And unfortunately for you, I want you to help me."

"Why me?"

"Because I need to carry out my investigation without attracting attention," Cholmondeley explained. "My supervisors will have to find out at some point, of course, but I want to keep this off the books as much as possible, at least until I have some evidence."

"I don't know about this," Leipfold said, hesitantly. "It sounds sketchy to me. Shouldn't you be assigned a job like this? You can't just investigate on your own."

"I have authorisation to do what it takes," Cholmondeley said.

"Let's just leave it at that. But we need to keep it off the books as much as possible. If word gets out to the wrong people, the whole damn investigation could be compromised. We don't know how deep the corruption goes. It could go all the way to the top."

"I see," Leipfold replied. The two of them were sitting in his office again, drinking coffee from the *I LOVE LONDON* mugs that Leipfold had bought from a shady guy in the Rose & Crown.

"So what do you think?" Cholmondeley asked. "Can you help me?"

"I can," Leipfold said. "But it'll cost you. Some of us have to make a living."

"I can pay," Cholmondeley said. "But it'll have to come out of my savings. There's no way I'm putting you on the books back at the station. No offence."

"None taken," Leipfold said. "I'm an ex-con."

"Not in my eyes," Cholmondeley said. "But in the eyes of the law, perhaps. You've served your time. Let's hope you don't reoffend."

"How could I?" Leipfold asked. He looked sad, remorseful. "I don't drink anymore. I don't even drive, come to think of it."

"Perhaps you should get yourself a motorbike," Cholmondeley suggested. Leipfold's eyes lit up as he considered the idea. Then they died again when he thought about how much it would cost to buy and run a vehicle.

"All right," Leipfold said, after giving the matter some thought. "I'll help you as much as I can. I'll need a list of names, of course. Everything you can tell me about the people that you suspect."

"Way ahead of you." Cholmondeley reached into his pocket and pulled out an envelope. He opened it up and reached inside, then withdrew a half-dozen sheets of paper that were covered with handwritten notes. "Here's a list I worked on. Start at the top and work your way down."

"Gary Mogford," Leipfold read, glancing over Cholmondeley's notes on the first cop on the list. "Who's he?"

"A new recruit," Cholmondeley explained. "Only been with us for a couple of months. Everyone loves him, but I've been getting bad vibes from him. I don't think everything is as it seems."

"All right then," Leipfold said. "Just leave it with me."

Leipfold took Cholmondeley through the motions, printed off a copy of his standard agreement and then got the policeman to sign it. Then he showed him to the door and promised that he'd be in touch.

The first stage of the investigation was to secure a little help. The only problem was that money was scarce, so Leipfold took some inspiration from Sherlock Holmes and paid the local kids a few quid to carry out some surveillance. They should have been in school, but Leipfold reasoned that it wasn't his job to make sure that they had an education. Besides, if they were going to skive, it'd be better for them to be engaged in something productive, even if it was just to carry out some clandestine surveillance on men of the law. They were the type of kids who liked to taunt coppers anyway, and Leipfold was just giving them an excuse to do what they normally did.

He called them The Rabble and asked them to report back to his office. In exchange, he paid each of them up front, with a £100 bonus for anyone who found evidence that could prove a cop's corruption. With this arrangement in place, he was able to spearhead the campaign from the office while he developed his second plan of attack.

He met with Cholmondeley the following day and updated him on his progress, which didn't take long because there wasn't much to say. Then he hit him with phase two, which would need his participation if it was to be a success.

"Here's the deal," Leipfold said. "I need you to leak some information."

"I can't do that, James," Cholmondeley replied. "It's more than my job's worth."

"Let me clarify." Leipfold grinned at Cholmondeley and took a swig of his coffee, then shuffled in his seat to get comfortable. "I'm not asking you to leak anything that could cause any trouble. Just start a few rumours. Tell different things to different people."

"And then what?"

"Then see what happens," Leipfold said. "See if anyone breaks cover. You said that your officers could be corrupt. How? Are they talking to the press? Taking payoffs?"

"A little bit of both," Cholmondeley said. "Or possibly neither."

Leipfold groaned. "Oh no," he said. "Is this another one of your hunches?"

"Let's not talk about that," Cholmondeley replied. "Let's just say that I have my reasons. What kind of stuff should I leak?"

"Make something up," Leipfold said.

So Cholmondeley did, and he took Leipfold along for the ride. It started when an informant provided him with some information on a lockup by the docks where a gangster was said to be storing something, although no one seemed to know whether it was drugs, guns or goods. Still, all he needed was the address, and that was enough to spread the rumour of a raid to a superior, a detective inspector who had a reputation for being a hard man, and not the type of man that it was a good idea to cross.

But Cholmondeley crossed him anyway, and the fake information must have had an effect because the shit hit the proverbial fan. Along with a half dozen of the street kids, Leipfold was keeping watch on the lock-up from a distance, and they got a front row seat for the whole performance.

The heavies arrived first, the fat-faced guys who wielded weaponry and beat men senseless on their bosses' orders. They were there to look good and to turn people away who didn't have their crooked best interests at heart. They were followed by a thin-faced Eastern European man in a smart, black suit. His swagger showed he was the guvnor, the man who ran things.

As Leipfold watched, they brought in a couple of lorries and parked them outside the lockup, then started to unload their contents. Leipfold watched impatiently and waited until the first of the lorries was full up and getting ready to leave, and then he dispatched one of his youths to phone in a code word to Jack Cholmondeley.

Leipfold had taken Cholmondeley's advice and bought himself a motorcycle on credit. It was the bike he'd fallen in love with after his release from prison, when he'd been interviewed by the mechanic for a position as a grease monkey. The mechanic had been unwilling to make the sale at first, but Leipfold had cooked up a scheme where the purchase was covered by a small business loan and the bike became the bank's asset until he finished paying them off. He'd had to write it off as an expense. He picked up his suit while he was there.

"You're lucky I kept the damn thing," the mechanic complained. "I had a feeling you'd be back."

"I came back for Camilla," Leipfold said.

"Camilla?"

"The bike," Leipfold said. "She has a name."

"She does?"

"Every bike has a name. You just have to get to know it."

"How come this one's a Camilla?"

Leipfold shrugged. "She just is."

Leipfold had fallen immediately in love with her. He had some experience with motorbikes, but not as much as he would have liked, and the race through the streets put his skills to the test. Luckily, the lorries weren't difficult to keep tabs on, and the bike could have outpaced them even on a bad day. The hard part was avoiding detection from the lorry driver. But Leipfold was unrecognisable in his leathers, and he kept a safe enough distance to track the lorry to another lockup on the east side of town. He got the address and location. That was all he needed.

*   *   *

Cholmondeley was busy the following day, but he met up with Leipfold the day after to give him a brief update.

"Thanks for being the eyes and ears, James," Cholmondeley said, helping himself to a seat in Leipfold's office. He nodded when the detective offered him a coffee and then tried to make himself comfortable.

"It's my pleasure," Leipfold replied. "I assume you got my message with the new address?"

"I did indeed," Cholmondeley replied. "Two raids in one day, that must be a new record. We caught all the players in the act, and they're looking at a hell of a lot of jail time. But it gets better."

"You caught the copper," Leipfold said.

"We did indeed," Cholmondeley replied. "He was there at the second lock up, handling illegal firearms at the address you gave us. We brought him in with the bad guys. Silly sod tried to tell us he was working undercover, but that's just the last roll of the dice for a desperate man. We got him."

"Great," Leipfold said. "One down. How many more to go?"

"There are nineteen more names on the list," Cholmondeley said. "Let's hope they're all as easy as this."

*   *   *

Leipfold and Cholmondeley continued to work their way through the names on the list, with varying degrees of success. After a week or so, they were checking in on number seven, one of the highest-profile names on the list: Max Medlock, the deputy police commissioner. Leipfold had heard of him before, but he'd never actually seen him. That all changed one fateful day when he teamed up with Cholmondeley to tail the man.

Leipfold spotted Medlock at the same moment that Cholmondeley pointed him out, and his reaction was quick and visceral. He grabbed Jack Cholmondeley by the lapel and whirled him around to pin his back to a wall.

"What the hell is going on?" he hissed.

"James, I—"

"That's him," Leipfold said. "The government guy from the Ledbury. The one who met with Awni el-Halim. I was tailing him a few years back and then the trail went cold."

"Are you sure?"

"Damn it, I never forget a face," Leipfold said. "If he's one of the Boys in Blue, or whatever the hell you want to call them, perhaps he had a hand in what happened back in Kuwait."

"Now, that's not what we're here for, James," Cholmondeley began.

"Spare me the lecture," Leipfold said, releasing Cholmondeley from his grip and starting to jog down the alley and back out on to the main road, where Max Medlock was at risk of receding into the distance. "We've got to catch up."

The man wasn't staying at the Ledbury this time, but he was living in similarly expensive surroundings at a private residence in the inner city. The two men tailed him back to it, swapping positions every now and then so that neither of their faces were around for long enough for him to recognise them.

Leipfold and Cholmondeley paused for a quick tête-à-tête at the end of Medlock's street.

"So what's the plan?" Cholmondeley asked.

"Do we need one?" Leipfold replied. "How about we go and knock on the son-of-a-bitch's door and ask him what he knows about the Boys in Blue."

Cholmondeley shook his head. "We can't do that," he said. "He's my superior officer. We need to handle this gently."

"Screw that," Leipfold said. "I'm not a cop and you're not on duty. And besides, I want to find out what he knows about Awni el-Halim."

"James, I—"

But Leipfold was already on the move. Before Cholmondeley knew it, he was a dozen steps behind him as he jogged down the road towards Medlock's front door. By the time that Cholmondeley had caught up with him, he'd already knocked at it.

The door swung open, and Leipfold surreptitiously jammed his foot in the gap so that it wouldn't swing closed again. It was his first close-up, full-frontal view of Max Medlock, but it was definitely the same man that he'd seen meeting up with Awni el-Halim all those years ago. Leipfold couldn't tell if the man recognised him, but in many ways it didn't matter.

"Who the hell—" the man began, but that was as far as he got before Leipfold's shoulder banged into the door and pushed them both back into the house. Cholmondeley followed quickly afterwards, sticking his head back out and looking up and down the street to make sure that no one was watching before pulling the door closed.

"What's the meaning of this?" Medlock was babbling. "I'll have you know, I'm the deputy police commissioner. You'll swing for this."

"I know who you are," Leipfold replied, calmly. "And capital punishment was abolished in the sixties."

"I'm terribly sorry about all this," Cholmondeley added.

"You," Medlock said, looking at the cop. "Don't I know you?"

"No, sir," Cholmondeley lied, hastily.

"Sit down," Leipfold said. Seeing no other alternative, the commissioner did as he was told. "Awni el-Halim. Does the name mean anything to you?"

"Doesn't ring a bell."

Leipfold slapped the man across the side of the head. It wasn't a blow that was designed to cause pain. It was designed to surprise, and it did just that.

"Jesus!" Cholmondeley exclaimed. "You can't just—"

143

"Be quiet," Leipfold said. "This is important."

He turned his attention back to the commissioner, who'd collapsed on to a chair and who was watching proceedings with a nervous expression.

"Tell me what you know about el-Halim."

"I don't—"

Leipfold struck him again, a little harder this time, causing Cholmondeley to take an involuntary step forward.

"I'll have you for this," the commissioner said.

"I'm sure you will," Leipfold said. "Now tell me what you know about el-Halim before I break your kneecaps."

"James, I really don't think—"

"Be quiet!" Leipfold hissed.

Max Medlock looked from Leipfold to Cholmondeley and back again, then seemed to arrive at a decision.

"Awni el-Halim was a traitor to his country," Medlock spat. Watching him was like watching water flow out of a tap. Once he started talking, he didn't seem like he'd ever stop. "And that made him a marvellous asset to ours. He did his bit back in the Gulf and we rewarded him with citizenship. Of course, he still has his contacts, and so we check in with him every now and then."

"But you're a copper," Leipfold said. "Why are you working for the military?"

Max Medlock chuckled, looking more at ease now that he wasn't being smacked upside the head. "Oh, my dear boy," he said. "You really do know nothing."

"The Boys in Blue," Cholmondeley murmured.

Medlock glared at him. "I *do* know you," he said. "You're Jack Cholmondeley."

"Busted," Leipfold said.

"When we get out of here, I'm going to have you working from behind a desk for the rest of your career," Medlock said.

"We'll see about that," Cholmondeley said. He seemed resigned to his fate, and while so far Leipfold had been running the show, he started to ask a few questions of his own. "Answer my friend's question, please. Why were the Boys in Blue in Kuwait?"

Medlock laughed. "You just don't get it, do you?" he said. "We were there because we had a job to do. Ours is not to question. From what I know, the orders came straight from the top. We were to provoke a skirmish with the Kuwaitis so we could authorise a revenge attack. The only problem was that the locals weren't too keen to get into a firefight, so we had to arrange something. A little friendly fire."

"Friendly fire?" Leipfold growled. He struck the man again, more forcefully this time, catching him with a solid right hook to the eyebrow. Medlock moved slightly at the last second, but there was nowhere for him to go. He took the punch and slid back into the chair. "My friends were killed."

"I'm sorry to hear that," Medlock said, and he did look it. He looked sorry for himself, too. His face was already starting to swell. "But you have to understand, it was for the greater good."

"The greater good being a revenge attack on an innocent opponent," Leipfold said.

"The Kuwaitis weren't innocent," Medlock replied. "Any more so than we were. And they had something that we wanted."

"Oil," Leipfold said.

"Exactly." Medlock spat on the floor, a bloody great glob of phlegm that seeped into the carpet. Leipfold thought it would leave a stain, but Medlock seemed like the kind of guy who'd have someone to clean up the mess for him.

"Why are you telling us all this?" Cholmondeley asked.

"Because your friend here kept hitting me," Medlock answered. "And because the truth can't be murdered and will always come out eventually. It won't do you any good. You have no evidence and it's your word against mine. Although I will admit that I'd prefer it if you didn't even try. You'd be making my life much more difficult."

"He's got a point, James," Cholmondeley said. "What are you hoping to achieve here?"

"I have no intention of going to the press," Leipfold said. "I'm here for something else."

"Pride?"

"Too many people have died," Leipfold said. He sighed. "Were the Boys in Blue responsible for my dismissal?"

"I wouldn't know," Medlock said. "But I wouldn't put it past them. If you were poking your nose into their business, it wouldn't be a surprise if they tried to chop it off."

"Plus you deserted your post, James," Cholmondeley added. "To search for the truth, no less, but perhaps that's not how your superiors saw it."

"What a waste," Leipfold murmured. For a second or two, he looked as though he was going to pass out. Instead, he lowered himself on to the sofa beside Max Medlock.

"It happens, dear boy," Medlock said. He sounded almost sympathetic. "There's nothing you can do about it now. Find something else to fixate on."

"I already have," Leipfold murmured, thinking about his motorbike and his fledgling business.

Cholmondeley cleared his throat theatrically and the two of them turned to look at him.

"What are we going to do about this mess?" he asked.

*   *   *

In the end, the trio found themselves in a Mexican standoff. Max Medlock agreed not to press charges, Leipfold agreed to let the dead lie, and Cholmondeley agreed to pretend that nothing had ever happened.

Over the next couple of weeks, Leipfold started to wonder whether Cholmondeley had jinxed them. Their investigations slowed down, although they still proved cases against a couple more cops and found reasons to suspect half a dozen more. It seemed like every name on the list was corrupt to some extent. Leipfold had spent several days compiling a comprehensive dossier on the lot of them, aided by the information that The Rabble provided. Then he calculated the final amount owed. It wasn't comprehensive, but it was good enough. And besides, Cholmondeley had been given carte blanche to do what he needed by his superiors. Leipfold reflected that either they were clean and had nothing to worry about or they were so sure that they'd get away with it that they were happy to sanction an investigation.

Leipfold called the report Rotten Apple because the job was like bobbing for the things in a barrel of water and because the police force was rotten to the core. Cholmondeley didn't see the funny side, but he had to admit that Leipfold's report had been worth what he paid for it.

Leipfold was rereading the report one morning, a couple of days after he'd submitted it, when there was a knock on the office door. He peered out at the visitor through the spyhole, but he didn't recognise the young man who was on the other side of it. He recognised the uniform, though. It was the same uniform that Jack Cholmondeley wore.

Leipfold opened the door and welcomed the policeman to his office. "Please," he said. "Take a seat."

"That won't be necessary," the man replied. "This won't take long. Do you know who I am?"

Leipfold shook his head.

"My name is Constable Gary Mogford," the man said. "And I expect you to remember that. You'll be seeing my face again, I'm sure."

"I'm sure," Leipfold murmured.

If Mogford heard him, he didn't react to it.

"I know what you're up to," Mogford said, leaning a little too close for comfort. "Don't think I don't. Stay away from the police force, you hear? This relationship you have with the boss. It's not healthy."

"I'm sure Jack Cholmondeley can make his own decisions."

"I don't care," Mogford growled. "If he orders you to check up on me again, I want you to turn him down. Politely. Don't bring my name into it. Just do it."

"Why?"

"Listen," Mogford said, raising his voice and backing away from Leipfold in a failed attempt to show that he wasn't a threat. "I have my flaws, but I'm not a bad cop. I can't be bought and you won't find my name in the books of any of the city's villains. I'm good at my job, and I take it seriously. I resent you for questioning my integrity."

"Don't blame me, pal," Leipfold replied. "I got paid to do a job, and I did it. That's all. I didn't put your name on the bloody list."

"Then who did?"

"I think you'd better speak to Jack Cholmondeley," Leipfold said.

* * *

The arrests came a couple of weeks later. Leipfold's report wasn't the only evidence, but it had acted as the catalyst for a formal internal investigation which made a lot of cops feel uncomfortable.

Leipfold had heard a little news from Cholmondeley, but it wasn't until the story hit the front page of *The Tribune* that he realised just how deep the corruption actually went. The police commissioner himself had been arrested, and Leipfold chuckled when he recognised the keen, fresh face of Gary Mogford on the front page as he made the arrest.

"Gary Mogford is a silly sod," he murmured to himself. "He reminds me of his father. I wonder how the old geezer's doing."

He expected to hear a lot more from Cholmondeley's new

recruit in the future if their first meeting was anything to go by. Then again, Leipfold thought, *there's nothing new about me having a cop for an enemy. And at least I also have a cop for a friend.*

*   *   *

Two days later, James Leipfold picked up a bouquet of flowers from a supermarket and rode Camilla to St. Editha's, where he parked and meandered around the back of the church and into the graveyard. It was incongruous this close to the city, but it was also a little piece of history that no authority had the heart to build over.

It took him twenty minutes to find Janine Taylor's gravestone. Once he was there, he laid the flowers at the foot of it and then sat cross-legged on the grass. He was silent for a moment or two. Then he started to talk, and he kept on talking until the sun went down.

The Break-In

THERE HAD BEEN A BURGLARY.

Leipfold knew it had happened as soon as he opened the door. The building on Balcombe Street was a relic of the Victorian era with long corridors and tall ceilings. The central hallway led to a downstairs bathroom and a graphic design company and then snaked up a flight of stairs to Leipfold's office on the first floor.

The first clue was the stack of mail in front of the door, or rather the lack thereof. The mail was stacked instead in the receptacle beside the door, and there were letters that hadn't been there when he'd left on Friday night. The designers rarely came in over the weekend, and Leipfold hadn't touched the envelopes. It could have been the landlord perhaps, but he usually let himself into the offices and took the mail with him, and he always gave a couple of days' notice.

Besides, there were scuff marks on the doorframe that suggested a tool had been used, an oily footprint on the carpet and a general bad vibe in the air that reminded him of when he was in the army and a shout rang out about a sniper. Something had happened, and he wanted to know what.

He walked cautiously up the stairs, bracing himself for fight or flight if he found someone. He wished he had a weapon, but all he had were the two built-in brass knuckles he'd been born with. The door to the office was closed, but it was on the latch and not the main lock, which Leipfold checked religiously every time he left the place. That was enough to prove that someone had been in there, but they hadn't forced the door like they did downstairs. They must have used a key or picked the lock.

It was hard to tell whether anything was missing. Leipfold cast his mind back to how he'd left it, reproducing it in his head in high definition, but everything looked the same as it had before. But that meant nothing. They could have copied down some information or booby-trapped the place.

That meant that the rest of his day was a write-off. He had to inch his way around the office, examining every part. He expected a bomb to go off at any moment. It reminded him of when he'd prowled the dusty deserts of Kuwait with his old army buddies. But there was nothing untoward, and it was mostly a wasted day. He found only one thing out of the ordinary.

One of his case files was missing. It was the file for a man called Bear who he hadn't seen since they'd been behind bars together in Reading Jail.

Leipfold finished checking the office, but there was nothing else for him to learn. Once he was satisfied, he picked up the phone on his desk and placed a call to Jack Cholmondeley at the Old Vic, one of the city's most prestigious and underfunded institutions. Leipfold told him all about the break-in—as well as what had been taken—and then asked the copper what he was going to do about it.

"I'll take a look at it," Cholmondeley said. "I don't suppose you plan to make a formal report?"

"No chance."

"That's what I thought," Cholmondeley said. "That makes things more difficult, but I'll do what I can. To be honest, James, you haven't given me much to go on. Do you have any idea who might be behind it?"

"None whatsoever," Leipfold replied. "Isn't it your job to find that out?"

"Listen, friend, I'd love to help," Cholmondeley said. "You know I would, but I haven't got the men to spare. I'll need something concrete. A proper lead."

"Hmm." Leipfold paused for a moment, mulling it over. "It could have been Bear, I guess. But why? And why now?"

Cholmondeley said nothing.

"Okay," Leipfold said. "I'll look into it and see what I can find out. If I get anything concrete, I'll bring it to you."

"Good lad," Cholmondeley replied. "If I were you, I'd start with your landlord. See if he can help."

"Oh no," Leipfold groaned. "I was afraid it might come to that."

*   *   *

Leipfold's landlord was a useless old man who'd retired young and lived a life of relative comfort in one of his properties. He paid his way with the money he made from his tenants, and he had a habit of cutting corners as a result of it. If he could fix the problem himself, he would do. If he couldn't, he'd leave it until it could no longer be ignored.

He wasn't very receptive. Leipfold reported the break-in for the second time, but the old man was unhelpful at best.

"What do you want from me?" the landlord asked.

"Good question," Leipfold replied. "I want you to install some security measures. CCTV cameras. They're all the rage these days. Some deadlocks for the doors. Maybe a burglar alarm."

"I can't afford that," the landlord said. He always had been a man of few words.

"Isn't it your duty as the property's owner?"

"To a certain extent," the landlord replied. "But I comply with the law. If you're unhappy with the current situation, you're free to leave."

"Can you at least fix my buzzer?"

"I'll add it to my list," the man said. Leipfold recognised it for what it was, a secret landlord code that meant "I'm never going to do it."

"What about if I foot the bill for the work?"

"If that's what you want, it's fine by me," the landlord said. "But you won't be getting a penny from me. You've already got me acting as your doorman."

"What do you mean?" Leipfold asked.

"That chap, that friend of yours," he said. "The one I let in last night."

"Woah," Leipfold said. "Slow down. Who are you talking about?"

"The well-spoken chap you sent down to your office," the landlord said. "It must have been Saturday, maybe Sunday. Early afternoon."

"What did he look like?"

"It's hard to say."

Leipfold turned to a clean page in his notebook and grabbed a pencil. "I'm going to try to draw him," Leipfold said. "But I need you to guide my pencil. Let's start with the shape of his head."

It took the best part of twenty minutes, and Leipfold could sense the man getting more and more irate as the time passed. But by the end of it, they had a reasonable sketch of what the man looked like, and Leipfold sensed it was the best he was likely to get.

The depressing thing, Leipfold thought, as he worked his way around the estate, *is how I could tell the landlord knew something. I don't* have *any friends.*

Leipfold was on a fool's errand. He'd made it his mission to take the drawing around every business in a one-mile radius of the office, hoping against hope that someone would recognise the man who'd been inside his office from his poorly rendered sketch. Unsurprisingly, the search was long, tedious and mostly unsuccessful. He was just about to give up when he got a match from the barista at Starbucks.

"Yeah," she said. "I remember this guy. He was in here over the weekend. Came in for a latte."

"What kind of time are we talking?"

"Must have been Saturday afternoon," she replied. "Maybe 3PM. Just after the lunchtime rush."

"Sounds about right," Leipfold murmured.

"Who is this guy?"

"Oh," Leipfold said. "Just some scumbag."

"This is exciting," the barista said. "It's just like a movie."

"Yeah," Leipfold said. "Something like that. Is there anything you can tell me about him? I'm trying to find him."

"Hmm," the woman replied. She thought about it for a moment. "He looked rough and ready, you know the type. Sat in the corner so he could keep an eye on the rest of the customers. You get those guys every now and then. You just need to keep your head down and wait until they leave. This guy, though. He was on another level. The worst part of it was his accent. Eastern European, Russian maybe. It was hard to tell, but whatever it was, it was terrifying. Scared the shit out of me, let me tell you."

"Wonderful," Leipfold said. "I love scary people. Can you do me a favour?"

"What's that then?"

"Call me," Leipfold said, scribbling the office's number on a sheet of paper in his notebook and handing it to her. "If he comes back in, I want to know. I need to catch this guy in the act."

"What's it worth?" the woman asked. Leipfold sighed and gave her a few notes from his wallet. Then he bought himself a coffee and went about his business.

His next stop was *The Tribune*'s office. He'd tried to book an appointment with Jan Evans, the paper's editor, but she'd palmed him off and hooked him up with a new reporter called Phelps instead.

"Make it quick," Phelps said, and so Leipfold did his best. He told the newspaperman about the break-in at his office, as well as how his useless landlord had failed to act on it. He also shared his suspicions that it was a case of organised crime and made a public pledge that he wouldn't rest until he tracked the man down. Then he shared his sketch with the man and asked if they'd be able to run it in the next issue of the paper.

"There's no story in it," the man said. "Our readers won't care. You could run it as an advertisement, I suppose."

Leipfold shrugged. "Whatever it takes," he said. "And I need you to mention something else. I need you to bait the hook."

"How's that, then?"

"Some of my notes were stolen," Leipfold said. "And we need to mention it. They were important notes on a case I've been investigating, and I have reason to suspect that they're the cause of the crime. Someone was looking for them, and they think they've destroyed my entire case. I need them to know that they haven't."

*   *   *

Leipfold started sleeping in the office. He wondered whether he was losing his mind. For the first time since his days on the bottle, his thoughts felt clouded and almost unusable. It felt like he'd switched heads with an idiot. He didn't like it.

He started to wonder whether it was all in his head. Perhaps there hadn't been a break-in after all, or maybe they'd targeted the graphic design company downstairs. Besides, what was it that the barista in the coffee shop had said? Something about an accent? Leipfold had made plenty of enemies throughout his career, but they were all from Brixton and Brentford instead of Belarus. Maybe it was all just a wild goose chase. Perhaps he was searching for an innocent man whose only crime had been to speak with a strange accent in the British capital. Perhaps the file hadn't been stolen. Perhaps he'd simply mislaid it.

But then he dismissed those thoughts as the ramblings of an impatient mind and continued to do what he did best.

A couple of days later, when Leipfold was in the middle of a meeting with one of his clients, the telephone rang. He excused himself for a moment and picked it up, then rattled off some instructions.

"Something's come up," he said, ushering the client out of the office as quickly as he could. "I'm sorry. I'll call you just as soon as I can to reschedule."

"You'd better," the client said, but Leipfold didn't hear them. He was already sprinting down the street towards the coffee shop, where the man with the bad accent was in the process of ordering another latte.

By the time that Leipfold got there, the man was nowhere to be found, but the barista who called him was able to point him in the right direction. He raced down the street until he hit the T-junction, then chose a direction at random and continued to jog down it.

Surely, Leipfold reasoned, *he can't have gone far with a hot cup of coffee in his hands.*

But there was no sign of the man. Leipfold returned to the coffee shop with a racing heart and an overwhelming sense of disappointment.

That night, when Leipfold was asleep in the office, he was awoken by the tinkle of glass. It came from the hallway, somewhere on the ground floor near the graphic designers' office. He pulled himself groggily to his feet and reached out for the two-by-four that he kept beneath his desk. With the wood in hand, he opened the door as quietly as he could and then snuck out onto the landing.

There was definitely someone down there. Leipfold could hear movement, but he couldn't make anything out in the darkness. He continued to work his way down the steps, skipping the third from the top because it squeaked when he put too much pressure on it. He made it to the bottom and then stood there in the darkness. The air felt heavy, invasive.

And then there was movement, and Leipfold swung the wood

through the air. A bone crunched as it made contact and a voice cried out in the darkness. Leipfold kicked out at the man and felt his foot connect, and then he hobbled over to the lights and turned the switch on. The light hit his eyes and blinded him momentarily, but the guy on the floor faced the same disadvantage and he had a minor concussion to contend with, too.

When his eyes adjusted, Leipfold took a good look at him. He was close enough to the sketch to be a match, but he was different enough so that Leipfold hadn't spotted the familial resemblance until the man was lying in a crumpled heap in his hallway.

"Christ," Leipfold said. "I know you. You're the spitting image of old Bear. He must be your father."

"I'm not saying nothin'," the man said. His voice was muffled by the swelling that had already started to kick in, and he spat out a couple of teeth at the end of the sentence like bloody punctuation marks.

"Ah," Leipfold said. "A double negative. So you *are* saying something?"

"Forget about it."

"Fine by me," Leipfold said. "Dear me, what was the plan? Does your father know you're here?"

"You can't do this," Bear Jr. replied. "You're not a copper."

"No, I'm not." Leipfold smiled unsettlingly and leaned in a little closer. "But I can call one."

*   *   *

It was a couple of weeks after Leipfold's citizen's arrest, and life was pretty much back to normal. He caught up with Cholmondeley over a soft drink in the Rose & Crown. Cedric wasn't pleased that Leipfold had brought a cop into his boozer, especially because they were both drinking soft drinks instead of beers and spirits. It was bad for business.

But Leipfold and Cholmondeley continued their conversation in blissful ignorance. If they felt the eyes of the landlord upon them, they didn't show it.

"So what's the story?" Cholmondeley asked.

"I want to press charges," Leipfold replied. "I want that kid behind bars where he belongs, just like his father."

"Oh," Cholmondeley said. "Haven't you heard? Bear's up for appeal. He might be getting out."

"We'll see about that," Leipfold replied.

"Why do you have it in for this kid, anyway?"

"Because he had it in for me."

"And why was that?"

Leipfold shrugged. "I had a file on him," he said. "And on his father, too. With his old man up for appeal, I guess he thought he was doing him a favour, getting rid of any evidence that could have kept him inside. He almost got away with it, too. But I know something he doesn't."

"And what's that?"

Leipfold grinned. "I had a backup," he said. "Here, I want you to take this."

He slid a plain-looking envelope across the table to Jack Cholmondeley.

"What is it?" Cholmondeley asked.

Leipfold grinned. "It's my notes on Bear. I always knew they'd come in handy. This is what the kid was after. It should be good enough to put the kibosh on any chance of appeal that he has. It might be enough to further prosecute."

"I see," Cholmondeley said. "And who exactly was the client here, James?"

"I was," he said. "Bear and I have a history. He was an ally once, back when we were serving time. Then we got out and went our separate ways. But we still ran into each other from time to time. I'll tell you about it someday. It seemed like a good idea to make sure I kept a little intel on him. He's a bad dude with a dark secret."

"I've heard rumours."

"The rumours are true," Leipfold said. "Bear still swears the photos they found in his cell were planted, but I'm not so sure. I think he was using them as currency, trading with the sex offenders in protective custody. Someone must have been running the photos for him. My money's on Simmonds, one of the screws. Then Simmonds lost his job, and Bear was left with the photos. Only someone beat the shit out of him before he had a chance to dispose of them."

"That's quite the story, James," Cholmondeley said, thoughtfully. He picked up the file that the detective had given him and flicked through it, giving it only the most cursory of glances. Then he whistled softly to himself.

"There's a lot for me to think about," he said. "If even half of this stuff checks out, your old pal Bear can say goodbye to his parole. He won't be back on the streets any time soon."

"Thank goodness for that," Leipfold said. "If he ever gets out, he'll want to see me. And if he comes to see me, only one of us is going to leave."

Leipfold finished his drink and tapped the folder, which Cholmondeley was holding close to his chest as though it was a newborn child.

"There's some serious shit in there," he said. "Don't read it on an empty stomach."

And so Cholmondeley didn't.

The Smuggler

LEIPFOLD HAD BEEN ASKED to investigate a theft.

There was nothing unusual about that, but it *was* unusual for him to turn a job down. He'd had to. According to his diary, he was fully booked for the next six weeks, and potential clients were ringing up on a daily basis. It must have been the adverts he'd taken out in the Yellow Pages.

This particular client looked disappointedly across at Leipfold from his perch on the plastic chair in reception. He was a Welshman in his late thirties, a diminutive man with gelled hair who looked like he ran an open mic night in a backwater pub.

"Look," Leipfold said, "I'm sorry. What can I say? I'm in demand. Why not go to the police instead?"

"I can't go to the police," the man said. "Someone stole my shipment."

"Your shipment?"

"Eight tonnes of marijuana," he said. "I can't exactly go to the cops and ask them to check lost property."

Leipfold whistled softly. "That's a lot of weed."

"I have money," the man said. "Money isn't a problem. I just need the expertise."

"Hmm," Leipfold replied. "Strictly speaking, I shouldn't. But strictly speaking doesn't pay my rent. You say that money's not a problem? I'll do it for triple my regular rates. In exchange, I'll give you full anonymity. As far as anyone else is concerned, the job won't exist."

"Good."

"But I need one more thing from you," Leipfold said. "I need to know the truth. I can't investigate if I'm not in possession of all the facts."

The smuggler sighed and said, "Very well. Eight kilos was a lie. It was more like half a tonne of premium skunk."

"Where was it coming from?"

"Holland," the man replied. "We bring it in by boat. It's got the fastest engine we could find and enough false compartments to store ten tonnes. Maybe twelve, on a good day."

"But you got caught?"

The man shook his head. "No," he said. "Nothing like that. It all went to plan, at least until we made it to the mainland. We unloaded the gear from the boat and into the back of a modified campervan. Same deal, with plenty of space to hide stuff. From there, it was due to be delivered to a safe house in Manchester, only the shipment never arrived. What do you make of that?"

Leipfold whistled softly. "What's the street value?" he asked.

"More than you'll earn in a lifetime," the man replied.

"No wonder you can afford to pay me."

"I was there when the boat was unloaded," the smuggler said. "And I had full trust in the two men who were responsible for delivery."

"I'm sure you did."

"No, you don't understand. I don't hire just anyone. People have to prove their loyalty before I bring them on a job like this. I doubt they did a runner with it, no matter how much it's worth. They're good lads. Besides, they know I won't rest until I track them down."

"You mean until *I* track them down," Leipfold said. "As for whether they're guilty or not...well, that's for me to decide."

"What's the plan?" he asked.

"You leave that to me."

*   *   *

Leipfold had a few connections up north through a friend of a friend, and he started by putting out a rumour that he was looking for an old model VW camper. His client had refused to provide him with any more information about the men who were responsible for the shipment, so Leipfold had to hope that somebody, somewhere, had spotted the campervan. It wasn't much, but it was all he had to go on.

Fortunately for Leipfold, he got a hit on the vehicle. It had been abandoned on an industrial estate in Salford, and he knew a guy who knew a guy who'd had to tow it away.

Small world, he thought. *Shame it keeps on getting bigger.*

The trail went cold in Manchester. Leipfold continued his enquiries as best as he could by calling people up and harassing them down the phone, but nobody had heard anything about the smugglers. Nor had they heard about the produce. If anything, Manchester was dry, rife with pills and cocaine perhaps but empty of hash and weed.

So Leipfold hopped on his brand new motorbike and headed north up the M1 and the M6. It was a long old drive to Manchester, a couple hundred miles, but he rode it all in a single sitting and used the journey to plan his attack. He talked to the guy who'd towed it and was directed to a scrap metal site. He was also told to hurry because it was just about time for them to shut up shop and there was every chance that the campervan had gone.

But it hadn't. Leipfold found it third in line for the crusher machine, the last vehicle on the day's roster. Leipfold ached from the long miles on the back of the bike, but he was also lit up with excitement. He knew that if he'd stopped, even for long enough to take a leak and grab a coffee, it would have been too late to find the vehicle until it was crushed into a patty.

The foreman at the yard let Leipfold look through the vehicle, but there wasn't much for him to find. He realised, too late, that he'd missed a secret panel where the manufacturers hid their plumbing, when the crusher hit its peak and a sticky jam of blood, plasma and excrement started to drip down on to the floor.

The foreman vomited on the spot, but Leipfold wasn't so lucky. He could still smell the stench two weeks later when he was tucking into popadoms at the Bombay Palace.

Still, he reflected, as he fled the scene and left it to the Manchester Metropolitan Police Force. *It could be worse. It could have looked like mango chutney.*

*   *   *

Leipfold wasted no time updating his client over the phone to begin with, before following it up with a journey back down south. He held nothing back.

"I've changed my mind," the smuggler said when Leipfold finished telling his tale and sat back to light a cigarette. "There must have been a rebellion. One guy killed the other and took the grass."

"They could have both been there," Leipfold said. "They got turned into Jammie Dodgers."

"Not with the grass still inside," the man said.

"Maybe," Leipfold replied. "Okay, here's the deal. I need you to do me a favour. Listen out for me. Keep your ears peeled. I want to know about any new suppliers in town."

"I'll get you a list of names and numbers."

*   *   *

The smuggler stayed true to his word, and Leipfold soon found himself knocking on a door in Bermondsey and inviting himself inside. He was met by a guy named Ken who was all body hair and tie-dye. Ken specialised in psychotropics, but he dabbled with grass as a way to make a living. He was what Leipfold thought of as a fake dealer, the kind of guy who sold just enough to feed his habit. He reminded Leipfold of himself when he was still on the bottle, but he didn't have Leipfold's background and so he quickly folded when threatened by the wrath of an ex-army private detective with nothing much to lose.

"You're in trouble now," Leipfold said. "I need you to tell me everything you know. If you don't, I'll call in the cops. Pretty simple, really."

"Fuck off," the dealer said. He cracked his knuckles threateningly and looked down at Leipfold, who was half a foot smaller than him and at least five years older. Leipfold barely batted an eyelid, he just drew back a fist and rammed it into the man's stomach. The dealer slumped to the floor, his face turning red as he desperately tried to draw some air into his lungs.

Leipfold kneeled down beside him and said, "Care to reconsider?"

Ken wasn't happy about it, but he had no choice, especially not after Leipfold took hold of his arm and twisted it up behind his back. He answered all of his questions then, all right. He started by pointing Leipfold in the direction of a northern gang, the Fists, who had a warehouse in Salford.

"That's where the drugs are stored," the dealer said. "I've been there. I buy from them. Let me get up, I'll give you directions."

Leipfold reduced the pressure on the man and allowed him to climb to his feet, then quickly jotted down the directions in his Moleskine notebook. He provided a little further information, including a reasonable description of the three men he'd met when he was last up there, but it was of little use to Leipfold. He left feeling confused, as though he'd unlearned something that he thought he knew.

Manchester was a long way away, and Leipfold had neither the time nor the inclination to head north again. Instead, he called his client, followed by Jack Cholmondeley at the Old Vic, who thanked him for the information.

So much for client confidentiality, Leipfold thought. *I always hated dealers.*

Leipfold knew that he was dealing with a conflict of interests, and that his client had specifically told him not to consult the cops. He knew that his clients needed to be able to trust him, and talking to the cops was bad for business. It was a good job that Jack Cholmondeley could be trusted to keep Leipfold's name out of the official records. He just hoped that the cop could come up with a good cover story to explain where he'd found the information.

He heard from Cholmondeley the following morning, at 5:35AM to be precise. The cops had raided the warehouse and found the grass, as well as one of the two drivers. Leipfold had a horrible suspicion that the other one had been turned into campervan jam. He hoped that the man had already been dead when his bones started to pop. No one deserved to be crushed to death.

According to Cholmondeley, the driver had been confused and disoriented, but there was no question about it. He'd been kidnapped and held against his will, and the Mancunian cops had managed to get him out of there and straight to the hospital, where he'd been placed on a drip and watched over by armed guards.

"Did he talk?" Leipfold asked.

"What do you think?" Cholmondeley replied.

Leipfold thought about it for a moment. "He's a con," the detective said. "They have their own moral code. I doubt he said anything."

"Bingo," Cholmondeley said. "Look, I've got to go. Lots to do, James."

"Great," Leipfold replied. "Thanks for the wake-up call."

It was an unfulfilling start to an unpleasant day.

That afternoon, when Leipfold was alone in his office, her heard a commotion from downstairs. He put the door on the latch and wandered out on to the landing, then looked down the stairs into the lobby. His client, the drug smuggler, was back, and he was telling the managing director of the graphic design agency where he could go and shove his head.

"Sorry," Leipfold called down. "So sorry. This is all my fault."

"You're bloody well right it is," the client shouted, running for the stairs with determination plastered across his face and eyes. Leipfold flashed an apologetic smile at the businessman downstairs and then retreated into his office. He held the door open for his client and closed it immediately behind him.

"Calm down," Leipfold said. "I did you a favour."

"A favour?" The smuggler took a swing at him, but Leipfold's reflexes hadn't slowed and he caught the fist with ease and then shifted his grip and threw the man to the floor with his own weight.

"I said calm down," Leipfold growled.

"My weed!" the man shouted. "It got impounded. They're going to destroy it. That wasn't what I wanted."

"No," Leipfold said. "But it's what you got. Besides, you got your henchman back. If they ever let him out of the hospital."

The smuggler struggled again, but Leipfold held him fast and the man soon saw that he wouldn't be shifting.

"What do you want from me?" Leipfold asked. "Revenge?"

"You're damn right," the man replied. "You betrayed me."

"And I'd do it again," Leipfold told him. "A thousand times. I hate dealers. Oh, and by the way. I expect payment within five working days."

"Payment? Forget it. I'm not paying you a penny."

"Yes, you are," Leipfold replied. "If you don't, I'll turn you in. I'm sure the cops would like to know what you've been up to."

"I don't believe you."

"Listen, Sonny Jim," Leipfold said. "I only agreed to work for you in the first place because I needed the money. You think I want to be wasting my time with dick munchers like you all day?"

"You've been planning this from the start."

"Nope," Leipfold said. "It was a late addition. I thought I could silence my conscience. I was wrong."

"But your conscience doesn't mind you blackmailing me."

Leipfold paused for a moment before continuing. "Funny things, morals," he said. "They're not binary. They're more of what you might call a spectrum. I don't like working outside the law, but I make an exception for scumbags like you. Sometimes the law fails us. When that happens, I have to look elsewhere. If I have to blackmail you to make sure the right thing happens, so be it."

"You wouldn't dare."

"I bloody well would," Leipfold said. He grabbed the man's arm again and twisted it. "How far do you want to push me?"

The man shrieked in pain and tried to throw Leipfold off, but the detective had an iron grip and showed no signs of letting up. Leipfold put a little more pressure on his limb and the man tapped out.

"Okay, okay," he said. "I'll pay your bloody fees. Let go of me."

Leipfold obliged. "If you fail to pay me, I'll find you."

"Yeah," the smuggler replied. "You said. And I told you that I'd pay you, just give me some time to get the cash. This isn't over."

Leipfold grinned at him. "That's what they all say," he replied.

The Case of the Missing Gnome

JACK CHOLMONDELEY WAS VEXED to say the least.

"One of Mary's gnomes has gone missing," he said.

Leipfold, who was sitting beside him in a booth at the local Wetherspoons, looked confused. "Her gnomes?" he parroted.

"Her gnomes," Cholmondeley confirmed. "She has a collection of the things. Those horrible little statues of old blokes fishing in ponds or holding tiny bloody signposts. They're her pride and joy, and now some scumbag has pinched one."

"Who'd want to steal a gnome?" Leipfold asked.

Cholmondeley shrugged and reached absentmindedly for his coffee, nudging it slightly and spilling a little without noticing. He took a sip of it and scalded his tongue.

"Shit!" he growled. He held his hand in front of his mouth and blew on it, then wiped it off on his trousers. "Where were we?"

"Who'd want to steal a gnome?" Leipfold repeated.

"Ah," Cholmondeley replied. "Who indeed? A drunk, perhaps? Some kid?"

"Perhaps."

"There's something else, though," Cholmondeley said. "Mary has dozens of the damn things, but only one of them went missing. Priscilla."

"Like the queen of the desert?"

"Exactly," Cholmondeley said. "Priscilla is her pride and joy. Her favourite gnome, if you can believe that. And I'm in the doghouse because she says I let it happen. She's making me sleep on the sofa until I find the bloody thing."

"I think I see where this is going."

"You've got to help me," Cholmondeley said. "If I don't find that damn gnome, my life won't be worth living."

Some men might have thought that Cholmondeley was overreacting, but Leipfold knew Mary and he knew what she was like.

"Tough break," Leipfold said. He thought about it for a moment. "Okay, so. Theories."

"What about them?"

"Have you got any?" Leipfold asked. Cholmondeley shook his head. Leipfold paused again. "Okay then. How about this? What if it was one of your enemies? Maybe they took it to kit it out with spy cameras? Or even something more sinister? Explosives?"

"Jesus Christ," Cholmondeley said. "You think so?"

"Not really," Leipfold replied. "But it's a possibility. You'll know for sure if it reappears again. Perhaps you should get your boys to have a look at the rest of the collection in the meantime."

"I'll do just that," Cholmondeley assured him. "Until then, I want you to put that brain of yours to use."

"I'm trying to run a business here," Leipfold reminded him.

Cholmondeley shrugged. "So what?" he asked. "You love a problem."

*   *   *

Cholmondeley asked his men to look at the gnomes as per Leipfold's suggestion, but they didn't find anything.

Unfortunately for Mary Cholmondeley, they also destroyed a baker's dozen of the things before she noticed they were missing and placed a panicked call to her husband. Jack was on duty and not best pleased to be interrupted by more of his wife's warbling about her precious collection. He broke the bad news over the phone and then held the receiver away from his ear as she shouted at him. He was glad that his colleagues couldn't see him.

"Listen, Mary," Cholmondeley said, trying to seize the initiative. "I'm at work, okay? I'll talk to you when I get home."

"Oh no, Jack," she said. "Oh no, no, no. You've gone too far this time."

"What are you talking about?"

"My gnomes!" she howled. "You know how much I love those things."

"I thought we might have been in danger," Cholmondeley said, making a mental note to give Leipfold a stern reprimand. "I can't help it if I put your safety first, darling."

"Don't 'darling' me, Jack."

"I'm sorry," Cholmondeley said. "But what's done is done. At least the boys didn't find anything."

"I almost wish they bloody well did," Mary growled. Amplified and distorted by a bad connection, her voice sounded hellish, almost satanic. It sent a shiver down Cholmondeley's spine and a cold sweat to his furrowed brow. "I'm serious, Jack. I make a lot of sacrifices to support your career. I don't ask for much from you. I just want my bloody gnomes. Is that so much to ask?"

"Of course not, dear," Cholmondeley said. "I'm sorry."

"Sorry doesn't cut it," she said. "You make this better or else you're in a lot of trouble. I'm going to go and spend some time at my mother's. It'll give you some space to figure out what's really important to you."

"You're important to me, Mary," Cholmondeley said. "You are."

But she'd already hung up the receiver.

*   *   *

"How could you have been so wrong?" Cholmondeley asked.

Leipfold was sitting in his office, a couple of miles away from Cholmondeley's throne in one of the Old Vic's private meeting rooms. He was glad he was out of arm's reach of the man. He was clearly having a tough time of it, and Leipfold didn't want to give him an excuse to lash out.

"I'll admit it was a long shot," Leipfold said. "But it's better to be safe than sorry. Besides, I always hated those gnomes. I did you a favour."

"A favour?"

"Yeah," Leipfold said. "I knew your tech boys would destroy them if they took a look at them. Don't pretend you're not glad they're gone."

There was a pause on the phone line, followed by a sound that Leipfold interpreted as a muffled laugh from a man who was holding a hand over the receiver.

"You make a good point," Cholmondeley said. "I always hated the damn things, too. Made my front garden look like bloody Narnia. But that's not going to help my marriage."

"I can't help you there, Jack," Leipfold said. "It's not my area. But I'll keep investigating the missing gnome to see if I can find something."

*   *   *

Jack tried his best to make it up to Mary. He bought her a dozen roses ("they remind me of death"), took her out to dinner at a fancy restaurant ("a waste of money") and bought her a hundred new gnomes ("not the same") that were delivered two days later by a Yodel truck. But it all seemed to make no difference. Mary was in a bad mood, and Cholmondeley was still on the receiving end of it.

A couple of days later, Mary came back from her mother's, and she took to skulking around the house in a black dressing gown and refusing to shave her legs. She made her husband sleep on the sofa.

"And all over a bloody gnome," Cholmondeley said. "I don't understand it, Mary."

"Fuck the bloody gnome," she said. Cholmondeley was taken aback and stunned into silence. It was the first time he'd heard his wife swear, and it ruined the illusion. It was like he'd caught her with her trousers down in the bathroom.

"What's wrong with you?"

"Sorry," Mary said. "I got a little carried away. But damn it, Jack. You know how I feel."

Mary paused for a moment. She looked down at her lap, even though she'd done nothing wrong. "Besides," she said. "It was never about the gnomes. It was about us, Jack."

"Us?"

"You never let me be myself," she said. "I'm just poor old Mary Cholmondeley, the homely wife of the keen cop. I always knew you hated those gnomes. So did I. They were bloody atrocious. But get this, Jack. You can get rid of the gnomes, I don't mind."

"Really?"

"Really," she said. "And instead, I'm going to collect plastic flamingos."

*   *   *

Cholmondeley hated the flamingos even more than he'd hated the gnomes, and that did a lot to fix the rift between them. Within a couple of weeks, Mary had two dozen flamingos out front and a dozen more in the back garden. She'd even pinned a flamingo air freshener up in his panda car.

By the time that Mary bought her fiftieth, Cholmondeley had almost forgotten about them. They were just a part of life that he tried not to think about.

Then he met the kid.

He was a wiry kid, the acne-faced youth from number twenty-six who Cholmondeley knew as a menace because of what he got up to on his mountain bike. Cholmondeley couldn't remember his name—David, Dean or Derek, perhaps.

The kid approached him with a bike between his legs while Cholmondeley was setting up Big Beaky, his wife's latest addition to the family. Big Beaky was like all of the other flamingos except he was eight feet tall and weighed the same as a piece of flat-pack furniture.

"Hi."

"Hey," Cholmondeley said. "David, isn't it?"

"No," the kid replied. "It's Jacob."

"Jacob!" Cholmondeley said. "Ah yes, I knew it. How can I help?"

"I wanted to say that I'm sorry, sir," Jacob said. "I feel terrible."

"You do? Terrible about what?"

"I stole your gnome, sir," the kid said. "A couple of weeks ago. I was drunk and it was a dare and, well…"

Cholmondeley started laughing, which was clearly not what the kid had expected. He flinched and leapt backwards like a cat that had been attacked, which only made Cholmondeley laugh even more. By the end of it, he was struggling to breathe and emitting loud whistles that sounded more like a kettle boiling than a human laughing.

"What is it?" the kid asked.

"You stole the gnome?" Cholmondeley said. "That's bloody priceless. You almost ruined my marriage."

"I'm sorry," the kid repeated. "I still have it if you want it. I could bring it back."

"Why the bloody hell would I want you to do that?" Cholmondeley asked. "Good riddance, as far as I'm concerned."

"What happened to the rest of them?" the boy asked.

"They've gone, kid," Cholmondeley said. "All thanks to you."

"Jeez," he replied. "I'm sorry, mister. Is there anything I can do to make it up to you?"

"As a matter of fact, there is." Cholmondeley smiled at him, the smile of a wolf in sheep's clothing. "You see those flamingos?"

"Yeah, I see the flamingos," the kid said.

"Good," Cholmondeley replied. "Do me a favour. I want you to start nicking those instead."

The Family Reunion

IT WAS LEIPFOLD'S least favourite time of the year. It was time for him to file his tax return.

He had a rudimentary understanding of mathematics, of course, and he kept his receipts as obsessively as he hoarded books after he finished reading them. But that didn't make the process any less arduous, and he hated that it took him away from his cases. That was why he had a man to do it for him.

Mr. Postlethwaite was a dull, unassuming man in a tweed suit that Leipfold had first hired through the Yellow Pages. He'd been doing a good job for a couple of years, although he did start to stress whenever Leipfold handed over his cardboard box full of receipts. They weren't even in chronological order, and Leipfold's sloppy handwriting in the company ledger was difficult to read at the best of times.

"How can I help you today, Mr. Leipfold?" Mr. Postlethwaite asked.

"I'm glad you asked," Leipfold replied. "I need you to file my tax return."

"Consider it done," Postlethwaite said. "And in return, Mr. Leipfold, I was wondering if you could do something for me. I have something I'd like you to investigate. You scratch my back, and I'll scratch yours. I'll waive the invoice for the tax return if you give me a couple of hours of your time."

"You can do that?" Leipfold asked.

"Of course," Postlethwaite replied. "I'm self-employed, I can do what I want. Well, within reason. You know how it is."

"I do," Leipfold said, and he did. He smiled. "Sounds like you've got yourself a deal. What's the job?"

"I'm looking for my birth mother," Postlethwaite said. "She gave me up for adoption when I was a baby. I haven't seen her since. She might not even be alive, but if she is then I want to speak to her."

"Why?" Leipfold asked.

For a moment or two, Postlethwaite looked offended, and Leipfold thought that the man was about to leave. Then he softened and a change came over him. Leipfold could see it in the way the man was sitting.

"Did I touch a nerve?" he asked.

"I'm sorry," the man replied. "It's not your fault. You weren't to know. Let's just say that I've got a growth on my lung that isn't good news. I'll be lucky if I make it to Christmas. If I can, I'd like to talk to her one last time."

"I'm sorry to hear that," Leipfold said. "But that's understandable. Have you got anything to go on?"

"I've got my birth certificate," Postlethwaite replied. "It has my mother's name on it, so that should help. And I was raised in the care of a chap called Mr. Oates at an orphanage. I have no idea if the place is still running, but I figured if anyone could find out, it'd be you."

Leipfold slid over his receipts and his ledger. "It's a deal," he said. "You reconcile this little lot, and I'll find out what happened to your mother. If there's something for me to find, I'll find it."

* * *

Oates's Orphanage was an imposing place that looked more like a gothic church than an orphanage. The building dated back to the 1700s and had once been used as a workhouse, which somehow felt appropriate. It felt like a prison and must have looked downright evil in the night, during a thunderstorm.

The building was still being used as a facility for children who needed care, but its funding had diminished and half of the wings were closed. Mr. Oates was long gone, and he'd been replaced by a young Hispanic woman called Mrs. Velasquez. She was a sour-faced matriarch with an unhelpful attitude. She told Leipfold that she was too busy looking after the children and running the facility to talk to him, which may well have been the truth.

"How about I make it worth your while?" Leipfold asked.

The woman shook her head, but she still took the thirty pounds that he offered her and slipped it into her back pocket.

"Consider that to be a donation to the cause," Leipfold said. "In return, I could do with a little information. I'm following up on a lead for a client. He was placed into care here as a child, and he's trying to find his mother."

"I can't give out that information," Velasquez said.

"I'm not taking no for an answer," Leipfold replied. "You're going to give it to me."

"Why should I?"

"Because if you give me the information I want, I'll double that 'donation'," Leipfold explained. "And because if you don't, I'll make a complaint to the council."

"You have no grounds for a complaint," Velasquez replied. "I'm simply following protocol. What do you hope to achieve?"

"I do my research, Mrs. Velasquez," Leipfold said. "You're coming up for a round of funding. My complaint might not stick, but it'll be enough to derail you."

"You'd do that to the children?"

"No," Leipfold said. "You'd do that to the children. Of course, you could just provide me with the information that I'm asking for."

Mrs. Velasquez spat out a stream of rapid Spanish that sounded, to Leipfold's ear, to be a string of curses. Then she said, "As you wish, Mr. Leipfold. But I want you to give me the money first."

*   *   *

Mrs. Velasquez led Leipfold through to an old storage room that was filled with their physical records from before they'd installed computers. She watched him like a hawk as he rifled through the musty information. It took the best part of an hour because the unholy mess wasn't alphabetised, but Leipfold was able to find the right record in the spidery handwriting of Mr. Oates himself in one of the old, leather ledgers from the mid-1960s.

Unfortunately for Leipfold, it told him nothing he didn't already know. The institute's records confirmed the client's story and backed up his place of birth: Good Hope Hospital, up north in Sutton Coldfield. Leipfold had been hoping the information was incorrect because a trip to the midlands would take time and money. It was starting to look like it would have been cheaper just to pay his accountant's fees.

But there was something in the thrill of the chase. Leipfold slept lightly that night and hopped on his motorbike as soon as the sun rose. It was just over 120 miles from door to door, but Leipfold covered the distance in an hour and a half. The conditions were great, and he'd missed the feel of the wind as he leaned towards it with the motorway passing by beneath his wheels.

He arrived at the hospital while most people were still on their way to work and introduced himself to the matron of the paediatric wards. She was in her late thirties and more than happy to welcome Leipfold.

"Hi," she said as Leipfold walked up to meet her outside the hospital's main entrance. She was holding a cardboard placard with Leipfold's name on it, as though she was picking him up from the airport. "Great to meet you at last."

"Likewise," Leipfold said. He looked her up and down and thought, *if only you lived in London*. "Thanks for agreeing to help me. You'd be surprised how rare that is."

"It's my pleasure," she replied. "Everyone should have a mother. If I can help your client to reunite with his, I'll have done a good job. If not…well, at least I tried."

"That's the spirit," Leipfold said. "So what have you got for me?"

"Well," the woman said. "We lost a lot of our records when we switched to a new system."

"I hear that a lot," Leipfold said.

"It wouldn't have done you much good," the matron said. "As much as I like to help people, there's such a thing as patient confidentiality."

"Then why did you bring me up here?" Leipfold asked.

"Good question," the nurse replied. "And it comes with a simple answer. You see, Mr. Leipfold, I might not be able to help you directly. But I can put you in touch with someone who can."

*　　*　　*

The matron of the hospital gave Leipfold the name, address and telephone number of a woman called Janet Way, a former midwife at the hospital who'd earned a reputation amongst the staff as the source of all gossip, the best person to speak to if you needed to know something.

Unfortunately for Leipfold, the address he'd been given was that of Sunnyvale Retirement Home, a private institution in nearby Tamworth. Leipfold parked his bike a respectable distance away so that the revs from its over-excitable engine wouldn't give some old geezer a heart attack.

It was a relatively open facility that allowed people to come and go as they pleased. Visitors weren't just allowed; they were actively encouraged. Janet knew Leipfold was coming over thanks to her old friend the matron, and the matron had also pre-warned Leipfold about the woman's unfortunate medical condition.

"I have early onset Alzheimer's, you know," the woman said by way of greeting.

Leipfold grimaced and tried to lighten the mood by saying, "I get tennis elbow."

The woman didn't smile, but she did shake his hand and invite him inside. Leipfold accepted her offer of a cup of tea and then interviewed her as best as he could about her time on the maternity ward. Janet Way remembered more than Leipfold expected, but she was mostly preoccupied with trivialities and meaningless stories of who kissed who at the Christmas party. When Leipfold fed her with some information about her client, she was less than helpful.

"Oh yes," she said, beaming like a kid with a new toy to show off. "I was working at the time. I remember because it was when Mrs. Monahan took a leave of absence after her husband walked out."

"Very interesting," Leipfold said. "So what can you tell me about the boy's parents?"

"Boy?" she asked. "What boy? No, her husband was no boy. He was a man. He joined the army, I believe."

Leipfold shrugged and wondered whether the trail was about to go cold. He couldn't tell whether it was her illness or whether she simply liked to talk in spiralling tangents that took him no closer to the case's culmination.

They talked for another hour or two, draining three more brews in the process, but the pages in Leipfold's notebook remained as empty as they were the day it came out of the factory. He decided to call it a day and to end the interview, but just as he was getting up to leave, the woman said something.

"Custer."

"Excuse me?"

"Custer," she repeated. "James Custer. He's the man you're looking for."

"The man?" Leipfold said. "But I'm looking for a woman."

"No," Janet said. "Not the mother. The father. James Custer."

Leipfold grinned. "That'll do nicely," he said. "Thank you for the information."

*   *   *

Leipfold found James Custer in the last place he thought to look. The old man had been dead for twenty years and was buried beneath a weeping willow in St. Mary's. The church was just round the corner in nearby Lichfield. Leipfold only found the grave thanks to a helpful caretaker at Tamworth's St. Editha's who was able to dig through the archives and point him in the right direction.

He'd only stopped by the church in the first place because he needed a place to sit down.

It's funny, Leipfold reflected, *how some of the best leads come when you least expect them.*

The caretaker didn't recognise the name, but he did suggest looking through the archives. Leipfold had been surprised to find that the church's records were computerised and that they were more in-depth than the archives of both the orphanage and the NHS. There was no record of his client's mother, but the father was listed right there in the records that had been shared by the council. After that, finding the grave was easy.

He'd been staring at the grave for so long that he'd forgotten where he was. He felt a curious emotion, something impossible to identify, as though he was connected to the dead man through some psychic bond, a shared adventure a score of years after Custer's death.

His concentration broke and he looked up. He was no longer alone there. Another mourner, a blonde woman dressed in black, was standing a couple of steps behind him with a bouquet of flowers in her hands. She was watching Leipfold with a curious expression on her face.

"Who are you?" she asked.

"I'm James Leipfold," he replied. "I'm a private detective. Who are you?"

"I'm Harriet Harper," she said. "Formerly Harriet Custer. That's my ex-husband that you're looking at. What are you doing here?"

"I'm on a case," Leipfold replied. "Harriet Custer, huh?"

"That's right," she replied. "I've been coming here every week for twenty years. He passed away when we were just kids."

"I'm sorry," Leipfold said. "Did the two of you have children?"

"Yes," she said. "A boy, many moons ago."

"But you didn't bring him with you today."

"What's it to you?" she asked, eyeing him suspiciously. "What are you doing here, Mr. Leipfold, really?"

Leipfold took a deep breath and then spewed out the truth of it. "Your son isn't here because you gave him away," he said. "I think your son is my accountant. He's the reason I'm here in the first place. He's looking for you. You're not an easy person to find."

"That's how I like it," the woman said. She paused for a moment. "You've found my son?"

"I think so."

"I never wanted anything to do with him," Harriet said. "I was always ashamed of my past. But everything's different, now."

"It is?"

"My husband is dead," she said.

"Your husband died twenty years ago."

She smiled thinly. "Not that one," she said. "Roger, my second husband. He passed away a couple of months ago."

"Then perhaps you're ready to confront the past," Leipfold said. "What do you think?"

The woman paused again. She gave Leipfold a look that he couldn't interpret, opened her mouth and then closed it again. Then she said, "Give me a week to think about it."

*   *   *

It took Harriet Harper a lot longer than a week to make a decision. In fact, Leipfold sensed she was stalling him for as long as possible. It wasn't until several weeks later that he finally convinced her to play her part in an impromptu family reunion. Even then, he'd had to resort to vague threats and insinuations, including a few hints that if she didn't come to meet her son in his office, he'd supply his client with her address and leave her to it. With no other choice, Harper had caved and agreed to a meeting in Leipfold's office on Balcombe Street.

Leipfold saved the surprise until Mr. Postlethwaite came in to deliver his tax return. When his mother entered the room and Leipfold told him who she was, the accountant started to cry. His birth mother awkwardly threw an arm around him and sat back to listen to her son's story. When he got to the part about the growth on his lung, she started crying, too.

Leipfold left the two of them to it and turned his attention to the reports that Postlethwaite had delivered. It had been the company's first successful year. Leipfold's business was officially running at a profit.

Married to the Job

LEIPFOLD WAS SORTING through his wardrobe, looking for his only good quality suit. He hadn't tried it on for a couple of years. It was a little tight around the stomach, but it'd do for a single night. He thought about the irony. Considering it was a blind date, he was putting a lot of effort into looking good.

The whole thing had been Jack Cholmondeley's idea. The woman he was off to meet was a friend of Mary's. That didn't bode well, and Leipfold had decided that if his date was anything like Mrs. Cholmondeley, he wouldn't be staying any longer than the starter.

I didn't even want to come in the first place, Leipfold thought.

It was true. Leipfold had initially refused to go. "I'm married to the job," he'd said to Jack Cholmondeley. "You of all people should know what that's like."

"Perhaps," Cholmondeley replied. "But I'm married to mine, and I still found time to marry Mary, too. What have you got to lose? Every strong man has a strong woman behind him."

"Bullshit," Leipfold replied. "Strong women don't need a man."

"Please, James," Cholmondeley said. "Mary will have my guts for garters if you don't take us up on it. Do it for me. I'll owe you one."

"You'll owe me one?" Leipfold repeated. He thought about it for a moment. "Ah, go on then," he said. "What the hell? But I won't forget it."

That's how Leipfold found himself heading along to The Ledbury, the brand-new restaurant that had opened up in London's Grosvenor House Hotel. There was a three-week waiting list, but Cholmondeley knew the owner and had managed to book Leipfold in with a nod and a wink.

His date for the night was called Jessica. He liked her straight away and was instantly smitten by her combination of class, good looks and good nature. She was a challenge, a little out of Leipfold's league, but he liked that. She reminded him of a crossword puzzle, and he couldn't wait to fill out her little boxes.

Jessica impressed Leipfold almost immediately by taking a keen interest in his work and professing her love for puzzles before she talked her way through the wine menu. Leipfold told her that he didn't drink. She laughed and replied, "Neither do I."

"Really?"

"Really," she said. "I've got a low tolerance, and I like being in control of myself. I like my wine from a distance."

Leipfold flashed her a rare smile. While the wine wasn't flowing, the conversation was. Jessica had put her hand on his and then left it there after he'd told an amusing story about a one-armed plumber, and they'd shared a kiss outside while they waited for her taxi.

"Can I see you again?" she asked, as the rain pitter-pattered down around them.

"Of course," Leipfold replied. He reached into his back pocket and pulled out his black leather wallet, then flipped it open to take out one of his business cards. He slipped it over to her and said, "Call me."

But he left it at that and didn't expect anything more. Unfortunately for Jessica, Leipfold had trust issues, and they manifested themselves in a flat-out unwillingness to entertain a future in which he was no longer alone. He liked her. He just didn't trust her. Not yet, at least.

So Leipfold decided to do what he did best. He decided to carry out a little investigation.

*　　*　　*

As much as Leipfold would have liked an excuse to ogle the woman from afar, he simply didn't have the time to get the job done. Instead, he gathered his team of local kids and set them on the woman's tail with explicit instructions to see that she didn't come to any harm. It didn't take them long to start reporting back to him.

The update was delivered by Gherkin, a kid with an unusual nickname who'd worked his way to the top of the hierarchy on the city's troubled streets. Leipfold always assumed that, like the Sue that Johnny Cash knew, the name had made him tougher. The truth was that nobody wanted the title. Being at the top made you a target, and Gherkin had already been stabbed four times with a screwdriver. It was just a part of life on the streets.

According to Gherkin, Jessica lived a relatively normal life. He gave Leipfold a breakdown of her activities for the week, and the highlight was a trip to the local soup kitchen. Leipfold paused him right there and looked up a number in the phone book, then put in a call to the church that ran the kitchen and asked a few questions. It didn't take him long to confirm the intel.

"There is one problem, though," Gherkin said. "I saw her with some geezer. Early twenties, maybe. I got an address for you, though. I can show you, if you'd like."

"Please do," Leipfold said, "I've got a window in my schedule. Besides, I might have another little job for you."

"Yeah?"

"Yeah," Leipfold said. "We're going to go and knock on his door, and I might need backup. Come on, you can ride on the back of the bike."

*   *   *

"Right," Leipfold said. "Are we clear?"

"Yeah," Gherkin said, "I'll knock on the door and ask the bloke how he knows your woman."

"That's the deal," Leipfold said. "But don't let on that you know me."

"Gotcha."

Leipfold watched apprehensively as the kid meandered his way down the street and up to the house's front door. It was painted black with a big white number nine on the front of it, and the chap that Gherkin had seen from a distance came to the door almost immediately.

From his distant perch, Leipfold couldn't tell what was being said, but he could tell from the man's body language that he wasn't happy. That much was obvious by the way he slammed the door in Gherkin's face. The kid wandered back over to Leipfold's spot amongst the oak trees that lined the street's perimeter.

"What happened?" Leipfold asked.

"He told me to piss off," the kid replied. "But don't worry about it. I get that a lot. I can be persistent."

"What did you do?"

"I said I'd keep ringing the bugger's doorbell until he told me what I wanted. He knows your bird, all right. He's her ex-boyfriend."

*   *   *

After that, Leipfold thought he knew all he needed to know, so he called off the kids and gave up on Jessica. Exes were complicated, especially when people were still seeing them, so he figured he'd let nature take its course. If she called him, she called him.

As nature would have it, she did call him, just over a week after their date at The Ledbury. She said she wanted to see him again and suggested a Vietnamese place that she knew, nestled along a little side street about a mile and a half from Leipfold's office. He rode there on the back of his motorbike.

The second date was a disaster. Leipfold wasn't exactly on his worst behaviour, but he was brashly and unashamedly himself. He was also worried about work, and he wasn't exactly communicative when she asked him questions about his personal life. Then she dropped the bombshell.

"So I hear you paid some kid to knock on my ex's door," she said. "That's weird. Who the hell does that?"

"I do," Leipfold said. "Apparently."

"Why?" she demanded. "If you wanted to know, you could have asked. Yes, I have an ex-boyfriend. Yes, sometimes I see him. We're just friends. But that's not the real issue here."

"It isn't?"

"Of course not," Jessica replied. "The real issue is that you went behind my back. What kind of precedent does that set for the rest of our relationship?"

"Right."

"How can I trust you if you're pulling stunts like this? Paying children to spy on me, James. Honestly."

"I'm sorry," Leipfold said. "I'm no good at this. I didn't even want to meet you in the first place."

"Charmed, I'm sure."

"I didn't mean it like that," Leipfold said. "I'm just not good with people. Well, I'm good with people, bad with romance."

"I thought you were doing pretty well," Jessica said. "At least, you were until you started to spy on me. Trust is important to me."

"It's important to me, too," Leipfold replied. "But I've never been any good at it. Especially with my history."

"Your history?"

Leipfold grimaced and tried to turn it into a smile. "I don't like to talk about that," he said.

"And that's exactly the problem," she replied.

The two of them parted on friendly terms, but they both knew that they'd never see each other again. It didn't need to be spoken aloud. It floated on the air between them and felt conspicuous by its absence.

Cholmondeley said it best when he found out about it.

"You ended it?" he exclaimed. "Jesus Christ. You really are married to the job. I thought you liked her."

"I did," Leipfold said. "Maybe a little too much. She's better off without me."

"She should be the one to decide that."

"There's nothing to decide," Leipfold said. "And besides, I'd rather be alone."

He meant it.

Bad Santa

LEIPFOLD *HATED* CHRISTMAS.

There was just something about it that made him want to vomit. Perhaps it was the food. Sprouts gave him wind, and he claimed to be allergic to stuffing, although he'd never tried it. More likely, though, it was the fact that he was utterly alone.

Leipfold's parents had died while he was serving time in Reading Jail, and the only friends he had were either people like Jack Cholmondeley, who had families of their own, or people like Cedric at the Rose & Crown who were busy hustling. But even the criminals and the gangsters had someone to spend the day with. Leipfold would be spending the holidays alone, without even the comfort of a bottle to get him through. He'd treated himself to a bumper crossword book as an early Christmas present, but it would only keep him going for a couple of days at best.

He'd even thought about buying himself a bottle, but he refused to allow himself anything stronger than a black coffee.

Meanwhile, Christmas was getting closer.

Leipfold waited until December twenty-second to get his shopping done. He didn't have much to buy, because he didn't have many people to buy for. He was after a bottle of brandy for Jack Cholmondeley and a new watch for himself, as well as whatever he could snare in the sales to help breathe some new life into his office.

When he finally got round to ticking it off his to-do list, he made the rookie mistake of going to Westfield. The place was absolutely rammed, and it was patrolled by more police than usual thanks to rumours of a bomb scare. The Good Friday Agreement had put an end to the fear campaigns of the IRA a couple of years earlier, but there were still loyalists on the fringes with a point to make. It didn't worry Leipfold. If a bomb went off, he'd deal with it. If a bomb didn't go off, he'd deal with that, too.

But he wasn't expecting to have to deal with Santa.

Leipfold was strolling casually past H&M when it happened. The jolly old fat man came tumbling down from the second floor of the shopping centre.

"Jesus Christ," Leipfold murmured. He ran over as quickly as he could and took a look at the wounded St. Nick. He was unconscious, but he was breathing. Leipfold found himself giving the man emergency treatment while he waited for reinforcements. It didn't take long. Thanks to the bomb threat, EMTs were already on the scene. Santa had been picked up and stretchered off into the back of an ambulance within ten minutes.

Santa wasn't looking good, but Leipfold thought he'd probably make it.

Not that he had much time to think about it. He was quickly shepherded away into a back office by the red-faced centre manager, who looked so stressed that Leipfold worried his head would explode. He guided the detective through a labyrinth of corridors and back rooms towards his private office.

Once they were inside, he offered Leipfold a seat on his plush leather sofa and wandered over to a drinks cabinet, where he pulled out a selection of whiskeys.

"Left over from our Christmas party," he explained. "I thought you could use a drink. You've earned it."

Leipfold smiled and waved the man away. "I don't drink," he said. "But thanks for the offer. A glass of water will be fine."

"Right," the man replied. "I'll see what I can do." He strolled back over to the door and barked out an order to an invisible PA, then moved back to his desk and sat down in his chair. "Thanks for your help."

"Don't mention it," Leipfold said. "But what the hell happened?"

The manager sighed. "Alas," he said. "Santa is a drunk. I should know. We've had problems with him before. He's worked here every Christmas for the last eight years. Old sod's on his final warning."

"Very festive," Leipfold said. "What's his problem?"

"He used to save it until after his shifts," the manager said. "But I've caught him with booze on his breath a couple of times in the last few weeks.

"It's a terrible thing," Leipfold murmured.

"Did you see how he fell?"

"I didn't," Leipfold admitted. "The first I heard was a scream. I ran over to see what was happening and saw Santa on the ground at a crooked angle. I ran over to him, cleared a space in the crowd and administered first aid. That's how you found me."

"I didn't see it, either," the manager said. "I bet he fell. Silly old drunk."

"I'm not so sure," Leipfold murmured. He rubbed his forehead absentmindedly. "What about your security cameras?"

"What about them?"

"Can you get hold of the footage?" Leipfold asked. "Perhaps we'll be able to see what happened."

"That's…actually quite a good idea." The man looked shrewdly across at him. "What did you say your name was?"

"Leipfold," he said. "James Leipfold. I'm a private detective. And you are?"

"Adams," the man replied. "John Adams." He offered him his hand and the two men shook. "A private detective, huh? Perhaps you can help me."

"Perhaps I can," Leipfold said. "But first, we're going to need to get hold of those tapes."

*   *   *

The two men were disappointed. John's staff had combed through the footage, but even with a few different angles, they could only see Santa falling and, after the impact, lying deathly still on the ground. But nothing had caught the moment that Santa had spilled over the balcony. Meanwhile, time was ticking on, and Leipfold still had his shopping to do.

"I'm going to have to go," he said. "But good luck with your investigation."

"Wait," John said. "I could use your help here. I need to prove that Westfield wasn't at fault."

"What if you were?"

"We weren't," John snapped. "And I need you to help me to prove it. How about taking us on as a client? We'll fund an investigation so that if that old fat bastard decides to litigate, we've got something to fight him with."

"And for your own peace of mind, of course," Leipfold added.

"Of course."

Leipfold sighed, but he reminded himself that a case was a case. Any new puzzle was good enough to pique his interest. So he took John through his rates and arranged for him to visit the office the following day to sign a contract. Meanwhile, John called his PA through and asked her to pull off a copy of the injured Santa's personnel record. He gave Leipfold a photocopy and told him to keep it to himself.

The detective finished his shopping that evening and then turned his attention to the case the following morning. From the personnel record, he picked out the man's address and followed the directions to what turned out to be a grubby little bedsit in Clapham. He wasn't sure what took him there, and indeed it would have taken a Christmas miracle for him to have been discharged already. Call it curiosity, perhaps. He'd been half a mile down the road for a meeting with a potential new client who wanted to hire him at the last minute to keep tabs on his ex-wife over the holidays.

With nothing better to do, and the promise of time and a half for a couple of days, he thought he'd probably take it on.

As expected, Santa wasn't in. But his landlady was, although she seemed put out by his disappearance and by the arrival of a stranger on her tenant's doorstep. Leipfold met her at the entrance of the building. By a bizarre quirk of fate, she happened to be inspecting Santa's room when Leipfold pushed the buzzer. She let him inside and agreed to answer a couple of questions.

They talked inside the apartment. The landlady took the only chair in the room and Leipfold took the sofa. He explained who he was and what he was doing there. The woman was only too keen to help when he promised to share what he learned with her.

"He hasn't paid his rent," she explained. "And as you can see, it's a mess in here."

Leipfold could see that, all right. The apartment was strewn with empty booze bottles and cardboard sleeves from microwave meals. Other than that, there were few personal touches. It looked more like a motel room than the room somebody lived in.

"So what's next?" she asked.

"I'll see if they'll let me go and speak to him," Leipfold said.

"Who?"

"Ah," Leipfold said. "About that. Santa is in hospital. It's not looking good."

*   *   *

Leipfold managed to blag his way into intensive care to speak to Santa, but the staff only gave him fifteen minutes. They were reluctant to let him in to begin with. Unfortunately, Saint Nick was still in a coma and hooked up to life support in a lonely hospital room.

But Leipfold spoke to him anyway. He told the man who he was and what his job was, and he left behind a half dozen business cards so that the man could find him if he woke up and remembered.

For the next couple of days, the case weighed heavily on Leipfold's mind. He found no new clues and Santa was still in a coma, although Leipfold visited him every day to see how he was doing.

And so Christmas Day rolled around, and Leipfold found himself alone in his tiny room, eating a microwaved Christmas dinner out of a plastic tray. He was using a plastic knife and fork to eat it so he could throw it all away in one trip to the recycling bin. He'd always been a fan of efficiency.

The phone rang, and Leipfold paused with his fork halfway to his mouth. He answered it cautiously, but he was back to his usual animated self within the first ten seconds of the conversation.

"Who is it?" Leipfold asked.

"It's Dave," the voice replied. "Dave Perkins. You might know me as Santa Claus. Ho ho ho and merry Christmas, Mr. Leipfold."

"Ah," Leipfold replied. "I wondered when I'd be hearing from you. How are things?"

"They're okay," the man replied. "I mean, as long as you don't mind hospital food."

Leipfold laughed. Having been there before, he could appreciate the man's gallows humour. It was funny, in a way. Funny because it was true.

"How did you find me?" Leipfold asked.

"You left your business card," the man reminded him. "And besides, I heard you."

"But you were unconscious."

"I was," the man agreed. "But now I'm not, and I remember. I thought I'd give you a call because truth be told, Mr. Leipfold, I don't have anyone else."

"I know that feeling," Leipfold said. "What happened at Westfield? Did you fall?"

The man paused. "No," he said, hesitantly. "I didn't fall. I jumped."

"Jesus, Dave," Leipfold said. "It can't be that bad, can it?"

"I have nothing and no one," he replied. "And I can't get off the bottle. I was drunk when I jumped, Mr. Leipfold. It does evil things to a man."

"Look," Leipfold said. "I get it. I really do. Are you still at the hospital?"

"Yes."

"Good." He smiled. "You wait there, Dave. I'm coming to see you."

*   *   *

How did it come to this? Leipfold wondered. *Off to see Santa on Christmas Day.*

The man wasn't in good shape. Without the outfit on, he looked more like a working-class pub wastrel than the jolly old fat man who lived at the North Pole. But Leipfold felt glad to see him in some strange way that he couldn't explain. The man's limbs were in casts, and his face was bandaged and battered. But he also looked like he had hope, which was refreshing. Leipfold hadn't been expecting that.

The two men sat and talked and traded cracker jokes, before tuning into the Queen's speech on the BBC thanks to the hospital room's small television set. When the speech was over, they turned it off and sat in a shared silence. It was the comfortable kind, but Leipfold was still compelled to fill it. So he told Santa about how he was naughty before he was nice and how he used to drink like a fish and get himself into trouble. He even told him about the accident and his stay in jail, despite the fact that the past was the past and he was trying his best to put it behind him.

"That's tough luck," Perkins told him. "And once you have something like that on your record, no one wants to hire you."

"Tell me about it," Leipfold said. "Why do you think I'm my own boss? No one else will have me."

"Have you ever thought about becoming a professional Santa?" the man asked. "It's the best job I've ever had."

"I don't think I'm ready for that just yet," Leipfold said.

"Suit yourself."

"What about you?" Leipfold asked. "What's your story?"

"Ah," Perkins said, smiling ruefully. "About that. I had a run of bad luck earlier this year. My wife passed away, I lost my job and then I lost the house. What little cash I had left, I spent on the bottle. This wasn't my first attempt at suicide. I can't even kill myself properly. All I can do is drink and hustle and repeat the cycle again and again until one morning I don't wake up."

Leipfold whistled. "That's quite the story," he said.

"Everyone has a story," Santa replied.

Leipfold laughed. "I suppose so," he conceded. "But listen, there's help out there. I go to meetings. Perhaps you'd like to come along sometime."

"I'll think about it," Perkins said.

"And I want you to look after yourself, you hear?"

"I'm not going to try to kill myself," the man said. "Not again. I have a friend now."

Leipfold smiled. "Good," he said. "It was nice meeting you, Santa."

*   *   *

After Christmas, but before the New Year, Leipfold made his way to see the centre manager with his findings. It wasn't a long meeting, but it did the job and convinced the man to pay his fees.

"As long as Westfield wasn't at fault, I'm happy," the manager said.

Leipfold furrowed his brow. "Santa tried to kill himself," he said. "You could be a little more sympathetic."

"I could," he said. "But I won't."

"Where's your humanity?"

"What humanity?" the man replied. "It's the busiest time of year. I don't have time to be compassionate at Christmas."

It struck Leipfold as just a little bit ironic.

*   *   *

It was New Year's Day, and Leipfold was back at the hospital. Perkins was about to be discharged, and Leipfold wanted to see him again before he moved on with his life. He wanted to remind him about the meetings and to extend the hand of friendship. And he wanted to give the man the £800 in fees that the mall owner had coughed up once Leipfold completed his investigation.

He found the man in his hospital room, sitting up in bed and squinting through a pair of glasses at a paperback copy of *Murder on the Orient Express*. He looked up at Leipfold as he walked into the room and flashed a weak smile at him.

"You're awake!" Leipfold said. He grinned. "It's good to see you, Dave. Here, I've got something for you."

"What is it?" the man asked as Leipfold handed him an envelope. Out of his costume and in the hospital bed, he didn't look in any condition to deliver presents. He was barely fit to receive them.

"Consider it a gift," Leipfold said. "Use it to get on your feet again."

"Are you serious?" the man said. "How do you know I won't spend it on the bottle?"

"I don't," Leipfold said. "How could I? But every drunk has a final bottle, and I think you've had yours. I'm giving you the benefit of the doubt, Mr. Perkins. Because no one ever gave it to me."

"But what if I don't want to stop drinking?" he asked. "And what if I *can't*?"

"You have to *try*," Leipfold said. "If you don't, you're a dead man."

Perkins thought for a moment. "Perhaps that wouldn't be such a bad thing," he said. "But I'll try, Mr. Leipfold. I'll try it for you."

Leipfold had wanted to go home as soon as he made the handover, but he couldn't bring himself to leave the man alone there. So he sat down in the chair beside the bed and talked with Santa about the day's news until the nurses came along and told him it was time to leave.

Silky's Cut

BUSINESS WAS DRYING UP, and Leipfold was worried about it. He was so skint that he'd soon need to dip into his savings account and withdraw the money he'd put by to pay the taxman. He was dicing with bankruptcy and he knew it.

Part of it was caused by the rise of the internet. Leipfold wasn't exactly a techie, but he knew enough to know that people were turning to Google instead of hiring a professional. The industry was changing, and, at age thirty-two, Leipfold worried he was too old to keep up with it.

Meanwhile, his credit cards were maxed out and the bank had refused him a loan. He could hardly blame them. He wouldn't have lent money to himself, either. But he needed to figure something out. The rent was due, and he was already a couple of months behind on it. If he wasn't careful, he might lose the office.

And so he treated the situation like only James Leipfold could. He treated it like a case that needed to be solved.

It started with a marker pen and a whiteboard. He listed out all the different ways he could think of to save some money, from giving up his bedsit and selling his bike to taking out payday loans and eating only instant noodles. He quickly realised it was the bedsit that was the problem, taking up 30 percent of his pre-tax income for a room that he rarely used. He put it at the top of the list and drew a big red circle around it.

*   *   *

Going homeless wasn't easy. There were all sorts of different considerations, like where he was going to wash. That particular quandary was solved when he signed up to a local gym, not so he could use the machines but so he could hit the showers. He knew the chap who owned it, although he couldn't remember where they'd actually met, and the membership came with the added bonus of free entry to the occasional exhibition match in the boxing ring.

Truth be told, the state of his hygiene and the state of his diet were minor concerns. He'd realised he could take toilet paper from public bathrooms, brush his teeth with his finger and live on a diet of pasta and rice, which he learned to whip up in the office's microwave. He didn't drink, so that wasn't a problem, but he'd smoked since he was a kid. So he bade goodbye to the tobacco plant and went nicotine-free through sheer force of will.

Then he took a visit from the landlord.

The sour old man was looking more tired and dishevelled than ever. He didn't seem pleased to be meeting up with Leipfold.

"You're behind on the rent, Mr. Leipfold," he said. "Three months behind. I need you to pay up by the end of the week."

"The end of the week?" Leipfold exclaimed. "I'll get you your money, but it's not going to be for a while."

"The end of the week," the landlord insisted. "Or you're out of here. It's your choice."

"Some bloody choice," Leipfold murmured.

*   *   *

Leipfold felt like he had no other option. There was only one place he could turn to in the hope of a loan. He put a call in to Jack Cholmondeley and arranged to meet him at the Rose & Crown.

"I need your help," Leipfold said, before Cholmondeley had a chance to order a drink. "I'm desperate."

"What is it, James?" Cholmondeley asked, catching Cedric's eye and signalling for him to bring a drink over.

"I'm not going to beat around the bush," Leipfold said. "I need some cash. I was wondering if you could loan me some."

"How much?"

"About four grand should do it," Leipfold said.

Cholmondeley whistled softly to himself. "That's a lot."

"It is," Leipfold agreed. "I owe back rent on the office. If I don't pay up by the end of the week, I'm out on my arse."

"Hmm," Cholmondeley murmured. He took a swig from his pint and set it back down on the table. "Well, we can't have that. I'll lend you the cash."

"That's it?"

"That's it," Cholmondeley said. He smiled. "Of course, I do need a little help with a case of my own. Now, I'm not saying I won't lend you the money if you don't lend me a hand, but…"

"Okay, okay," Leipfold said. "Point taken. As long as this isn't a pity case."

"It's not a pity case," Cholmondeley insisted. "A hopeless case, perhaps, but if anyone can solve it then it's you."

Leipfold sighed. "What do you need me to do?"

"I need you to track someone down for me," Cholmondeley said. "He's a big name in the underworld. Dangerous chap. Don't mess with him. Goes by the name of Silky. That's about all we know."

"That's it?" Leipfold said. "That's not much to go on. How did you even come across this guy?"

"We've heard the name from a couple of informants," Cholmondeley said. "He's a dealer, we think. But he's also something more than that, the big black spider in the middle of the web."

"Not the kind of man to mess with, then," Leipfold said. "Nice of you to ask me to find him."

*   *   *

Leipfold started to work his contacts. He didn't have many of them, but the ones that he did have were good at what they did, which was basically nothing. They earned cash doing odd jobs, and providing information to Leipfold was just one of them. He paid well because he passed the costs on to his clients. Jack Cholmondeley was going to have an expensive surprise waiting for him when the investigation was over.

He got lucky. A chap called Darren, who he remembered from his heavy drinking days in the Rose & Crown, was able to give Leipfold a phone number. "Tell him I sent you," he said.

So Leipfold did. He made the call from a payphone so that Silky couldn't track the call.

"Am I speaking to Silky?" he asked.

"Yeah," the man replied. He had a deep, languorous voice with a vaguely foreign accent. "Who's this?"

"My name's Jay," Leipfold lied. "Jay Little. I got your number from Dodgy Darren."

"Yeah? What do you want?"

"I'm looking to score."

"I don't know you from Adam," Silky said.

"Does it matter?" Leipfold asked. "My money's as good as anyone else's."

Silky laughed. "You sound like my kind of customer. I'm going to give you a set of instructions. I want you to follow them closely."

*   *   *

Silky's instructions led Leipfold to an underpass on an East London housing estate. The deal went down without a hitch, and Leipfold was soon the not-so-proud owner of just under a gram of cocaine. Silky had to take his cut, after all. He walked off one way and Leipfold walked off in another, but the detective soon doubled back and started to track the dealer as he looped back around and cut through alleyways and across busy roads to throw anyone who might be trailing him. He was good, but he wasn't *that* good. Nobody was.

Leipfold followed him back to the shit-heap of a council house that he lived in and made a note of the address. Then he paid a visit to Jack Cholmondeley.

*   *   *

Jack Cholmondeley was dead impressed. He hadn't expected Leipfold to come up with anything, and so the address that he'd provided was a pleasant surprise. Inadmissible in court, of course, but a good sign to guide the rest of their investigation.

"And to think I thought he was just a rumour," Cholmondeley said. "Well done, old boy. I'm impressed."

"I have that effect," Leipfold said. "I also have a bill for you."

Cholmondeley glanced down at it. It was more than he'd been expecting, but it wasn't so much that he couldn't afford it. He paid it happily.

"Who is this kid, anyway?" Leipfold asked. "Silky. Bloody stupid name, if you ask me."

"My money buys silence," Cholmondeley said. "That's the deal, right? I'm taking this out of my savings. I'd, ah…prefer it if you didn't mention it to anyone. If Mary finds out, she'll give me hell for it."

"I see," Leipfold said.

But Leipfold wasn't the type to stay silent. He wanted an answer, and he also wanted the thrill of excitement that came from wearing an undercover camera while meeting a gangster.

So he wore an undercover camera and went to meet a gangster. Silky was only too happy to sell Leipfold another gram, and Leipfold was only too happy to follow him. It was boring to begin with. He just headed home.

It was much more interesting once Jack Cholmondeley showed up.

Leipfold almost had a heart attack. Cholmondeley was sitting nonchalantly on the wall outside a corner shop with a hat pulled down low over his eyes. Stranger still, he was there with a friend. No, not a friend. He was there with Mary Cholmondeley.

Leipfold watched from a distance as the Cholmondeleys knocked on the door and somebody answered it. Even from his distant observation spot, he could see it was Silky. He moved a little closer, as casually as he could, then strolled slowly past on the other side of the road. The goal was to get an idea of what was being said, and he succeeded at that.

All he caught was a short snippet from Mary Cholmondeley. It sounded like she'd said, "What would your mother think?"

In that moment, Leipfold figured it all out. But he had no one to talk to, so he made an anonymous call to the police hotline and let them deal with it. He'd always hated drug dealers.

*   *   *

And that, Leipfold thought, was that. He put the case to the back of his mind and turned his attention to an upcoming one. He'd been hired by a rare book dealer to investigate the provenance of a manuscript that he'd been offered on the black market. If the manuscript was genuine, he intended to take it. Leipfold thought that the man would be disappointed.

Several weeks later, he was staring at the crossword in *The Tribune* while jabbing himself in the gum with a toothpick when he was interrupted by the shrill ringing of his telephone. He frowned at it as though it had done something to offend him and then he picked up the receiver.

"James Leipfold," he said, gruffly.

"Ah, James, it's me." There was no need for him to ask. He would have recognised the voice of Jack Cholmondeley anywhere. "Can't stop to chat, old friend."

"You called me," Leipfold pointed out.

"Quite," Cholmondeley replied. "Listen, James, someone tipped off one of our anonymous hotlines. Silky is in custody. I don't suppose you happen to know anything about that?"

"Not a thing," Leipfold said.

"Hmm," Cholmondeley replied, and Leipfold could tell that he didn't believe him. Not that it mattered. "He matches up with the description you gave of the chap you told me about."

"The one that you and Mary met up with?" Leipfold asked. There was a shocked silence on the other end of the line, and Leipfold could tell that his comment had hit the mark.

"You know about that?"

"I have my methods."

There was another sigh from the other end of the line, and Leipfold could almost hear the cogs turning in the old man's head. In the dead air, he could also hear the background susurrus that he'd come to associate with the Old Vic.

"Silky is Mary's nephew," Cholmondeley said. "An estranged nephew. His mother died when he was a lad and Mary hasn't seen him since. That's why I had you track him down."

"Well, I hope I helped you to find some closure."

"Closure?" Cholmondeley growled. "I should be so lucky. No, James, as far as I'm concerned, this is still an open case."

"How so?"

"You didn't catch the end of our conversation, did you?" Cholmondeley asked. "That little drug-dealing bastard isn't Silky. He isn't Mary's nephew."

Leipfold cursed softly to himself. "Then who the hell is?" he asked.

"Like I said, James," Cholmondeley replied. "The case isn't over. I have more questions than ever."

"Don't we all?" Leipfold replied. "But at least I know one thing."

"What's that?"

"I know how I'm going to pay my rent," Leipfold said.

Call it Blackmail

"SO WE HAVE A DEAL, THEN?"

"We have a deal," Leipfold confirmed. The man he was looking at had an angry leer on his face, and he seemed unimpressed by the detective's fees. But perhaps it was just a side effect of the case he was being asked to investigate.

The new client's name was Wilson. He'd asked Leipfold to follow his fiancée and to report back on whether she was loyal or whether she was seeing someone else. Cases like this were what made Leipfold the bulk of his profits. There was always some rich guy with a young girlfriend who he suspected of adultery. Wilson was just the latest in a long line of men with a sensitive job for Leipfold to work on.

"For cases like this," Leipfold said, "I usually ask for a deposit."

"That's fine," Wilson said. "I've come into a little bit of money. I won the pools."

"Congratulations," Leipfold said. Secretly, he got the feeling that something didn't add up, but money was money and it didn't matter where it came from.

For the next two weeks, Leipfold and his gang of youths from the local estate tracked the woman across the city. She was beautiful, a vision in blonde who turned heads wherever she went. Leipfold started to understand exactly why his client was so paranoid, but he didn't see evidence of any wrongdoing.

Their job was helped by the boyfriend, who was working closely with Leipfold and his team to keep tabs on her. He was a paranoid soul who rarely allowed her to leave the house on her own except for when she had to go to work, and he dropped her off and picked her back up again. That meant he was able to call the detective every time she went somewhere. He was even able to give him a heads up, offering up a time, a day and a location so he could allocate resources.

Leipfold invited Wilson back to the office for a catch-up meeting and to ask the man for a favour.

"Please," Leipfold said, "let her live her life a little bit. Give her some freedom. Let her do what she wants to do."

"Don't tell me how to manage my relationship," the man said. "I'll treat my fiancée how I want to."

"But how do you expect me to catch her out if you don't give her a chance to act against you?"

"Touché," the man said.

"You have to cut her loose."

"Not on your life."

"Trust me on this one," Leipfold said. "This is what I do for a living. You need to give people enough rope for them to hang themselves with."

The man grunted but said nothing.

"Here's the deal," Leipfold said. "I can't take the case on unless you're willing to work with me. If you want my help, you need to do as I say. It's your choice."

Privately, Leipfold hoped that the man wouldn't call his bluff. He'd caught up with his rent and he had a little cash squirreled away somewhere, but he couldn't afford to turn down work without a good reason. He held his breath until the man replied.

"Okay," he said, reluctantly. "I agree to your terms, Mr. Leipfold. But you'd better come up with the goods for me."

"I'll do my best," he said.

Once Wilson had left, Leipfold washed his hands. The man was scum through and through, a slimy scuzzball who treated his fiancée like a possession. The man clearly had control issues and all the signs were there for an abusive relationship. He hoped to God that the woman wouldn't actually marry him.

Unfortunately for Leipfold, he was being paid to do a job. He didn't need to like his client to take the money.

A couple more weeks passed, but the only man she met turned out to be a half-brother from her mother's side of the family. When Wilson found out about it, he was far from happy.

"Bloody bitch," he growled. "She lied to me. Said she was going to meet one of her girlfriends."

"It's hard to fault her for that," Leipfold said. "You wouldn't have let her go if you knew she was meeting a family member. You're a control freak, a manipulator."

"You're damn right I wouldn't," Wilson said. "They poison her and try to turn her against me. I won't stand for it."

"Mr. Wilson," Leipfold said, "I have the final report for you right here. But I'm not sure you're going to like what it says."

"Why?"

"She's in the clear," Leipfold said. "She's not seeing anyone else."

"Thank God," the man said.

"Unfortunately, that's only the start of it," Leipfold replied. "She's planning on leaving you. That's why she was meeting her brother."

"Bitch," he repeated.

"If you say so," Leipfold replied. "It's not my place to judge. But don't you think you're a little…oh, I don't know, controlling?"

"No," the man said. "No, no. You've made a mistake. I'm not paying for this."

"I assure you," Leipfold replied, "there's no mistake. You asked me to uncover the truth. That's what I did."

"Whatever," the man said. "I'm not paying your fees." He started to walk towards the door.

"Hmm," Leipfold murmured, tracking the man's progress across the office while affecting an air of nonchalance. "I beg to differ."

*　　*　　*

The following day, Leipfold was visited by the woman. She looked the same as she had when he'd first started following her, except now she had a shiner on her eye and a horrible bruise running down the side of her face.

"Don't ask," she said. "I walked into a door."

"I'm sure you did," Leipfold replied. They were sitting on the uncomfortable chairs in the office's poky reception area, cradling hot cups of coffee. There was an awkward silence.

"Look, Mr. Leipfold—"

"It's okay," Leipfold said. "You don't have to say anything. Just tell me how I can help."

"You've helped me a lot already," she replied. "Thank you for the tip-off. I should have known he'd have someone follow me. I'm just lucky that it was you."

"It was nothing."

"I want to get away," she said. "Far away. Somewhere he'll never find me. Can you help me?"

"It's not really my line of work," Leipfold said. "Can't you go to the police? I can put in a word for you with Sergeant Cholmondeley at the Old Vic if you'd like."

"No," she insisted. "Not the cops. Please." Her voice broke on the final word, and Leipfold's heart went out to her. He usually tried not to get emotionally involved, especially with his clients. But this woman wasn't a client, and so he decided to break the habit of a lifetime.

"Okay," Leipfold said. "I'll help. What do you need?"

"Money," she replied. "And a ticket out of here."

"Lady," Leipfold said, "I'm skint."

"Use the money he gave you."

"Your fiancée?" Leipfold asked. "He didn't pay me."

"He will." She smiled for the first time since entering his office.

"I'd like a little vengeance. And perhaps we can get your money while we're at it."

*   *   *

Leipfold was on the hunt again. This time, he was following his former client.

The man's soon-to-be-ex fiancée had told Leipfold all about his cocaine habit. She'd given him a description of the dealer and told him when he bought and where they usually met. Leipfold watched from a distance and took a few photographs of the men making the deal. He had a specialised lens to zoom and focus on what he wanted to photograph. He just hoped that it was good enough to catch the little baggie as it passed between their hands.

When the exchange was over, Leipfold followed his mark as he walked back home. He had the address and had taken the time to scout it out. He knew the perfect place to make his move. It was a little walkway halfway down a cul-de-sac that cut through the back of the estate and offered a seventy-foot stretch where Leipfold could catch up to the man and have a chat with him. He did exactly that.

Leipfold tailed the man at a distance but sped up a little when he reached the entrance to the alleyway. By the time that he heard the footsteps, Leipfold was ten paces behind him and accelerating. He turned to run, out of instinct more than anything, but the detective had a head start, as well as momentum on his side. He took his ex-client down with a flying rugby tackle, using the man's body as a shield to protect himself from damage when he landed.

They were both panting. Leipfold was out of breath from the sprint, and his mark had been winded by an elbow when they hit the floor. Tired as he was, Leipfold summoned his final reserves of strength and hauled himself on top of him. Then he pinned the man to the floor.

"You're in trouble now," Leipfold said. "I have all the evidence I need."

"So what?" the man wheezed. "It's just a bit of coke."

"It's a *lot* of coke," Leipfold replied. "And it's not the first time, either. Is that why you hit your fiancée? Did you do a line and feel like a big man?"

"If you're trying to threaten me, it won't work. I don't care."

"You will, though," Leipfold promised. "When I talk to your parents, your boss and your landlord. When I talk to the police and tell them about the gear, as well as that unpaid invoice of yours. Your life is going to come crashing down around you. Unless, of course…"

"Unless what?"

Leipfold grinned. "Two things," he said. "First, I want you to pay my invoice. And second, I want you to leave that fiancée of yours alone. She deserves better than you, and she won't struggle to find it."

"Is this blackmail?"

"Sure," Leipfold said. "Call it what you want."

"You'll pay for this."

"No," Leipfold replied. "*You* will. Where's my money?"

*   *   *

It was the following day, and Leipfold was pawing through *The Tribune* at the office. He was interrupted after just a couple of pages by the clatter of the downstairs letterbox. He didn't usually listen out for it, but he was expecting a little something and so he had the door open to keep an ear out.

He took the steps two at a time and surprised the receptionist from the design agency downstairs by yanking a sheaf of letters from his hand and sorting through them. There, as expected, was a letter with his name on it. Inside it there was just a single cheque without a note, but that was all the detective needed.

Now we see whether it clears, he thought.

He went back upstairs to the office and closed the door, then dug around in the bottom drawer of his desk for the little bag of white powder that he'd seized from the man who hit his fiancée. When he found it, he carried it across to the kitchen sink and tipped it in there, then rinsed it down the drain with water from the cold tap.

That's the coke gone, Leipfold thought. *I'll keep the photos, though.*

He went back to the crossword in *The Tribune* and finished it off, then flicked through the rest of the paper before heading off to the bank to cash the cheque.

He laughed when he saw the tiny article, half way down page seventeen. The information he'd provided to *The Tribune* had made it to print—and it looked like he wasn't going to keep the man's secret after all.

And it serves him bloody well right, too.

Bad for Business

THE OFFICE DOWNSTAIRS had been broken into.

It shouldn't have been much of a concern for Leipfold, but he had a bad feeling about it and thought he ought to investigate. After all, there was always the chance that the intruders had targeted the wrong office and that they were after him and the files that he held on the city's criminal underworld.

So Leipfold did what he did best. He headed downstairs to meet Otto Watson, the owner of the agency, to form a strategic partnership to secure the building. Leipfold had his secrets, but evidently they had theirs too.

"What have we got so far?" Leipfold asked.

"Not much," Watson replied. "They came during the night. We know that much. They got in somehow and removed our machines. Computers, printers, you name it. They even took the fax machine. Anything missing on your end?"

"Nothing obvious," Leipfold said. "I'm not missing any hardware, but mine's not worth much to begin with. I'm more concerned about my data. Someone could have made a copy without me knowing."

"We've got to call the police."

"Way ahead of you," Leipfold said. "I called my old buddy, Sergeant Jack Cholmondeley. He's already on his way over here. He's a cop, see. But cops can't work miracles. I think we should look into this ourselves."

*　　*　　*

But it wasn't as easy as all that. Cholmondeley arrived with a couple of his colleagues and they gave the place a once over, but they didn't find anything of note. With no clear damage to the building, the best guess was that it was an inside job. Watson suggested speaking to their landlord. Cholmondeley took the address down and led the way out of the building and back to the cop car. Leipfold didn't have much hope for a result.

Worse still, the insurance company refused to pay up. The agency was covered by two different policies, one held by themselves and one held by the landlord, and both of them refused to pay a penny until a point of entry could be confirmed. There was always the possibility that human error was at fault, and neither policy paid enough to cover that.

And so Watson and Leipfold teamed up to investigate, with Leipfold providing the brains and Watson providing the money. Leipfold gave the man a discount, but not a big one. Watson barely even noticed. Unlike Leipfold Investigations, their business was booming. They paid Leipfold's fees up front.

"Whatever it takes," he said. "Do what you've got to do. This isn't about the money anymore. It's about the principle."

Leipfold nodded. "The first thing I'll need to do is to interview each of your employees. We need to find out if they spotted anything suspicious."

*   *   *

The interviews were long, tiring and unproductive. Leipfold learned nothing new despite spending two days working the case. He had thousands of words of written transcriptions and absolutely nothing of value to show for it.

Bloody typical, he thought.

So he came back at night, armed with a set of tools that could have landed him in a jail cell if Jack Cholmondeley had found them. He approached the offices from behind and tried to stay out of the light from the streetlamps. It wasn't difficult.

But that was as far as he was able to get. Their landlord might have skimped on cost, but apparently he'd still got hold of quality. The lock was unpickable and the bars over the windows made them unusable as an entry point. He circled the building a couple of times and even climbed on to the roof via the fire escape of a neighbouring building, but there was no way in. Not without causing damage, at least. They could have smashed the windows and forced the door without a problem, but not without leaving any evidence.

And so he retreated from the place, disappointed, and went back to his little bedsit to mull things over. He thought about Occam's razor and how the simplest solution was usually the correct one.

"It would've been hard to break in without doing any damage," Leipfold murmured. "So they must have used the key. And that can only mean one thing. It was an inside job."

*   *   *

Leipfold spent the next couple of days trying to identify a likely suspect, but the truth was that all of Watson's employees were paid well and pretty lucky in life, even if they did work occasional unpaid overtime. There was only one man who could have had a grievance against the company, a Polish programmer called Andrei, and it seemed as though the finger of guilt was slowly pointing towards him.

But Leipfold wasn't convinced. He thought that Andrei was an unlikely suspect. He had a new job lined up, and Leipfold saw no reason why he'd want to risk it, especially as he was being given redundancy pay.

When asked about it, Watson said, "Andrei was fired. He was a waste of space. We don't carry dead weight here. Besides, he used to steal from us. Little things, at first. Then some of our tech started to go missing and we all knew who was to blame. If anyone broke into our office, it was Andrei. He's already stolen from us before. He's got form."

And yet when Leipfold asked Andrei the same question, he'd said, "I quit. I found a better job. They offered a better salary and part equity. It was hard to say no."

"Watson said you stole from him," Leipfold had said.

But Andrei had looked offended and shook his head. "That was nothing to do with me," he said. "Everyone stole from that place. I was one of the only ones who didn't. Sure, I took the odd pen home here and there, but I have nothing to do with any thefts and nothing to do with any break-in."

Leipfold didn't know who to believe until he called the number for Andrei's new company and asked a couple of questions of their HR department. They confirmed his story, or at least the part of it that involved them, and Leipfold was back at square one again, trying to figure out who might have held a grudge against the company or its owner.

It was a small list, a list to which he once again applied Occam's razor. That only left one name to investigate: Otto Watson.

And so Leipfold met with the owner again, this time inviting him up to his office for a little privacy. It was a mess and it was unwelcoming, but it had the effect of putting the man on edge. It was a welcome effect, as far as Leipfold was concerned.

"How can I help?" the man asked.

"You can tell me the truth," Leipfold replied.

"The truth?"

"That you were behind the job," Leipfold said. "There *was* no burglary. You think I'd fail to notice that? No damage to the building, no evidence of forced entry? Sure, it could have been one of your employees. I dare say it could even have been the landlord. But it wasn't, was it? It was you."

"I have no idea what you're talking about," Watson said.

"Then perhaps you'd better refresh your memory," Leipfold replied. "And fast. The police are going to know what you've been up to. It's fraud, you know. I called up every storage facility in town and managed to track down your unit. What's the bet that the missing machines are inside the container that you registered two days before the break-in?"

"I...I, uh—"

"I thought so."

"Don't tell anyone, okay?" he said. "I don't want any trouble. Business is booming but cash flow is a problem. I just thought I could bring in a few quid to tide us over. I thought I'd claim the machines on insurance and then just bring them back in once the storm had blown over."

"By committing a crime," Leipfold said. "And worse still, by wasting my time. You'd better pay my fees."

"I'll pay your bloody fees," the man said. "As long as it buys your silence."

Leipfold considered it for a moment. "Deal," he said, reluctantly. "But with one condition."

"What's that?"

"You move out of this place and get yourself a new office," Leipfold said.

The businessman looked confused. "I don't understand," he said. "Why?"

Leipfold frowned at him. "It's bad for business to share a building with a conman," he said.

As he walked away, he muttered, "And I should know."

The Same Flight Home

IT WAS TIME for a rare holiday.

Well, maybe not a holiday, but Leipfold was leaving the country for the first time in the best part of a decade and in his line of work, that was close enough.

He boarded the flight to Amsterdam at Heathrow Airport at 6:10AM in the morning. He was tired, so tired that even coffee couldn't save him, and the bags under his eyes were starting to look more like trash cans. He was hoping to catch some sleep on the flight, but it was an ill-conceived hope, a hope that life would never quite live up to.

The two seats to his left were taken by a couple of middle-aged women who were having a heated debate. At first, Leipfold had no idea what they were talking about, but he couldn't help himself from overhearing. Or more precisely, from listening in.

He paid little attention to the names, but the story was easy enough to follow. Someone had stolen the younger woman's bracelet, and it was the only thing she had left from her former lover. Leipfold had been listening for long enough to absorb the full story. He'd been taken by sickle cell in his early thirties, and she'd been single and unhappy ever since. He'd only ever given her one thing: the platinum bracelet that had disappeared.

He sighed and turned around in his seat, all hope of catching some sleep long forgotten.

"Excuse me," he said, addressing the two women and interrupting their conversation. "I couldn't help overhearing you. Perhaps the two of you could use a little help."

"I don't think you can help us," the older of the two replied.

"Martha, right?" Leipfold said. He turned to look at the younger woman, who was sitting beside Martha in the aisle seat. "And you must be Amy."

"How do you know our names?" Amy asked.

"I just listened to your conversation," Leipfold said. "There's no mystery there. And, Martha, I'm pleased to say that I think I *can* help you, no matter what you say. I'm a private detective."

"A private detective?" Amy repeated.

"Amy," Martha said, "We don't know this man. Can we trust him? All we know so far is that he's nosy."

"I'm a private detective," Leipfold said. "It's my job to be nosy. That's what I do."

"I suppose it is," Amy admitted. "Okay, sir. I'll tell you my story."

She started from the beginning and repeated a lot of the information that Leipfold had already heard, but she also told him about her new husband, a man who mistreated her and who liked to play games to keep her guessing.

"I wouldn't be surprised if *he* stole it," she said. "He's stolen from me before."

"Possessions?"

Amy shook her head. "No," she replied. "He took my money."

"What a gentleman," Leipfold said.

"There's something else, as well." She rolled up the sleeves of her shirt and showed Leipfold a couple of nasty bruises. One of them was a lurid purple and the other had faded slightly but still looked the colour of charcoal. He could tell from a glance that they were historic. He could also tell something else. The bruises were self-inflicted.

"It's true, you know," Martha said. "Her husband is a brute. It's awful, some of the things he does to her."

"Have you ever seen him hurt her?"

"That'd be difficult," she said. "I've never met the man."

"Well, that tells a story in itself," Leipfold murmured.

"What do you mean?" Amy asked.

"It's easy," Leipfold said. "Your husband didn't hit you. Your husband doesn't even exist. You made him up."

"Why would I do that?"

"Beats me," Leipfold said. "Why does anyone do anything?"

"This is preposterous," Martha said.

"Perhaps," Leipfold replied. "It's nothing to me. All I know is the truth. You know exactly where the jewellery is."

"That's not true."

"It's with the person you sold it to," Leipfold said. "Isn't it?"

"Jesus," Amy said. "You're good. Well, what's the harm? Martha saw it was missing so I spun a tale."

"You lied to me?"

"Oh, get over yourself."

Amy scowled at Leipfold and mouthed a sarcastic "thanks" across at him. He shrugged and said she should seek some help. It sent her into a rage, and so she did the only thing that she could do in the situation. She called the flight attendant and asked if she could switch seats with another passenger.

"Ooooh," the woman replied. She was called Lyndsay. "I'm sorry, ma'am. You have to stay in the seat you were assigned. I'm afraid it's company policy."

"I'm sure it is," Amy replied.

The three of them spent the rest of the flight in a stormy silence.

*   *   *

When the plane landed at Amsterdam's Schiphol airport, Leipfold didn't need to hang around to wait for his case to be ejected from the conveyor belt. He travelled light and carried everything he needed in a rucksack on his back.

It was a big airport, but it wasn't hard for Leipfold to find his way around. He was soon on a shuttle train into the city. He found a seat and opened up his notebook to review his notes on the case so far.

Leipfold was in the city of sin to track down a client's ex-girlfriend. It was the kind of work that he resented but which paid well, and so he'd decided to take it on. But at least he'd blagged an all-expenses paid trip to Amsterdam.

And it wasn't like he had much to go on. All he knew was that she was a junkie and a stripper in a city of junkies and strippers. He had his work cut out for him.

He started by wandering the city, ambling through the side streets and up and down by the canals. For a city that was known for its drug culture, it was a surprisingly clean place. People flew past him on pushbikes, and trams wound their way through the picturesque streets. He saw no sign of heavy drugs, and the smell of marijuana only floated out from the licensed coffee shops that dealt the herb to locals and tourists alike.

His hotel was in the south of the city. He took a detour to wander down to it and to check into his room before heading to the Rijksmuseum. He wandered idly around the exhibits, scribbling notes here and there, before taking the tram into town to start work.

When dusk fell, the atmosphere in the city started to change. It was a slow, subtle shift to begin with, but by 10PM it was a different place entirely, as Leipfold couldn't fail to notice when he wandered through the Red Light District, perusing the human wares in the windows. He'd been given the name of a gentleman's club where his mark was rumoured to work.

So Leipfold went along and paid for the peep show. It wasn't his kind of thing, but he couldn't deny that the women were beautiful, empowered creatures who nevertheless looked like dope fiends and crack addicts. The woman he was looking for didn't make an appearance, but the other girls were pleasant enough. He waited for the show to finish and then headed off to speak to the leading ladies.

Most of them wouldn't talk to him, but he found a couple of girls called Silver and Summer who took him over to a corner and who agreed to talk to him in exchange for a little hard currency.

"Money first," Silver said.

"Hell no," Leipfold replied. He opened up his wallet and flashed them a glimpse so that they could see he had some notes in there. "I'll give you your money after you give me some information."

"There's no trust in this world," Summer said.

"There isn't," Leipfold agreed. He showed them a photo of the woman he was looking for. "Have you seen her?"

"Yeah, I've seen her," Summer said. "Candace. She dances here sometimes. Not tonight, though."

"Why not?" Leipfold asked. "Where is she?"

"She's at The Blue Room," Silver told him. "It's a brothel. It pays better than this dump, but the shifts are less reliable."

"I can imagine," Leipfold said. "Where can I find The Blue Room?"

The girls gave him directions, and Leipfold thanked them and then followed them. They took him down a couple of side streets and right down by the river, along an alleyway and up a flight of stairs into a tiny little brothel that looked like it was for locals and not for tourists. The journey reminded him of the commute to his office on Balcombe Street, another country away.

The Blue Room was drab, dingy and unashamedly functional. Leipfold was greeted by a middle-aged madam who listed off their services. He showed her the photo, asked for Candace and was told that it wouldn't be a problem, as long as he had the money. They haggled and Leipfold paid up front for a couple of hours, then followed the madam into a back room where his mark was ready and waiting. She was scantily clad and wearing much more makeup, but it was definitely the woman from the photograph.

"What'll it be?" she asked.

"I want you to come home with me," Leipfold replied.

"You're crazy."

"Perhaps I phrased that badly," Leipfold said. "Listen, there's someone who loves you and who wants you back. I think you know who I'm talking about."

"I do," she replied, reluctantly.

"He's why I'm here," Leipfold said. "I'm a private detective. He sent me to track you down and bring you home."

"By force?"

Leipfold shook his head. "That's not my style," he replied. "Besides, if I brought you back by force, you'd jump ship at the first opportunity. He can't keep you locked up forever. No, you need to *want* to return. I mean, look at you. Look at where you are. Is this really what you want?"

"I don't know what I want."

"Then come home," Leipfold said. "You won't have to do this to earn money. You'll have everything you could possibly want."

"I wouldn't have my freedom."

"You would," Leipfold insisted. "It's just a different kind of freedom. It has to be better than this."

They talked for the rest of the two hours, sparring with words like two fencers until they were both too exhausted to deliver the killing blow. Leipfold thought he'd made some headway, but it was hard to tell.

"You have to go, Mr. Leipfold," she said. "Your two hours are up. Here, take this." She took a paper towel from the adjoining bathroom and wrote something on it with an eyeliner pencil.

"What is it?"

"It's my address," she told him. "Visit me in the morning and I'll have a decision for you. In the meantime, if you'll excuse me, I have a shift to finish."

* * *

Leipfold met her in the morning at the address she'd given him. By the cold light of day, she looked like a different person. It wasn't just the outfit. She'd removed all traces of her makeup and looked younger, almost innocent. She held herself differently, too. She held herself like someone who'd been waiting for a train for two hours and who didn't know if they could hold on any longer.

"Thanks for coming to find me, Mr. Leipfold," she said. "I've come to a decision. I'm going to leave the city. But I need a couple of days to get my affairs in order. Can you give me them?"

Leipfold whistled softly and looked around the shithole apartment that she was living in. He didn't think it'd take her two days to pack up her meagre belongings. But what was another forty-eight hours?

"I'm here for three more days," Leipfold said. "I'll see if I can book you on the same flight home. Can I trust you to come with me?"

"I can give you my word, if that will help?"

"I suppose it'll have to do."

Candace and Leipfold shook on it, and he left her to get on with things. He had admin of his own to do, including calling his client with the good news. The client was ecstatic and told Leipfold as much, and he wired over the money for the flight as soon as he got off the phone. The flight itself was almost fully booked, but Leipfold was able to get a ticket for a single seat at the other end of the aircraft, which was good enough.

He spent the next couple of days enjoying his time in a strange city.

*   *   *

On the day of the flight, Leipfold went back to the address to pick Candace up. There was only one problem. She was nowhere to be found.

226

Well, that wasn't quite true. He could make out the silhouette of a body on the floor on the other side of the glass door.

Leipfold panicked. He didn't know the number for the emergency services, so he flagged down a stranger to put the call in while he tried to kick the door down. It broke on the fourth boot. Leipfold spilled inside with the stranger in tow, but it was clear that they were too late to help her. Her skin had turned blue, for a start. And Leipfold's eyes lit up on the needle in her arm.

"Holy shit," Leipfold said. "We've got to get out of here. There's nothing more we can do."

He turned around, but the stranger who'd called the police had already disappeared.

Leipfold disappeared shortly afterwards. He had a plane to catch and some bad news to deliver.

The Case of the Optometrist

LEIPFOLD HAD A VISITOR.

It was an elderly man with a bad toupee and hunched shoulders. Leipfold had hurried him into a seat for fear that he'd collapse and die of a heart attack right there in the office's poky reception area. The man took the seat gratefully and wheezed for a minute or two before he was ready to talk.

"Sorry about that," he said. "Bloody stairs. Can't you get yourself a lift?"

"Fat chance," Leipfold replied. "The landlord won't even fix the intercom. My name's James Leipfold, private investigator. But you probably know that or you wouldn't be here. How can I help?"

The old man coughed and wheezed a little again. Then he took off his glasses and polished them absentmindedly on his shirt. He spoke to Leipfold while his glasses were still circling around in his hands.

"I keep losing things," he said. "My wallet. My glasses. My mobile phone."

"Your glasses are in your hands," Leipfold said.

"Not *these* glasses," he said. "Do you think I'm an idiot? My *other* glasses."

"I see," Leipfold said. "And you're sure you're not just misplacing them?"

"I'm sure," the man replied. "You think I'm losing my mind, don't you? I can see it in your eyes."

"Well, maybe," Leipfold admitted. "But that doesn't mean I'm not going to take the case. There must be a rational explanation for all this."

"Well, until you find one, consider yourself hired," the man said. His body creaked as he leaned forwards and used a frail hand to remove a leather wallet from his trouser pocket. He opened it up and took a sheaf of twenty-pound notes from within its folds.

"This is all I've got for now," the man said, "but there'll be more where that came from if you help me to get my stuff back."

Leipfold grinned. "Well, in that case," he said, "let's do it."

Besides, he thought. *There's a good chance he'll forget all about it.*

*　　*　　*

But the client didn't forget about it, and Leipfold soon found himself actively investigating the case. He'd tried to put it off at first, but the old man called him every day to check his progress. He knew he'd either have to come up with something or take his phone off the hook.

He started by getting the client to keep a diary of his day-to-day life, with a particular focus on what he was doing around the time that the items were going missing. It turned out that the man already kept a journal, and so he was able to check his entries and to backfill the log until the point at which the disappearances first started. He even provided Leipfold with a cash valuation for each of the missing items.

He faxed a copy of the final document over to Leipfold, who flicked quickly through it before reading through it again while taking notes with a highlighter. It was a curious mix of objects, from luxury watches and expensive technology to bananas, bottles of water and even a stuffed bear that he'd won at the fair and planned to give to his granddaughter.

He spotted a key consistency and called his client to ask for some clarification.

"Who's Dr. Applegarth?" Leipfold asked.

"She's my optometrist," the man replied. "My eyes aren't what they used to be. I'm not getting any younger."

"No, you're not," Leipfold agreed. "You seem to see her a lot."

"I have cataracts. I'm undergoing treatment."

"Are you now?" Leipfold said. "Interesting."

"It is?"

"It is," Leipfold confirmed. "Perhaps it's time for me to get my eyes checked."

*   *   *

When Leipfold booked his optometry appointment, he asked for Dr. Applegarth. If the staff found it unusual for a new patient to ask for a specific doctor, they didn't mention it. Leipfold was glad. His cock and bull story about a personal referral must have worked.

His appointment was at two o'clock on a Thursday, and he showed up to it wearing his best (and only) suit. He'd styled his hair and borrowed a fake Rolex from one of his contacts, then carried himself like a man with money. He acted as though he owned the world and everything in it, including the dingy little optometry clinic in Walthamstow.

"Mr. Leipfold? Could you follow me please?"

Leipfold assumed that the woman was the optometrist he'd heard so much about, but she turned out to be a receptionist called Gemma who was on her second day in the job. Dr. Applegarth was waiting inside a side room and Leipfold walked straight in to meet her.

"Please take a seat," she said. Leipfold did so. She started the appointment by asking him to talk about his history, which he did, and followed it up by getting him to look at an eye chart. Leipfold squinted at it and read out the letters, throwing his score to average around 70 percent. And then he did something quite extraordinary.

He fell asleep right there in the seat while he waited for the optometrist to process his records and write out a prescription. For a while, it seemed like Dr. Applegarth hadn't even noticed. Then, as cool as a cucumber, she sidled across to where Leipfold sat and reached towards the clasp of his watch.

His hand flew up in a flash and wrapped itself around her wrist. He yanked her roughly, and she fell sprawling to the floor.

"What the hell do you think you're doing?" Leipfold roared.

"I thought you were asleep!"

"I can bloody well see that," Leipfold replied. "You've been stealing from your customers. Worse, you've been stealing from the most vulnerable."

Leipfold had been expecting her to deny it, and perhaps even to threaten him with a lawsuit. He hadn't expected her to burst into tears, which is what she did. Leipfold had never been good at offering comfort, so he merely sat there and watched until the tears started to slow and she was ready to speak to him.

"I'm sorry," she said, her words slurred by the occasional sob and her chest still rising and falling. "I know I did wrong. But you don't understand. It's a compulsion."

"Then get help," Leipfold said. "Don't indulge it by stealing from your customers. Good lord, I'm amazed you're still in business."

"We won't be in business for much longer if news of this gets out," Dr. Applegarth replied. "I'll never do it again, Mr. Leipfold, I swear to you. And I'll return the goods that were taken."

"I don't believe you."

"You have to believe me, Mr. Leipfold," she protested. "This job is my livelihood."

"You've got two days to return the belongings," he said.

"If I do that, will you let me off the hook? I don't want to go to jail."

Leipfold frowned. "We'll see," he said.

*　　*　　*

Leipfold's elderly client came in a couple of days later with the good news. He was over the moon, full of life and walking with the stride of a man ten or twenty years younger. Dr. Applegarth hadn't just returned his possessions; she'd also returned his self-confidence.

"You did it, Mr. Leipfold," the man said. "My God, you actually did it. I never thought I'd see my belongings again. How can I ever repay you?"

"By paying me," Leipfold replied.

"Oh, don't you worry about that." The old man reached into a pocket and pulled out an envelope that was stuffed with cash of different denominations. "In fact, they had a bit of a whip round at the optometrists. They asked if I'd be good enough to hand it over."

Leipfold gratefully accepted the envelope and counted out the cash. "Christ," he said. "This'll keep me going for a couple of weeks."

"It's not the money that matters, Mr. Leipfold," the man said. "I'd pay anything for peace of mind. Believe it or not, I'm glad she took my stuff."

"You're glad?"

"Of course," he replied. "I thought I was losing my mind. Are you sure there's nothing else I can do to repay you?"

"Well," Leipfold said. "I guess there *is* one thing."

*   *   *

Alan Phelps, *The Tribune*'s crossword compiler and backup researcher, took less than an hour to get to Leipfold's office. He didn't know why he'd been summoned, but he did know that Leipfold only called him when something exciting was about to happen.

Leipfold and his client sat the newspaperman down in the reception area and then drew up chairs beside him. Leipfold brought a round of drinks out and gestured for the client to take the lead. The old man was only too happy to tell his story again, and Leipfold was able to augment the tale with a detail or two of his own. When he got to the part where the optometrist asked him not to tell the cops, Phelps laughed.

"Sneaky," he said. "That's why you're telling me instead."

"That's partly true," Leipfold admitted. "But I wanted to ask you a favour as well."

"What is it?"

"When you publish the article," Leipfold said, "I'd like you to deliver a message from me."

"What's the message?" Phelps asked.

Leipfold took a deep breath and then slowly exhaled it. "It's simple," he said. "I don't think she's going to stop. I never claimed to be a cop and I don't want to see her arrested, but the woman's a kleptomaniac. She won't stop stealing unless she's made to stop, and someone needs to give her the help she needs."

"I see," Phelps said, although he didn't. "And you thought that sharing her story with *The Tribune* would be a smart way to achieve that?"

"Precisely," Leipfold said. "She needs to confront her issues head on."

Mr. Phelps grinned and tipped him a wink. "Excellent," he replied. "Trial by press. I like it."

The Game[2]

MAILE O'HARA WAS BORED, and she was also easily distracted. With Leipfold out of the office and with nothing to do until he came back to give her an update, she busied herself by trying to find something—anything—to do. She updated Leipfold's blog with an in-depth article about behavioural analysis and the practicalities behind using it to track down a missing person. She scheduled a couple of social media posts and defragged his computer. Then she swept the floor, spritzed the kitchen with disinfectant and made herself a cup of coffee.

She set the coffee on her desk and sat down.

I'm still bored, she thought.

With nothing better to do, she took the time to check her stats on her favourite MMORPG and to see where she ranked against the big boys. Then she logged into IRC and messaged Mayhem, because Mayhem was the kind of guy who was always working on something. She asked him what he was up to and he sent her a sketchy-looking link and told her to check it out.

"What is it?" Maile asked.

"Don't worry," Mayhem replied. "It's legit. Some new fad that people are talking about."

"Sweet."

After scanning it for malware, just in case, Maile clicked the link and waited for it to load. It led her to a simple site with a

---

2 Unlike the preceding stories in this collection, which take place before *Driven*, the events of this story take place between *Driven* and *The Tower Hill Terror*.

single page. She'd seen sites like this one before. They were virtual puzzles, online treasure hunts. Kind of like a crossword, but with infinitely more possibilities. She'd read about one that no one had been able to solve and another which had turned out to be a tool to recruit code-breakers for a government agency.

This one, though, was a new one. Maile had never heard of it, and Mayhem said he only knew about it because a friend had sent the link to him. They dug a little deeper and found no mentions of the site on social networks, and it didn't even rank in the results pages when they searched for the exact URL.

Someone's made an effort to hide it, Mayhem wrote, updating her on an instant messenger. *They've blocked search engines from crawling it, for a start. And check out the web address.*

It's just a series of letters and numbers, Maile replied.

Exactly. The guys on Reddit have found something in the source code that tells us a little bit more. There's a cash prize for whoever makes it to the end. There was another message in binary, too. Krypt0 sent over a transcript. I won't bore you with the details, but it says that there's also a job up for grabs for whoever's first to reach the finish line.

So what? Maile said.

I could use a job, Mayhem replied. *A proper one, I mean. The landlord's put the rent up and modding phpBB forums doesn't pay what it used to.*

How do you know they'd let you work remotely?

I don't, Mayhem said. *Hell, it might be local to me. Who cares? It's not like I have anything keeping me here.*

So where do we stand?

Mayhem went silent for a minute or so, but Maile knew he was still there. He was still logged into the chat network, and the interface said, *Mayhem is typing...* Then he pressed the enter key and the text flew through the tubes and pipes, across the ether, into the router and out on to her computer screen.

My guess, the message began, *is that they change the URL every couple of days, probably based on some sort of mathematical formula. They want to make sure that you can only find it if you know the right people and you go to the right places. It's a shit filter, designed to stop your Average Joe from finding the site. Want to team up on it? If we can't solve it, no one can.*

Maile paused for a moment and mulled it over. It didn't take her long to arrive at a decision.

I'm in, she said. *What's next?*

Mayhem told her.

*   *   *

When Maile got home, she headed straight into her room to boot her laptop up. For her, that was unusual. She usually skipped the laptop and went straight for the console. But that evening, she had work to do, and it was extra work, work that she couldn't justify when Leipfold was paying her an hourly rate.

While it was loading, she nipped into the kitchen and nodded at Kat before hunting through the snack drawer. Maile was the only one who topped it up because Kat was on a perpetual diet, but she was pretty sure that the diet had gone out of the window because someone had been stealing the pickled onion Monster Munch. Maile grabbed a bag of pretzels and popped the seal, then started absentmindedly munching at them as she made her way back into her bedroom.

She messaged Mayhem as soon as the machine loaded up, but he was away and so she said she'd catch up with him later. He was a couple of hours ahead of her, so for all she knew he'd given up for the day and gone out for a few drinks. Instead of sitting around and waiting for him, she started looking into a few ideas of her own. It was a pure type of research, unencumbered by any suppositions or presumptions from Mayhem's own work.

The web page seemed simple enough, with just a hundred words or so of copy explaining the rules of The Game. Simply put, there were a series of clues scattered online and off, and the winner of The Game would be the first person to reach the end of the trail. It ended with the phrase, "Game on."

That led Maile to believe that The Game, whatever it was, had already started, although there was no real indicator either way. Other than the brief set of instructions, it was a bare, boring website, a badly designed one-pager that looked like a throwback from the 1990s. The casual observer might have dismissed it as a relic, a derelict, but Maile knew better. The only way to make something that ugly was to design it to look like shit, and she confirmed its age by running a whois on the domain name. It had been registered just a couple of weeks earlier by a Mr. A. N. Onymous. She cringed.

Maile dug deeper, scanning through the site's source code for inconsistencies. But she found nothing, so she set up a crawler to scan the site for hidden links and directories. It was a piece of software that Krypt0 had created for finding the admin areas of high-security websites, and Maile suspected that the idea had already occurred to Mayhem. But he was still set to away, and Maile was in no rush. She was enjoying the thrill of the chase.

She dipped her hand back into the pretzels and filled her mouth absentmindedly as she watched the software pull the results in. It took a while because her home internet was somehow slower than Leipfold's office line, even though she paid more for the privilege, and she found herself drifting off into thought.

I wonder what the boss would make of this. The thought made her smile. Leipfold loved a puzzle, and it was possible (if not likely) that he could have helped her to look into it. But at the same time, after Maile had offered to teach him to be more computer literate, he'd told her he was computer dyslexic. When she'd first joined the company, the security had been shocking, and she'd taken it upon herself to update Leipfold's systems and to install some decent software to catch viruses and malware.

Leipfold had an idea of what she could do, of course. He just didn't know the extent of it. Before she'd spotted the ad that had brought her to his office, she'd been looking into how to get a job with MI5 or the American Secret Service.

Technology is the future, she remembered thinking. *There are the good guys and the bad guys. I've got to pick a side.*

The crawl of the mysterious website came to a slow and satisfying stop, and Maile pored over the pages while absentmindedly humming a Nightwish song. She clicked a few of the links, browsed through the source code and scanned the pages for irregularities, but she came up blank.

Then she opened up a CSS file, which would usually be used to specify the site's look and feel. This one, though, was in isolation, unlinked to and unused, just sitting there on the server and waiting for someone to find it.

Maile examined it closely and clapped her hands in delight. It contained instructions for the next step of the treasure hunt. At least, she *thought* that was what she was looking at. It was hard to tell.

The whole damn thing was cyphered and unreadable.

*   *   *

Maile and Mayhem were at an impasse. They hadn't given up on the puzzle, but they *had* hit a dead end. Maile had shared the link to the CSS file, and Mayhem had pored over it at length. So had Maile, for that matter. They'd even recruited Krypt0, Brn0ut, KAOS and ProfSyntax. Krypt0, as his username suggested, had a love of cryptography, but even he couldn't make any sense of the material.

Maile hadn't *meant* to get her boss involved, but it had almost been inevitable. She was part of a team now. Leipfold had her back whether she liked it or not, and that meant he was even willing to help when she was bunking off the work he was paying her to do to take part in an online treasure hunt.

And besides, he'd caught her using the printer and snatched the sheet of paper with the CSS file's source code before she was able to pick it up.

"What's this?" he asked.

"It's a long story," Maile said.

"I've got time."

And so Maile told him, explaining her progress so far and the way that she was working with the IRC boys to identify the next step in the digital treasure hunt. She'd expected him to be bored, perhaps even angry that she was trying to solve the puzzle from his office. But no.

"That's amazing," Leipfold said. "Let me have another look at it."

"Go ahead," Maile replied, handing him the printout.

Leipfold grinned and pored over the document. He read it from start to finish a couple of times, then went back over it more slowly with a highlighter. Then he started to scrawl different letters and characters.

"Interesting," he murmured.

"It is?"

"Yeah," Leipfold said. "It's double encoded. I can solve the cypher—it's pretty basic—but there's some other logic behind it."

"How do you know about this stuff?"

"When I was a kid," Leipfold said, still making little markings across the paper, "I wanted to be a spy. You know, like James Bond, but without the Aston Martin. Back in my day, we didn't have the internet to keep us busy. We had little pocket books with puzzles in them. If we couldn't figure out the answer, we had to send off a letter with some money in it."

"I get it," Maile said, "you're old. So you learned all this in a book?"

Leipfold nodded. "You'd be amazed at what you can learn from books," he said. "That's how I learned to pick locks."

"I learned that from YouTube," Maile said. She grinned. "So what have we got?"

"Still working on it," Leipfold said. "But don't worry, we'll get there. I've cracked the first level, so now we just need to figure out the second. Only…hmm."

"What?"

Leipfold was staring intently at the markings he'd made on the paper. He'd stopped writing, but his brain was still whirring like an overheating computer and a million and one possibilities were running through his mind.

"I think I've got it," he said. Then he grinned. "The second layer of the cypher. It's not in code at all. It's a set of numbers. And I think I know what they represent."

"You do?"

Leipfold nodded. "They're coordinates," he said. "I've seen it done before. Better key them into your computer and see where they take us."

*   *   *

Maile was at the office, holding the fort while Leipfold made the rounds on the back of Camilla. She had work to do, but it was boring work, nothing stimulating enough to hold her attention. And so instead of building a better spreadsheet for the boss to track their finances on, she logged into IRC and caught up with Mayhem and the team.

Leipfold's discovery of the cyphered coordinates had led them to a small suburb of Istanbul. So far so good, but nobody had the time or the inclination to go there, so Krypt0 took it upon himself to find someone to do it for them.

I've got just the guy, he explained, when Leipfold asked Maile to check for updates. *He's called Kareem, a taxi driver. He said he'll take a look for us if we send him the fare.*

Then do it, Maile said. *I'll pay for it, if you want.*

I've got it covered, Krypt0 said. *I convinced him to take bitcoin. He's on his way over there now.*

Get him to stream it, Maile said. *Send him a walkthrough or something if you need to. I want to see what he sees.*

Already on it, Krypt0 said, sprinkling in a couple of emojis. Then he sent her the link and Maile opened it up and dragged it over to her other monitor. She watched in silence, staring blankly at the grainy video that was being beamed across the globe from a Turkish dashcam. After ten minutes of tedium, which Maile endured by distracting herself with Leipfold's spreadsheet, the car started to slow before pulling up at the side of a dust-covered street in the back end of nowhere.

Kareem got out of the car. Maile watched his back as he crossed the road and began to look up and down for something, anything, out of the ordinary.

Why didn't he take the damn camera? Maile asked.

Krypt0 sent another string of emojis before adding, *He'll be back for it, if he finds anything.*

Kareem meandered up and down the street, peering into windows, looking into mailboxes and examining the graffiti on the sides of the food stalls. He looked closely at the posters that promoters had plastered on the walls and picked up a couple of scraps of paper that were rolling around in the breeze. Maile was getting impatient. From where she sat, it looked like the search had so far been unproductive.

Then he came back and picked up the dashcam at the same time that Krypt0 posted in the group chat. *He's on the phone to me. He said he found some markings in chalk. They're old and scuffed. Looks like they've been there for a couple of weeks.*

The feed bounced spasmodically as Kareem walked back along the dusty street. Then it shook again, more violently this time, as he flipped the camera over in his hands and tried to focus it on a small patch of the dusty ground. There was something there all right. Paint or chalk or blood or something. Maile squinted at it as Kareem tried to hold the camera steady.

What is that? Krypt0 asked.

Maile punched the air in delight before dashing off a quick response.

It's a QR code, she said. *Or at least, part of one. I wonder what it leads to.*

*   *   *

The Istanbul QR code was incomplete, but that didn't stop Maile and the boys from feeling convinced it was the next step in the treasure hunt. Kareem said it had been daubed on the floor with waterproof chalk and that it looked like it had been there for a while. It almost certainly predated the domain name.

With the video as a record, as well as some stills that had been taken at the scene, Maile and the boys had been able to clear up the distortion and to enhance the photo, but it still wasn't perfect. About a third of the code had been scrubbed away, if it had ever been there in the first place. Maile suspected it was another test, and she'd been able to propose an elegant solution in the group chat.

We just need a piece of software, she explained. *Mayhem, you could code it in an hour or so if I send over a couple of diagrams. We need to take what we have and augment it by adding one pixel at a time, then scan the results until we get a match.*

It sounded impressive, but Mayhem had quickly pointed out that it was impractical. *There are too many possibilities,* he said. *Each missing pixel makes it less likely that we'll get it.*

Have you got a better idea?

*   *   *

Somewhere across the North Sea, Mayhem disappeared to code up a piece of software to automate the process. After a couple of days, the software had failed to produce results. He was worried that if they didn't find it soon, the code would expire and they'd be too late, but their luck was about to change.

Mayhem grew so bored while waiting for a hit that he built a bot to alert them all. When it finally went off, trolling the lot of them with the first few bars of a Rick Astley tune, they all assumed it had malfunctioned. That was until one by one, they scanned the code with their phones to test it.

Fuck me, Mayhem said. *Looks like we've got a result. We've got a working code that sends us to a URL that looks pretty similar to the first one. All letters and numbers and shit.*

Good, Maile said. *Send me the link. I want to check it out.*

Will do, Mayhem replied. *But there's a problem…*

What is it?

Better see for yourself, he said. He sent Maile the link and said he'd be right back. Maile opened it up and stared at the screen in disbelief.

The URL resolved all right, but it loaded up a web page with nothing on it.

At least, Maile mentally corrected herself, *nothing I can see.*

*   *   *

Maile dug deeper into the site's source code, expecting to find another message cyphered deep within another file, but she'd been unable to find anything. Leipfold, meanwhile, quickly lost interest when it became apparent that this step of the investigation needed Maile's skills and not his. And so Maile turned to Mayhem and the rest of the IRC crew.

What we need, Maile explained, *is another variation on Mayhem's software. This time, we need to crawl that site in as many different ways as possible. There's something there. There has to be. We just need to find it.*

I'm out, Krypto wrote. *This is taking too long. Why are we even doing this?*

For the thrill of the chase, Maile wrote.

And for the reward, Mayhem added.

The new software took a couple of days to develop and relied on brute force attacks, reloading the site as many times as possible with different filenames and folder variations. If there was something hidden on the site, no matter where it was hosted, Mayhem's software was designed to find it.

Maile had launched the software on her work computer and her laptop so that it could double the programme's processing power. So far, there hadn't been a hit, but she hadn't given up hope. She was rewarded that morning with the little ping of a 200 OK result for one of the queries. That meant that there was a page there and that it loaded, which also meant that she might have the next clue in the global treasure hunt.

Of course, they'd already come across half a dozen false positives and there was no telling whether this one was the real deal. She figured she'd waited so long that another ten minutes wouldn't hurt, so she finished off what she was working on and allowed the software to continue scanning.

When she was ready, she saved her work and clicked on the link. It popped up on the screen like a banner ad for a porn site, but it was empty and blank, like the homepage. And like the other half dozen pages that they'd already found and scanned without success.

Maile sighed and viewed the page's source code, not expecting to find anything, but there *was* something there. It was the next clue, just looking her in the eye like a demented clown from a horror movie. She sighed again, a little less forcefully this time, and scooched forward on her chair to take a closer look.

There on the site, buried in the source code for the page and invisible to the casual observer, was the next clue in the global game of hide and seek.

This new message was cyphered again, but the code had changed since last time and Maile couldn't make any headway. Luckily, she knew a man who might be able to help, and he happened to be sitting in the same room as her.

*   *   *

The investigation crawled to a stop again. Leipfold spent most of the evening poring over the latest cypher. While it felt like the solution was right there on the tip of his tongue, it was slow to come forward, reluctant. It was starting to give him a headache.

And so he did what all good investigators do when they're not sure what to look at next. He outsourced it by putting in a late-night phone call to an old acquaintance, a friend from the estate who'd managed to escape his austere surroundings and who'd made a name for himself in the field of forensic cryptography.

"Bill Buckley," Leipfold said. The man answered the phone with a terseness that suggested he was either getting ready to sleep or already well on his way. "How the devil are you?"

"Tired," the man said, pointedly. "What do you want, Leipfold?"

"A favour," he said.

"No chance."

The man put the phone down, so Leipfold called him back repeatedly until Buckley took the hint and picked it up.

Buckley sighed and said, "You're going to make my life hell unless I help you, aren't you?"

"Yes."

"Bastard," Buckley said. "All right then, what is it? Make it quick."

Leipfold told Buckley the story so far, from Kareem and the street in Istanbul to the cypher that Leipfold had cracked and the second one that he'd made no headway with.

Buckley sighed again and said, "Send it over and I'll have a look." Then he cut the call.

Leipfold smiled and emailed it over, then started a timer on his phone and settled back to read his book. Buckley called back after eleven minutes with an answer.

"It's simple stuff, old boy," he said. "I'm surprised you couldn't solve it. Perhaps you don't have the eye for it."

"Yeah, yeah," Leipfold growled. "Get to the point."

"Not before I've had my fun," Buckley said. Like Leipfold, he loved a good puzzle, and his fun consisted of explaining exactly how he'd solved it. Leipfold listened patiently.

Then Buckley dropped his bombshell. "You were looking at it wrong," he explained. "It was part cypher, part equation. You just didn't see it because you're a words man."

"Numbers, schmumbers," Leipfold said.

Buckley laughed for a moment and then rattled off a long list of digits.

"What's that?" Leipfold asked.

"That's your answer," Buckley said. He repeated the numbers, more slowly this time, and Leipfold wrote them down.

"But what does it mean?" he asked.

"No idea," Buckley said, cheerfully. "That's for you to find out. But either way, it's your answer."

Leipfold paused for a moment, deep in thought. "We know the answer," he murmured, "but we don't know the question."

He tapped his pen against the paper a couple of times, then slowly but intently counted the number of digits. A little light came on behind his eyes.

"It's a number," he said. "A phone number."

"No," Buckley replied. "There aren't enough digits."

"That's what you think," Leipfold said. He grinned. "Typical Bill Buckley, you're looking at it like a numbers man. It takes a words man to tell you to add a zero to the front of it."

Maile answered the phone in a foul mood.

"You were working on it without me?" she growled. "You suck. How would you feel if I filled out the crossword before I handed you the paper?"

"I'm sorry," Leipfold said. Maile softened almost immediately. "I'm going to put you on speakerphone and use the other line. Listen in, okay?"

Maile agreed. She listened as Leipfold keyed in the number on his desk phone and the call connected. The line was silent for a while, except for the static as it tried to connect. Then there was a haunting, screeching sound and an automated message. She'd expected Morse code, an ethereal, robotic voice or for the call to not connect at all, but she hadn't expected this. It was like she was listening to the mating call of a rare animal, played backwards with the reverb turned up. It was a shrill sound, but it had a deep timbre that carried across the airwaves despite the fact that the speaker and the mic were sitting a couple of feet away from each other.

"What in the hell is that?" Maile shouted. "Turn it off!"

Leipfold did as she asked but said nothing, absorbed in thought as he tried to figure out what to make of it. Maile asked him for the number and jotted it down, then told him she'd call back once she'd had a chance to look into it.

Maile keyed the number into a search engine and was rewarded with an empty results page. She searched on social networking sites with the same result, which helped to convince her that they were the first people to get this far.

So far, so good, she thought. *But what's next?*

She started by setting up a VOIP line from her machine and booting up some software to record its audio output. She dialled the number and hit the record button, then left the machine unsupervised for a while to have a chat with Kat. Maile's housemate was tired from a long day at work, but she was always happy to gossip about her colleagues, and Maile needed a distraction from the hellish noise that was whining its way through the ether and out of her headphones.

Twenty minutes later, armed with a fresh cup of coffee and a cookie that Kat had brought back from Waitrose, Maile went back into her room to cut the call. Then she exported the audio and shared a copy with the IRC boys and set her status as away so she could focus.

Maile started by analysing the audio to see if it looped, which it did. That meant she could isolate the exact clip that was pumping down the phone line so that it didn't skew her data. The next step was to scour the file for inconsistencies. At first, it seemed utterly random, but Maile was able to identify several spikes in the waveform that seemed to repeat themselves at regular intervals. But when she listened to the audio, she heard nothing.

Or rather, she heard everything. It sounded like the message had been designed to overload the senses, and it was certainly doing a good job of it. It was stuck in Maile's head like a bad ringtone, and she started to hear echoes of it even when she shut the playback off. But she persevered, switching to headphones after Kat came in and told her to "shut that racket up," and Maile put in a couple of hours behind the keyboard to try to clean the audio up.

It was slow, tedious work, but she was making steady progress, and Mayhem was able to recommend a couple of filters to speed the process up. But it was still so dull that she almost called it a day and gave up on it.

Screw this stupid treasure hunt, she thought. *I could be playing Skyrim.*

By the time that she called it a night and tried to get some beauty sleep, she'd been able to identify something barely audible that was hidden beneath the audio and largely in line with the unusual peaks and troughs in the waveform.

Behind the jumbled cacophony, the acid trip audio that would be stuck in her head for the next three weeks, there was something else. Something that went *beep beep beep.*

*   *   *

It was a couple of days later and, what with one thing and another, Maile hadn't had a chance to follow up with the treasure hunt. But Mayhem was bugging her for a solution. Even though she knew what that solution was, she hadn't had time to properly look at it. She'd been too busy helping Leipfold to computerise his old case files to dedicate any attention to it.

But at last, she'd finally finished. She wasn't in the mood to go home and she didn't have any work left, so she had to find a way to occupy herself.

She switched from her work computer to her laptop and loaded up the audio file, then spent twenty minutes or so finalising a few filters to make the audio as clean as possible. Then she hit the export button and played it back again.

Beep bip beep beep. Beep beep beep. Bip bip beep. Bip beep beep beep beep bip. Bip beep bip. Bip. Beep beep bip. Bip beep beep. Bip bip. Beep bip. Beep beep bip. Beep bip beep bip. Bip beep bip bip. Beep beep beep. Bip bip bip. Bip. Bip beep bip beep bip beep.

Excited, Maile started to transcribe it. Krypt0 could have done the job weeks ago, but he'd bailed on the project. Mayhem could have learned how to do it, but he was a lazy son-of-a-bitch and the job was still stuck there somewhere on his to-do list. That only left her.

She thought about running the sequence through an online Morse code translator, but then she had a better idea. It would take a little longer, but it would also bring a smile to someone's face. So she took a photograph of the sequence and emailed it over to James Leipfold.

She received a reply within the hour, and she punched the air when her hunch was proved correct. The start of the message read, "*You're getting close.*" She read the message a couple of times before forwarding the email to Mayhem.

Look at this, she said. *It's another set of coordinates. I ran a search for it and found out what we're looking at. It looks like some sort of industrial estate in Dagenham.*

Where?

Not far from me, Maile said. She sent him a second screenshot, this time of the route from Leipfold's office to the industrial estate. It looked like someone had grabbed a pen and scribbled disjointed little circles winding their way slowly towards the northeast of the city.

What else does it say? Mayhem asked.

It just says to be there, Maile said. *And then it gives a date and time. Hang on a sec.* She pulled up her calendar and consulted it, then said, *Soon. Less than a week.*

What are you going to do?

Isn't it obvious? Maile asked. *I'm going to go and check it out.*

But what if it's a scam? Mayhem said. *Or worse. What if someone tries to hurt you?*

If someone tries to hurt me, I'll hit them in the face, Maile told him. *I've got my pepper spray, too. And besides, what's the worst that can happen? No one ever got hurt by the internet.*

Famous last words, Mayhem replied.

*   *   *

It was a Thursday, and Maile had always hated Thursdays. She thought of herself as a modern-day Arthur Dent, only instead of wearing a dressing gown and carrying a towel, she wore all black and carried pepper spray.

It was also the day of her appointment in Dagenham, at least if her translation of the Morse code was anything to go by. It told her to be there at 9AM, but she made her way to the complex at 8:30, just in case. She dressed conservatively, still in all black but in a black dress with black leggings, black nail varnish and black hair that seemed to suck all the light from the gloomy sun that barely bothered to shine on the city.

The coordinates that she'd discovered weren't exactly specific. They took her to the right area, but she still found herself crawling up and down a sketchy street in East London while the bin men collected garden waste from an area where no one had a garden. She walked up and down the street, covering the distance two or three times before she found what she was looking for.

The truth was that she didn't know *what* she was looking for. It turned out to be a painted mark on an asphalt drive that led to a nondescript door at the end of a winding path between two houses. She waited until 9AM exactly, killing time by catching Pokémon on her phone, and then she knocked on the door. It was answered almost immediately.

She found herself facing a small man in a sharp suit. He had a well-groomed goatee and a mole on his cheek, and Maile noticed he was wearing a pair of white Nikes that caught the eye. Rather than detracting from the suit, they enhanced it. The man looked smart regardless, radiating an aura of comfort and sincerity. He offered his hand and she shook it.

"Thom Scott," he said. "It's a pleasure to meet you."

"Yeah," Maile said. "About that. What's the deal?"

"I think you'd better come in," he said. She sucked air through her teeth and tightened her grip on the canister inside her handbag, but she followed him inside despite the qualms that had her palms sweating. He led her past an overweight woman who was working the security desk, through a set of double doors and then into an elevator. He slid a plastic card into the slot and punched the button for the third floor.

"Don't worry," he said. "I'll explain things shortly. Follow me."

251

When the lift slowed to a stop on the third floor, he grabbed her firmly by the arm and steered her to the right, then in through another door with a passcode, along another military grey corridor and into a small white room. Everything was white, even the carpet, and it reminded Maile of John Lennon's "Imagine" video. It kicked her anxiety off, and she started to wonder if someone was going to shoot her.

The man, Thom Scott, offered her a seat on a white sofa, opposite a white fireplace with a plain white canvas hung above it. Maile took it, but she didn't make herself comfortable. She sat up in her seat like a plaintiff at a hearing, like a meerkat on watch while the rest of the world was sleeping. She didn't trust him, and she said as much.

The man smiled. He told her that he didn't trust her, either. He said that was the whole point of the experiment. Then he told her who he was again, except this time he said who he worked for. It was a company that had recently gone through a successful IPO. He also told her about the £5,000 prize that he was authorised to give to the first person to crack the riddle.

He talked to her about projected growth, monetisation and expansion. He took her through a few charts to back up his claim, and he even gave her a one-to-one demo of their new beta, an updated application that wasn't due to be released until the summer. It allowed users to solve complex puzzles and equations to earn virtual currency that could be exchanged for cold, hard cash.

"What is it that you actually *want*?" Maile asked

"It's not what I want," the man said. "It's what I can give you."

He handed her a large white envelope and told her to open it up and look inside. She did as she was told.

"It's a contract," Maile said.

"It's a job offer," the man replied. "You managed to solve our riddle. We could use someone like you."

"I had help," Maile said.

The man shrugged. "So you're resourceful. You're also intelligent, a problem solver. Too many new hires bring nothing but problems. We need a solutions man."

"I'm a woman."

Scott shrugged again. "Figure of speech," he said. "Apologies if I made you feel uncomfortable. I think you'll find we offer generous remuneration."

"It's not about the money," Maile said. "At least, not this time."

"We offer a different challenge every day," Scott said. "There's that."

"Already got it," Maile said.

Scott sighed. "You know," he said, "when we first came up with the idea of our little treasure hunt, we didn't think it was going to be this difficult. We thought that if someone took the time to solve it, they'd be willing to take the next step when they reached the end."

"You know what they say about assumptions," Maile replied. "It's a nice idea on paper. But people don't always fit into little boxes."

"Do you?" the man asked.

"What the hell do you think?" she growled.

"I get it," he said. "It's just a shame that it had to be this way. So you're not going to take the job?"

Maile grinned innocently across at him. "I never said that," she told him. "Let me think on it."

*   *   *

Maile's heart was beating fast. She had a phone call to make, and she hated making phone calls at the best of times. This time, though, she also had to be an adult, which was ever so slightly worse than having to make a phone call.

Mr. Scott picked up the phone on its third ring. Maile thought he might have been at the office, but wherever he was, it was noisy.

It had its own special kind of meandering hubbub and sounded like the kind of place where people got things done and where they enjoyed what they were doing while they were at it.

"Hi," Maile said. "It's me."

Scott recognised her voice immediately. "Milly!" he exclaimed. "How are you?"

"Maile," she said, automatically. She didn't bother to answer him or to ask him the same question. "Listen, let me cut to the chase. I've made my decision."

"You have?"

"I have," she confirmed. "I'm sorry. While it's an incredible offer, it's just not what I want to do."

"I understand," Scott said. Maile could picture him on the other end of the line, probably wearing some stupid suit and drinking Peruvian coffee. "To be honest, I was expecting you to say as much."

"Don't get me wrong," Maile said. "I just prefer the thrill of the chase to the prize at the end. Although the cheque that you gave me will come in useful."

"Glad to hear it. What are you going to spend it on?"

"I'm going to share it with the rest of the guys who helped me," Maile said. She stared moodily into space for a second. "I guess I'll spend my cut on some new hardware. There's a VR headset I've got my eyes on."

Thom Scott chuckled at the other end of the line. "Are you sure we can't tempt you?" he asked. "You'd be a perfect fit."

"Positive," Maile said, "but I might be able to offer you an alternative."

"Who?"

Maile laughed. "There's a guy I know," she said. "A guy called Mayhem. Don't ask me for his real name because I don't know it. I think he's Dutch, maybe, or Norwegian. Nice guy."

"But it was you who solved the puzzle."

"Yeah," Maile scoffed. "And look how that worked out. Mayhem helped me every step of the way. In fact, Mayhem told me about the first clue. If anyone has a right to the job, he does."

"Hmmm." Scott paused on the other end of the line. Maile could almost hear the cogs whirring as he turned it over in his head.

"Let me guess," she said. "You sunk a lot of time and resources into this treasure hunt and never considered the possibility that your winner would turn you down."

"That's about the size of it," Scott admitted. "We made the reward very clear. Why would someone follow it through to the end if they didn't want the job?"

"For the thrill of the chase," Maile said. "So now you need to make a hire to satisfy your stakeholders. Otherwise someone's going to get the sack. Who's going to get the sack, Mr. Scott? You?"

"No comment."

"Mayhem's looking for a job," Maile said. "And you're looking to hire someone. Sure sounds like a good fit to me. Of course, he'd have to relocate, or perhaps he could work from home. Perhaps you give him just a couple of hours a week. Just enough to make it look like he solved your scheme and now he works for you. Just enough to pick up a little press coverage. Just enough to make you guys look like heroes."

"We were hoping for word of mouth," Scott mumbled. "Press coverage is just a part of that."

Maile laughed and then paused for a second. She could hear Scott on the other end of the line, breathing softly and waiting for whatever she was going to say next. She pictured him there, still sitting in that unknown office with his stupid suit and his expensive coffee.

Not my scene, she thought.

"So when does Mayhem start?" she asked.

Leipfold Inc.[3]

"WHAT THE BLOODY HELL is this, then?"

The postman had just arrived—late as usual, Leipfold observed—and pulled his usual half-arsed trick of leaving the mail downstairs instead of bringing it up to the office. Leipfold had to sort through it every damn day and to throw out the promo materials that still arrived for the graphic design studio downstairs, even though they hadn't been there for years.

Maile meandered slowly over to him and took a look at the letter he was holding. It had an impressive-looking seal on it, and Leipfold was absentmindedly crumbling the wax and sprinkling it over the floor.

"Who's it from?" she asked.

"It's from a lawyer," Leipfold replied. "On behalf of some company. Leipfold Inc."

"What's Leipfold Inc.?"

"Damned if I know," Leipfold said. "Never heard of it before."

"What do they want?"

"Well," Leipfold said, slamming the door behind him and marching forcefully across the room. Maile raced after him and stood beside him as he flopped into his chair and threw the letter down on the desk in front of hm. "Well," he said again.

"Well what?"

"Well," Leipfold repeated. "Apparently I'm being sued for copyright infringement. It's a cease and desist notice. Look."

---

3   The events of this story take place between *Driven* and *The Tower Hill Terror*.

Leipfold slid the letter across the desk to her and leant thoughtfully back in his chair.

"Leipfold Inc., huh?" Maile said. She scanned through the letter a couple of times. "What's that all about?"

"It's my bloody name, for God's sake." Leipfold looked frazzled, but he also looked concerned. He looked like he was starting to question whether he really was who he thought he was.

"So what are you going to do about it?" Maile asked.

"What can I do?"

"You could hire a lawyer," she suggested.

"Pah!" Leipfold exclaimed, banging his fist on the desk hard enough to make his coffee cup wobble. "I could, I suppose, if I pooled my resources and stopped paying you. But I'm not going to do that."

"Then what are you going to do?" Maile repeated.

"I'm going to fight it with everything I have, of course," he said. "I need you to find out what you can. Look them up online and find a website, a phone number, whatever you can get. I want a full report with as many details as possible. Nothing's too minor. If it's out there, I want to know about it."

"Sure," Maile said, flashing him one of her good-natured grins. They made an appearance every time he briefed her on something she couldn't wait to sink her teeth into. "I can do that."

"Good," Leipfold said. "Get started right away."

*   *   *

Leipfold left the office shortly afterwards, and Maile held the fort in his absence. For once, they had a little walk-in traffic. Nothing significant, just three people who asked for a quote and one guy who thought it was a restaurant and wanted to use the toilet. But it kept her on her toes when she wasn't working or refilling the kettle.

Before he left, the boss had asked her to follow up with her research into Leipfold Inc. Maile was more than happy to get stuck into it. She'd already done some preliminary work, consisting of putting the company name into a search engine and feeling disappointed when no hits were returned, and had moved on to her second batch of ideas, the ones that took a little more legwork.

She had what she wanted within the hour, after spending twenty minutes on the phone to a kind young lady from Companies House. She'd introduced herself as Lucy and talked in an annoying, whiny voice that set Maile's teeth on edge. The woman reminded her of the kids that used to bully her at secondary school, back when she cut her own hair and drew band logos on the sides of her Converse.

"What was the name again?" she asked.

"Leipfold Inc.," Maile told her for the third time. "L-E-I-P-F-O-L-D."

"Got it," Lucy said. "I-N-K, right?"

"Are you shitting me, Lucy?" Maile growled. "L-E-I-P-F-O-L-D. Space. I-N-C. You need me to repeat it again?"

"I think I've got it," Lucy said. If she was bothered by the outburst, she didn't show it. "Yep, looks like I've got a match for you. What do you need to know?"

"What can you tell me?" Maile asked.

Lucy from Companies House turned out to be surprisingly useful when she finally understood what Maile was looking for. She couldn't tell her everything, of course, but she did manage to list off a couple of the key directors, Thomas Fox and Derryn Shah, as well as a registered address in Bristol.

"Is there anything else I can help with?" Lucy asked.

Maile shook her head, then remembered that the woman couldn't see her. "No," she said. "But thanks. You've been surprisingly helpful."

"It's what we do," Lucy replied. Maile could detect a little hint of sarcasm and, as she cancelled the call and put the phone down, she wondered how the woman could stand the tedium of answering the same questions in the same office day after day after day.

Maile turned her attention back to the internet. She ran another search for "Leipfold," this time omitting the "Inc." Then she scrolled through the results pages, steering her mouse lazily down the screen and clicking the occasional link. On the sixth page, where she'd never thought to look before, she spotted an obscure reference to her boss's name on some sketchy-looking listings site.

It was a list of copyrighted terms and their rights-holders, and the word "Leipfold" was right there, on page 21,924 of the site's listings. It was owned by Leipfold Inc.

"Son of a bitch," Maile murmured. "What the hell is going on?"

She picked up her phone and gave Leipfold a call. He didn't answer, so she left a message.

"Boss, you need to see this," she said. "I've got some news for you." She paused, struggling to figure out how best to summarise the results of her investigation.

She settled on, "You need to get a lawyer."

*   *   *

Leipfold had a meeting. Maile had found a lawyer online, basing her decision on who had the best Yelp reviews. If Leipfold had been left to his own devices, he would have checked the telephone directory and called the guy who came first alphabetically. Maile's way worked better.

The lawyer was a man named George Gilbert. He was a stocky man of middle age with short, unruly hair. His suit was expensive and well-maintained, but his shoes were worn and in need of replacement. Leipfold found that reassuring. It told him that the man was good enough at his job to make a living from it, but not so good that he'd charge a fortune.

"Hello, Mr. Gilbert," Leipfold said when he opened the door to the office and led the man across to the plastic chairs in reception. He gestured for Gilbert to take a seat and then sank slowly down himself. He made a mental note to look into replacing the chairs with something more comfortable. If he could afford it.

"Hello, Mr. Leipfold," the lawyer said. After he took his seat and dropped his briefcase down to the side of him, he shook Leipfold's hand. "Better make this quick. I'm not in the habit of making house calls, but I've made an exception for you. I like the colour of your money. How can I help?"

"I've got a problem," Leipfold said. He gave Gilbert a brief lowdown of the cease and desist command from Leipfold Inc., as well as what Maile had learned about the trademark. "They've got my bloody name," he finished. "I need you to help me to take it back."

"Hmm," Gilbert said. "It sounds like you've got a case. There must be a precedent for something like this. It's fair use. I'll bet my hat on it."

"You're not wearing a hat."

"I know," Gilbert replied. "I don't own one. But that's not the point. Can you share your research so far?"

"Sure, but I don't have much. I need a little guidance on where you want me to look."

"Let's start with the letter you received," Gilbert said. Leipfold handed it over. The lawyer gave it a cursory glance before reading back through it more thoroughly. "Hmm."

"What is it?" Leipfold asked.

"The signature at the bottom," Gilbert said. "Leipfold Inc. is being represented by Filthy Phil. That rat bastard."

"Who's Filthy Phil?"

"He's called Phil Reed in the courtroom," Gilbert explained. "But outside of it, he's Filthy Phil. I don't trust him. He gets up to all sorts of shenanigans. If you ask me, he's lucky to be on the streets. He'll have to defend himself one day, you mark my words."

"Uh-huh," Leipfold said, making a mental note. "So you think I should look into this guy?"

"If you go looking for dirt, you'll find it," Gilbert said. "God, I'd love to nail that guy."

"Then represent me," Leipfold said. "Give him his day in court."

"You know," the lawyer said, "I might just take you up on that."

Leipfold laughed and clapped the man on the shoulder. Then they started talking terms. Leipfold took notes as they went, and he set himself a mental reminder to get Maile to type them up for him and to augment them with a little more research.

"So," Gilbert said, eventually. "Now that you're clear on my pricing structure, I've got one final offer to make."

"What's that?" Leipfold asked. He was nervous, mainly because the man's fees added up to about three weeks of his own time, and that was assuming he was being paid for that time in the first place. He was already having big, bad daydreams about having to sell Camilla to pay his way.

But the lawyer wasn't worried about all that. "This one's personal," he said. "If we win, you can pay my rate from the damages. We'll have those bastards for libel. And if we lose...well, we're not going to lose. But if we do, you don't have to pay me a penny."

"You can afford to do that?"

"No win, no fee," the lawyer replied. "And besides, I've always wanted to bring that son of a bitch down a peg."

*   *   *

Maile was sitting at her desk, absentmindedly squeezing a lump of blue stress putty with one hand while she navigated her computer with the other. She had a little time to fill, and Leipfold had already briefed her on the next step in the attempt to reclaim his name from Leipfold Inc.

"We're looking for a man called Filthy Phil," Leipfold said. "Phil

Reed, a lawyer. He's the guy who's representing the case."

And so Maile started out by simply plugging the names into a search engine to see what she could find. Most of the results were positive, listings for legal organisations and coverage of his work on *The Tribune*'s website. He was active on a couple of social networking sites, but Maile found nothing there that might bring his character into question.

But then she noticed something else, a little box that told her that results had been removed due to a right to be forgotten request. She'd always hated those things. Designed to help people to request unflattering search engine results with their name in them to be removed, she thought they were little more than a form of censorship.

The angle of her research changed, and she looked into the different options for uncovering the hidden data. One of them was to file a freedom of information request, which she did, but she didn't have much hope for it. Another was to switch search engines to try to find one that didn't hide the results from her. But she quickly abandoned that when she realised how much data there was. She'd still have to filter through each of the results and figure out which links were the redacted ones, knowing all the time that they might not be there at all.

That was when she hit on an idea. With the help of a couple of different tech tools, she was able to generate and download the results from hundreds of search engines, all exported as lists of links in CSVs. Then she designed a script that would scan through them all and rank each link based on how many times it appeared.

After barely an hour, when the script was finished, it took less than ten seconds for her to execute it. In no time at all, she was examining the results, starting with the least common links and working her way up. She started to find stuff that she hadn't seen before. Nothing concrete, but there were certain indications from online reviews or legal opinion pieces on specialist sites. Something was shady about this guy. She could feel it. She could taste it.

And then she hit the jackpot. If this wasn't the result that had been hidden from her, she'd eat her metaphorical hat.

The website popped open in another window, and Maile immediately recognised the interface. It was a piece in *The Daily Mail*, naming and shaming people that they claimed were convicted sex offenders living near danger zones. The headline referred to them as "paedo scum," but Maile knew from experience that *The Daily Mail* was about as reliable as a faulty socket. Of course, they didn't reveal their sources.

According to the paper, Filthy Phil was a very bad boy indeed. He'd served time for a sex crime back in the 1990s, and now he was living four hundred feet away from a primary school.

The man wasn't a paedophile, which was probably why the page had been removed in the first place. But he was a sex pest, as well as a convicted criminal. Maile smiled. If the case went to court, they'd make mincemeat of him. She was starting to hope that it would, just so she could see the look on the man's face.

*   *   *

Leipfold was out on the streets, dressed in a smart suit and carrying out a little recon. He was posing as a bored businessman, and indeed he was working on his finances while he watched his mark from a distance.

Filthy Phil looked ridiculous. Even with Leipfold's unashamed lack of fashion sense, the man looked like a muppet. He was wearing a salmon pink suit with a black tie, and he'd grown and styled his beard with some unidentified substance that clogged the hair and made it look like seaweed stuck to coral. When he sneezed, he made a sound like a gun going off. People stared at him uneasily every time he made a sudden movement to sip his coffee.

They were sitting in Leipfold's favourite coffee shop, and the fact that he was known there was enough to set his nerves on edge. He figured that the lawyer probably knew what he looked like, but Leipfold was a master of lurking in the shadows, even in the middle of a brightly lit room. He wasn't a tall man, and hiding his ginger hair with a baseball cap was enough to make him look less like a private detective and more like a tired labourer who was stopping off for a brew before heading back out on the road. But he still worried that the staff might recognise him and try to strike up a conversation.

Leipfold watched from around the edges of the spreadsheet, but Filthy Phil was boring the pants off him. He was just sitting there, tapping away at his laptop computer without a care in the world. He ordered a second cup of coffee and nipped to the toilet, but Leipfold resisted the temptation to check his screen out. He hated computers at the best of times, and the man could be back at any moment.

The detective was about to give up and go back to the office— his spreadsheet still incomplete—when another man entered the coffee shop. He was the polar opposite of the lawyer in his salmon pink suit. The new man was dressed in a dull brown suit and wore Ray-Ban sunglasses to hide his eyes. He looked like he was trying to be inconspicuous, which made him conspicuous. And Filthy Phil stood out like a marble obelisk in a grassy plain.

The meeting was short and to the point, and the two men talked for less than ten minutes before shaking hands and leaving within a couple of minutes of each other. Leipfold couldn't hear what they were saying, but he did know that it wasn't good news. He didn't need to follow them down the street to know that they'd separated, the classic move of two crooks up to no good, quickly meeting and disappearing again in the daylight. It reminded him of something his father used to say: When crooks meet by day, you'd better lock your doors by night.

It never even entered his mind that Filthy Phil and his sketchy-looking business associate could be up to something legit. And there was a reason for that. Leipfold had seen the second man somewhere before. It was during an investigation that he'd worked on in the murky early days of the agency's history.

He was called Gun-Hand Sammy, and he'd earned his name from being good at his job. He was a hired hand for a local gang, and Leipfold had helped to put his boss away.

*   *   *

Alone at home, bored out of his skull in his tiny bedsit, Leipfold spent the rest of that evening mulling over his impending court date with Filthy Phil Reed and Leipfold Inc. Just the thought of it made his blood boil. He felt like a horde of angry soldier ants was inching its way across his cerebrum. The unfairness of it all!

Leipfold knew what was happening, of course. He'd followed the man a couple more times and observed another meeting with Gun-Hand Sammy, and this time he'd inched close enough—by queuing up to buy a pint that he wouldn't drink—to overhear their conversation. Cocky as ever, the lawyer was making no attempt to keep his voice down. Sammy spoke slowly, more quietly, but his low rumble carried across the background noise like a clap of thunder across a mountaintop.

"The boss wants this over quickly," Sammy was saying. "A quick case to make a statement. The bastard is on the brink of bankruptcy. This will push him over the edge."

"It's a good job I'm your lawyer."

"Why's that?"

"No one else would take the case," the lawyer said. "Believe it or not, most of us have morals. Me, though, I work for the highest bidder. What did this Leipfold chap ever do to you?"

Leipfold shrank back at the sound of his name and left the pub shortly afterwards, leaving the untouched pint on the table at the whims of the local drinkers. Someone would have it, he was sure.

He didn't stick around to figure out why they were fucking with him. He already *knew* why. Gangsters hold long grudges, and they also get bored when they're serving the time that they owe to society. Gun-Hand Sammy worked for a man who wanted nothing more than to see Leipfold fall, preferably from a large height, and who had the power and the resources to reach him from a jail cell.

"Butch Johnson," Leipfold murmured. He lay back in his tiny bed and stared thoughtfully up at the ceiling. "I know it's you, Butch. It has to be."

Inspiration hit him like a battering ram, and he leapt out of bed and rushed over to his wardrobe. Inside, at the bottom, there was a wicker hamper with a lock on it. Having lost the key many moons ago, Leipfold picked the lock and pulled it open. His old notebooks were all still in there, as he'd expected them to be.

He picked them up at random, flicking through one after another to figure out when he'd kept them and what he'd used them for. The nostalgia was almost overwhelming, and he found himself thinking about all the cases he'd worked on throughout the years.

Finally, he found the notebook he was looking for. It was an old blue Moleskine that was filled from cover to cover with his thin, spidery handwriting. It was one of his earlier books, from back when he gave a damn about how tidy the inside of it was. He found the notes he was looking for towards the end of it.

It was his notes on the original Butch Johnson investigation. He'd laid out everything he thought he might ever need to know, and there were at least a dozen pages on Johnson alone, as well as notes on Gun-Hand Sammy and a` couple of others. Leipfold remembered all of them, as clearly as if the case had concluded just a couple of days earlier. It was one of the advantages of his damn near eidetic memory.

The case was one that stuck out in his memory, involving a missing guitar case, a flamenco dancer, two murders, a revolver with the serial number filed off and a mobster called Butch Johnson, who Leipfold had inadvertently turned into an enemy after getting a few of his boys sent down when he shared his findings with his client, who'd subsequently told the police.

He also remembered Jake the Squib, who'd earned his name thanks to his temperament. He was like a firework that could never be lit. Johnson had recruited Jake to the gang because he was the best damn racketeer this side of Moscow. The Squib turned out to be one of his most loyal henchmen, refusing to give evidence against Johnson at his high-profile trial. Despite this, the mobster thought that Jake, now rechristened Jake the Snake, had been involved in his arrest. He'd sent Jake a message to show that he wouldn't be forgotten. He arrived home one night to find that his pet cat had been chopped in half and nailed to the front of his house. His loyalty to Johnson had evaporated on that day, and Leipfold hoped that it had never returned. He also hoped that the number he had, an old landline with a London area code, was still in service. And he hoped that Jake the Whatever would be happy to take his money in exchange for information.

Shivering slightly, Leipfold picked up his mobile phone and dialled the number.

*   *   *

The court date rolled slowly around, and Leipfold splashed out to get his only suit cleaned and pressed so that he'd look his best. He polished his shoes, shaved the thin rash of ginger beard that had sprung up without him noticing and then hopped on the back of Camilla to ride through the streets to the courthouse.

Leipfold met Maile outside, and they just had time to grab a quick coffee before heading off to find their lawyer. Gilbert was already inside, hobnobbing with his fellow professionals and trying to represent his client as best as he could. It was important—no, it was *vital*—for Gilbert to appear as professional as possible. Their strategy relied on showing Filthy Phil Reed up as a charlatan, and the best way to do that, they'd decided, was by showing what a real lawyer should look and act like.

But that was only one side of the strategy, and Leipfold felt confident as he wound his way through the streets on the back of the bike. He'd done everything he could to prepare himself, from scoping out the enemy lawyer to digging deep into Gun-Hand Sammy's shady history. He had photos of the two of them in both the coffee shop and the pub, but the photos proved only that the men had met. In the eyes of the court, that was unlikely to mean a thing.

Mr. Gilbert greeted them with a smile and a handshake each, lurking outside the courtroom while they waited their turn.

"The other guys aren't here yet," he said. "Maybe they're not going to show up."

But they did show up, just a couple of minutes before the session was opened. The waiting plaintiffs were led inside the court room.

The judge was a dour-faced man who made it clear that he wasn't in the mood for any bullshit. He also made it clear that he wasn't in the mood for theatrics. He wanted a good, clean trial. When Maile whispered something to Leipfold towards the start of the hearing, he shot her a look that shut her up for the rest of the session.

Phil Reed took the stand first, and he kicked things off by outlining the history of Leipfold Inc. and the importance of its trademark to their ongoing business operations. He talked the talk and he walked the walk, and he looked smugly self-satisfied when he sat back down again.

Then it was Leipfold's turn. While Mr. Gilbert took the lead on proceedings, he cross-examined the detective in such a way that a narrative was created. Leipfold was, of course, the hero. Gun-Hand Sammy was the antagonist's sidekick, and Filthy Phil was an unwitting pawn in a criminal game.

And then Mr. Gilbert played his trump card. He called Jake the Squib to the stand, and the former gangster played his part in the case with all the ease of someone extending their middle finger. He owed Leipfold a favour, like half of the city's underbelly, but he would have testified for Satan himself if it would have helped him to get his own back on his erstwhile employer. Gilbert asked him question after question—at least, until the judge said he'd heard enough—and Jake rattled off his answers like an actor immersed in his lines at the final rehearsal.

It didn't take long for the verdict to be delivered.

*   *   *

It was a couple of weeks later, and Leipfold was in the office. He was wearing his suit again, not because he needed to but because he could. He had a debriefing lined up with Mr. Gilbert, and Leipfold knew that he owed the man some professional courtesy. He'd helped him to win the case, after all.

Gilbert arrived ten minutes late, but he came bearing coffee and some good news, which he explained almost as soon as he was over the threshold. Leipfold was still clearing old case files off the chairs in reception to create a space for him when he started to speak.

"Good news, Mr. Leipfold," he said. "There's no further action needed on your part."

"I know," Leipfold said. "We won the case."

"We won the case in court," Gilbert corrected him. "But that doesn't always mean game over. There's always the potential for appeals, retrials and all the other fun stuff that makes the legal system what it is. But you don't have to worry about Filthy Phil anymore."

"How come?"

"He's dead," Gilbert said. "Shot himself, if the rumours are true."

"Or maybe someone else did the job for him," Leipfold replied. "The man was an egotist. Men like that don't kill themselves. They're too proud, too self-assured."

"I suspect you're right, Mr. Leipfold," Gilbert said. "But either way, it's no longer our concern. In the eyes of the law, justice has been served. Leipfold Inc. has been declared insolvent. That means you're free to use your own name again. I strongly suggest that you copyright the term as soon as possible so you can prevent this from happening again."

"And I'm guessing you can help me with that."

"I certainly can," the lawyer said. "For a fee, at least. And that brings me on to the next point for discussion."

"Yeah?" Leipfold flashed him a suspicious glance, but he stayed silent. He wanted to hear what the man had to say for himself.

"Yeah," Gilbert confirmed. "See, we were awarded damages. Now, as you'll recall, I agreed to take the case on a no-win, no-fee basis."

Leipfold did indeed recall it, and he found himself wondering how much the man was about to ask him for. His glum cynicism must have showed in his face because the lawyer shook his head and clapped him on the shoulder. They were both sitting down, their perches amongst the paperwork looking like the reading section of some overpopulated library.

"Don't worry about it," the lawyer said. "The settlement will more than cover my fees, not just for the court date but for the copyright case, too. You'll still have a little cash left over."

"How much?" Leipfold asked.

The lawyer told him, and Leipfold's eyes opened wide like those of a condemned man on the electric chair. The figure that he'd quoted was equivalent to a month's work, and Leipfold had barely done a thing to earn it. He'd just been caught up in a crooked attempt to game the system, and now he was reaping the rewards.

Leipfold grinned. "Go ahead and copyright my name for me," he said. "It could come in useful one of these days."

"That it could," the man said. He shook Leipfold's hand and made a little small talk, then started to gather his things and to walk towards the door. He paused on the threshold.

"Just one more thing," he said, lowering his voice as though he was afraid of being overheard. He leaned a little closer to Leipfold.

"What is it?"

"I've got a proposition," the lawyer said. "Between you and me, sometimes my clients could use a detective. Sometimes *I* could, for that matter. So what do you say about a partnership?"

"That depends what it involves," Leipfold said.

"It's simple," Mr. Gilbert replied. "I bring you work and you do it. You give me twenty percent off your fees and I give you twenty percent off mine if you ever need me again. What do you think?"

Leipfold smiled and offered the lawyer his hand. They shook on it, and then the lawyer left the office to make his way to another meeting. Leipfold closed the door behind him and then turned his attention back to the mound of paperwork.

The Marshall Stack[4]

LEIPFOLD WAS ALONE in the office when the visitor came in. She was an imposing-looking woman who towered over him by at least six inches, and she wasn't even wearing heels. Instead, she was dressed conservatively, which made her age hard to place. Leipfold guessed she was around his age, maybe even a little older.

She hadn't called in advance to make an appointment. She'd simply walked in from the street on the assumption that he'd see her. Her assumption had turned out to be correct. The business was doing well, but it wasn't doing so well that he could turn people away at the door. Instead, he led her up the stairs into his office and offered her an uncomfortable seat in the reception area. She accepted the offer gratefully and introduced herself as Mrs. Marshall.

"Well, Mrs. Marshall," Leipfold said. "It's a pleasure to meet you. How can I help?"

"It's my son," Mrs. Marshall explained. "I'm worried about him."

"That's not unusual," Leipfold said. "It's a mother's job to worry about her children."

"Perhaps," she said. "But most of them don't have a son like mine. The boy is nothing but trouble. He's one of those drug fiends you hear so much about. And he's involved in something."

"What kind of something?" Leipfold asked.

"I'm not sure," Mrs. Marshall replied, shaking her head sadly. "That's what I was hoping you could help me with. All I know is

---

4   The events of this story take place between *Driven* and *The Tower Hill Terror*.

that he's spending time with the wrong people, making friends with the wrong crowd. They're of the class that takes things before they go missing."

"Thieves," Leipfold murmured.

"Exactly."

The woman paused for a moment and made a dramatic show of thirst by sucking at her teeth and coughing politely. Leipfold took the hint and popped the kettle on, and he poured her a glass of tepid tap water in the meantime. She drank greedily from the cup and sucked at her teeth again, then gestured for Leipfold to sit down while the kettle boiled.

"What I want to know, Mr. Leipfold," she said, "is whether you'd be willing to do a little research. I don't want him to know that I sent you.In fact, I'd prefer it if you kept your distance altogether. But I simply have to know what he's planning."

"I can do that," Leipfold replied. "But I can't promise you'll like what I discover. It's my job to chase the facts, Mrs. Marshall."

"Call me Vera," she said. "And that's a risk that I'm willing to take. I'm at my wits' end."

Leipfold nodded. "Well, Vera," he said, "I can certainly try. Do you have a recent photograph that I could use?"

Wordlessly, Mrs. Marshall rooted through her handbag and came up with a passport-sized photo that she kept inside her purse. She handed it over to Leipfold.

"His name's Mikey," she said. "Mikey Marshall."

The kettle had finished boiling and Leipfold poured out a couple cups of coffee while he talked fees and suggested a retainer of a day's work a week. The woman agreed before he'd even finished explaining it all, and Leipfold realised that she was desperate as only a mother could be. In a moment of madness, he said he'd give her a day and a half at the same rate.

Mrs. Marshall smiled and shook Leipfold's hand before scrawling her John Hancock at the bottom of one of his client onboarding forms. He dropped the clipboard and the contract on his desk, grabbed his notebook and sat back down beside her.

"Now, Vera," Leipfold said. "I need you to do something for me."

"What's that?" she asked.

"I want you to tell me everything you can about your son."

*　　*　　*

While Leipfold was out of the office, Maile played a few tunes from her computer and pottered around. At first, she focused on giving it a clean. Leipfold was a tidy man with a tidy mind, but tidiness and cleanliness are two different things. The only thing she didn't touch was the toilet, which had so much grime caked on it that she thought it'd be best to remove the whole damn thing and to pay for a new one.

Still, she cleaned the insides of the windows and bleached the sink in the kitchen, and she even ran a hoover around the place and did her best to reach the eaves with a three-foot feather duster. The office had a high ceiling, a remnant of the Victorian design that had escaped the building's inevitable refurbishments, and so she had to climb onto a chair to reach the cobwebs. In some places, they were so thick that she was half afraid that even if she managed to reach them, they'd stand their ground and send her tumbling to the floor.

After the best part of an hour and a half, she sat back down at her desk and admired her handiwork. It was kind of depressing because she'd barely made a dent in it, but it was a start, and if Leipfold noticed, perhaps he'd dig up some cash to pay a cleaner to finish the job.

With that out of the way, Maile turned her attention to the Marshall case. Leipfold had given her the briefest of briefings and a name, Mikey Marshall, for her to look into. It was a simple enough job, by the sound of it. He just wanted her to find the guy and to report back on what he was up to.

It didn't take her long to find him, despite how common his name was. She used a few geofilters and added a couple of extra search terms, then built up a catalogue of everything she'd found. There was a lot of noise for her to cast her eyes over, but she tracked him down on a couple of social networks and an image search pulled up some photos that were more recent than the one that his mother had provided.

"Christ," Maile murmured. The guy didn't look well at all. He had big bags under his eyes, a strip of acne scars across his cheek and the kind of haunted expression that she was more used to seeing in ol0d paintings than in person. He had shoulder-length hair, which was matted and knotted like he was trying to grow dreadlocks, hair which must have been grown in the couple of years since he'd renewed his passport and given the remaining photos to his mother. In one of the photos, he was smoking a cigarette. One thing was for sure, though. It was definitely Mikey, even if he had let himself go over the years.

Maile dug a little deeper and managed to get a contact number, as well as a rough idea of where he was living. But that wasn't what she found most interesting. No, she was more interested by his activity in the local selling groups, the online equivalents of car boot sales and market stalls. Mikey Marshall was all over them, and he was selling everything from jewellery to electronics. He even had a bunch of games for Maile's console, and she thought about making a bid for them before she remembered that he was part of an active investigation.

But then, she thought, *why the hell not?* If nothing else, it would be a good way to get in front of him. If he turned out to be a criminal, she could claim the cash back on expenses. If he wasn't, she'd get some new games at a bargain price.

Maile bit her lip and took the plunge. She sent the man a friend request and messaged him to say she was interested in a couple of listings. She hesitated before she pressed the send button, trying to decide what Leipfold would think when she told him that she'd used her initiative. He'd either be happy or mad, and Maile wasn't sure which it would be.

But she figured there was only one way to find out.

* * *

That evening, Maile went to meet Mikey Marshall. Leipfold approved of the plan and had wanted to go with her, but she'd argued that his presence would only put the man on his guard, and neither of them wanted that.

"Besides," she'd reminded him, "I can defend myself. Remember Tom Townsend?"

"Yes," Leipfold had replied, a darkness passing across his face like the shadow of an eagle across the plains as it hunted for food and water. "I remember Tom Townsend. Be careful."

But Leipfold needn't have worried. Maile met the man in the Rose & Crown, and the place was thick with drinkers and petty criminals. Besides, in Maile's experience, men didn't like it when other men raised their fists to a woman, especially one as short and insubstantial as she was, so if Marshall turned violent, he'd have a riot on his hands. And she always had the canister of pepper spray in her handbag to fall back on.

Mikey Marshall looked even worse in person than he had in the photographs. Maile couldn't help wondering what kind of poison was working its way through the man's veins. He was an addict—there was no question of that—but it was hard to tell whether his drug of choice was heroin, coke or crystal meth. She wouldn't have been surprised if it was all three. Either way, she figured he mainlined. While they talked, he scratched relentlessly at the track marks on his arms, and he was making no attempt to hide the scars of his habit.

"Maile, right?" he said, as he sat down beside her in one of the booths. He pronounced it Mah-ill-ee, but she let it pass without correcting him.

"And you're Mikey," she said. "Nice to meet you."

"Yeah," he said. "Yeah. So what you saying?"

"Excuse me?"

"How can I help?" he asked. He had the kind of husky voice that came from smoking too many cigarettes, half Tom Waits and half Keith Richards.

"I saw the games you had for sale," Maile said. "Did you bring them?"

"Course I did," the man said. He laughed, and it sounded like a car backfiring or the tortured scream of a rusty bolt as someone slid it home. He reached into a battered rucksack with a broken zipper and pulled out a stack of console games. He dropped them on the table and then dove back in, this time coming out with a couple of controllers. "Here's what I've got. You interested?"

"Hell yeah," Maile said. "How much?"

"How much you got?"

"Twenty?"

Marshall shook his head. "Thirty," he said. "Come on, love. You're looking at over a hundred if you go to the shops."

"If I go to the shops, they give me a receipt and a money-back guarantee," Maile said. "Twenty-two."

"Twenty-eight."

"No," Maile said. "Twenty-five."

"Twenty-seven."

"Twenty-five," Maile repeated. "For the games and the controllers."

Mikey Marshall shot her a look that seethed venom, the kind of look that a rattlesnake might give to a field mouse. Then he lowered his eyes, and Maile knew in that moment that she had him where she wanted him. He needed the money, just like he needed a fix.

"Twenty-five or no deal," Maile said.

"Fine," Marshall spat. "But this is daylight robbery."

"I'm sure it is," Maile replied. "But who's the victim?"

* * *

The following morning, Maile took the bunch of games that she'd bought from the crook in the Rose & Crown and handed them reluctantly to Leipfold.

"You take good care of them, okay?" she said. "I haven't had a chance to play them yet."

"They're evidence," Leipfold reminded her, but he was smiling. He handled them as carefully as he could, like an executive chef carrying a cake over to the guests of honour. He laid them out on his desk, then excused himself for a moment to head into the storage room. When he came back, he was carrying a police-issue ultraviolet scanner.

"What the hell is that?" Maile asked.

"It's an ultraviolet scanner," Leipfold said.

"Where the hell did you get it?"

"Cholmondeley," Leipfold said, simply. His expression said that he'd prefer not to say any more, so Maile shrugged and left him to it.

Leipfold held the scanner like a giant fountain pen and passed it carefully over each of the games in turn, first over the cases and then over the discs and the interiors. With each game, his excitement grew, until he finished up with a lupine grin spread across his tired, chiselled face.

"Anything?" Maile asked.

"I think so," Leipfold replied. "Give me a minute."

Leipfold picked up the phone on his desk and placed a call, and Maile listened unobtrusively to one side of the conversation. It was pretty easy for her to follow it.

"Good morning," Leipfold began. "My name's James Leipfold, and I was wondering if—"

He paused for a moment, presumably listening to the voice on the other end of the line, before continuing. "No," he said. "Nothing like that. In fact, I think I might be able to help you."

Another pause. Maile flashed him an inquisitive look, but he waved his hand impatiently and she turned her attention back to her computer screen.

"It's okay," Leipfold said. He paused again, almost imperceptibly, before adding, "It's about a burglary, I guess. I'm not sure, you tell me. Have you been the victim of a recent crime? Specifically, a crime involving a selection of games for a console?"

Leipfold rattled off the list of games and paused again. He held his hand over the mouthpiece and whispered, "I think we're onto something." Then he removed his hand from the receiver and repeated the list of games again.

"That's right," he said. "Well, I'm a private detective, but close enough. I was following up on a lead and…well, one thing led to another and I found myself in possession of a stack of games."

Maile flashed him a glare from behind her computer screen, but if he noticed, he didn't dignify it with a response. She was still bitter that she hadn't had a chance to play them.

"Ultraviolet," Leipfold continued. "Looks like someone wrote your number down in the slot where the discs click in. Smart move. We wouldn't have found you otherwise. Can I ask you for your name and address, please? I'd like to pop over and ask you a couple of questions."

Leipfold paused with the receiver in one hand and his pen in the other. He sketched a small bird in his notebook while he waited to take down their information.

"Uh-huh," he said. "No, don't worry. It won't take long. And I can bring your games back while I'm at it."

Maile looked up again at that and shot her boss the middle finger. He covered the mouthpiece again and mouthed something across to her.

It looked like he said, "Expenses."

*   *   *

Leipfold's visit to the burglary victims was short and uneventful. The family was unwilling to talk, and he was kept in check by its bull-headed patriarch, a man in his late thirties who looked ready to rip the head off a kitten and to stick it in a blender. He'd answered Leipfold in monosyllables and cut off the rest of his family whenever they tried to elaborate. Leipfold left disappointed, but he did at least learn a little.

The house had been burgled in the dead of night less than a week earlier. The family had been away for the weekend. They'd come back to find their porch door forced and most of their gear gone. There was jewellery missing too, but they were unwilling to tell him exactly what had been taken. Without that, he was unable to check it against Marshall's online fire sale, but it was suggestive at the very least. They recognised the games that he'd sold as the ones that they'd lost, and they took them off his hands without so much as a thank you.

That lead had proved to be a dead end, so Leipfold followed the only other angle he could think of. He got Maile to give him Marshall's number, then gave the man a call to offer up some bait. It was a short call, over in less than two minutes, but Marshall said he'd be able to help. Leipfold had told him he was looking for some high-end audio equipment, a Marshall stack, and the irony wasn't lost on him. Marshall, ever the opportunist, told Leipfold that he was in luck. He'd get something over to him the following day.

To Leipfold, that meant he was planning to strike that evening, and he wanted to catch the man in the act. He also wanted Maile to come along with him.

"Two heads are better than one," he'd said. "Especially when you're trying to follow someone."

Leipfold said that they'd only have one shot at it, but he also had a good idea of where the man was likely to strike. Maile had been able to narrow down his address to a low-income estate in Hounslow, and Leipfold was willing to bet that he'd keep his crimes local, like most criminals. The man was a junkie, for God's sake. He wasn't about to go on a long drive out of town for a minor crime. The nearest music shop was just over a mile away, so Leipfold stationed Maile at the shop and took it upon himself to cruise the streets of the estate until he saw his mark.

It didn't take him long to pick up the skeletal figure of Mikey Marshall, even without the advantage that Maile had of meeting him in the puke-grey flesh to buy the computer games. It didn't matter. The estate was full of uncouth youths and mean-looking sons of bitches, but Mikey was the first person he'd seen that could have squeezed himself sideways through the bars of a jail cell. He was riding a pushbike. Leipfold tailed him as best as he could, keeping a reasonable distance and looping around here and there so that the man didn't notice his motorcycle. But he needn't have bothered. Marshall had only two things on his mind: getting the job done and getting another hit once it was over.

Marshall followed the exact route that Leipfold expected him to take, taking basic precautions to throw off any scent he might leave by doubling back a couple of times and taking the long way round. Still, he honed slowly but surely in on Evans's Music, the only place in an eight-mile radius that could be relied upon to stock a Marshall stack, and Leipfold grinned behind the visor of his helmet as he realised it.

When they were a quarter of a mile away and counting, Leipfold pulled over and sent Maile a message to tell her to be ready. Then he revved up Camilla and took the back route to the music shop.

*　　*　　*

Mikey Marshall paused for a moment outside the music shop to clear his head. It was murky inside his skull, and it had been for as long as he could remember. It was hard to think straight, to plan ahead. But he had enough sense to check that his driver was there, and he was relieved to see his dodgy friend Darren behind the wheel of a stolen Subaru. Like all good thieves, they planned not to waste a single thing. After Mikey picked up the grand or so he'd been promised, they'd strip the car for parts and then burn it out in a country lane somewhere.

After he'd smashed and grabbed as much as he could carry and then scored another couple dozen hits, of course.

Marshall lurked outside the shop for a moment, watching the passers-by and trying to get a feel for the footfall in the area. It wouldn't do for him to be caught by a vigilante. He knew that the place was likely to have a live link to the police station and that an automated call would be made as soon as he broke the glass or forced the door, but he also knew that if he made a clean getaway, he'd have enough loot to fund himself for at least a month, maybe six weeks at a push.

He didn't notice Leipfold as he chained Camilla up further along the street, nor did he notice Maile as she leaned oh-so casually against the wall outside Tesco, affecting an air of bored nonchalance as though she was waiting for someone who was running an hour late.

The two of them watched as Mikey Marshall made a decision and headed down a small side street to the shop's rear entrance. It played out exactly how Leipfold was expecting, and he and Maile took their positions with all the efficiency of two army commandos, albeit two commandos who were effectively unarmed.

Marshall didn't even make it inside the building. He pulled out a long, thin knife from the inside of his baggy coat and tried to slip it through a crack in the doorway. The blade made it inside, but he was still trying to jimmy it when Leipfold pounced on him from behind. He wrapped a thick arm around the man's scrawny neck and pulled him away from the door, sending the knife clattering to the ground. Marshall tried to bite him, but his teeth were turned away by the leathers, something that Leipfold would later be grateful for.

Marshall kicked back at Leipfold, and the detective grunted as the man's boot connected with his knee. He lost his grip for just a moment, but it was enough. Marshall wriggled free and lunged for the knife, fear and anger and anguish all rolling into one and turning him into the hominid equivalent of a rabid dog. From outside the alleyway, the mingled sounds of the busy road made their way over to them, but the rear entrance to the music shop was still unobserved, still silent.

Marshall whirled around and rushed at Leipfold, who backed away without taking his eyes off him. He got a little closer, then closer still.

Maile came at Marshall from his blind side and hit him in the back of the head with a bunched fist. Marshall turned on her, and Leipfold dove at him. Amidst the chaos, Maile brought her other hand up and hit the trigger on the little canister she carried around in her handbag.

Mikey Marshall was about to find out why they call it pepper spray.

*   *   *

Even blinded, emaciated and outnumbered, Mikey Marshall had put up a good fight. In the end, they'd been able to subdue him. Leipfold held the man's hands behind his back while Maile looped plastic cable ties around his wrists to hold them together. Leipfold had pulled them from his wallet like it was nothing, and when Maile called him out on it, he'd simply shrugged and murmured something about it being a trick that he'd learned in the army.

"They're cheaper than cuffs," Leipfold said. "And less conspicuous."

"But how are we going to get him back to the office?" Maile asked.

Leipfold grinned and pulled out his mobile phone. "We're going to put a call in," he said.

Vera Marshall arrived just over twenty minutes later after an uncomfortable period in which Marshall, Maile and Leipfold sat around in silence, all three of them hoping that no one would interrupt them in the alleyway. It would have been difficult to explain it to even the most gullible of passers-by, and Leipfold wasn't in the mood to lie to people. He would have been more likely to tell the truth, which would have led to the police being called, and that would be the end of the case as far as he was concerned. Justice might have been served, perhaps, but he wouldn't have been paid for it.

Mrs. Marshall drove a mini, which caused a problem, but they were able to bundle her son into the back seat while Maile rode shotgun, her head twisted around like an owl so she could keep her eye on the man while covering him with the nozzle of the (now half-empty) canister. But she needn't have worried. His mother's presence, or perhaps whatever he'd taken before he left the house, was enough to keep him in check. He just sat there with his head hanging against the window throughout the entire journey. At first, Maile thought he was planning on making a break for it, but then she remembered that they were riding in convoy and that Leipfold was behind them with Camilla's chrome handlebars shining bright beneath the streetlights. Even if he got out of the vehicle, he wouldn't get away from them.

Leipfold had let himself in for a shaky ride. As he pulled into the road, he was almost mowed down by Mikey's getaway driver, who'd decided he'd better make a getaway. But before the car was out of sight, Leipfold committed the number plate to memory. He made a mental note to call it in to Jack Cholmondeley.

They pulled up outside Leipfold's office at the same time, but it was dark enough for them to enter the building unobserved. The clocks were yet to spring forward for the summertime, and that was a boon for the criminal class because it gave them more darkness to work in. It was also a boon for Leipfold because their unusual convoy attracted little attention from passers-by. It was the work of a couple of minutes to shepherd Marshall upstairs and into his office.

When they sat Mikey down in the reception area beside his mother, he started to shake. He was mumbling to himself, but the mumbles quickly grew into murmurings and grumblings and then finally into ravings and raging.

"This is against the law," he babbled. "False imprisonment. I'll have you, whoever the hell you are. I'll call the cops."

"Be my guest," Leipfold said. "Here, I'll lend you my phone."

He keyed in the triple digits of the emergency services and handed the phone to Mikey Marshall, whose hands were cuffed but who still had enough freedom of movement to jab the dial button. He chose not to.

"As I thought," Leipfold said. "Don't worry, my friend. You can call this a citizen's arrest."

*   *   *

Over the next hour or so, Leipfold's office turned into a scene from the Jeremy Kyle Show. Vera Marshall started crying, then Mikey Marshall started crying, and then Leipfold started shouting and Maile put the kettle on to calm everybody down. It was no easy task. They were all talking at once. It wasn't until Leipfold slammed a heavy fist into his desk and sent coffee cups clattering to the floor that everyone shut up and turned to look at him.

Silence reigned.

"Thank you," Leipfold said. "Let's start at the beginning. Mr. Marshall, do you deny that you have a drug habit?"

"Course not," he replied. "I love drugs, me. I'd be off my face all the time if I could afford it."

"That doesn't end well," Leipfold said. "Believe me."

For a mad moment, Leipfold thought about sharing his own story, but then he remembered the promise he'd made to himself over a decade ago. It was like a scab that was waiting to be picked, and if he started to worry at the wound, the metaphorical pus would pour out. He had no desire to get it infected.

Instead, Mrs. Marshall stepped forwards and slapped her son across the side of the head. She drew back and struck him again, then went for another swing before Maile was able to grab her by her bony wrist and yank her aside.

"You stupid, stupid bastard," she shouted. "After everything your father and I did for you. After all of the sacrifices. And you're throwing it all away."

"I never asked for any of it," the man said. "It's my life, not yours. Let me do what I want with it."

"So that's how you want to play it?" Mrs. Marshall looked for all the world like an industrial cleaner who'd just pulled a dead rat from the U-bend of a public lavatory. For a moment, Maile felt sorry for her. Then her expression changed and she took on the appearance of a shrewd old harpy who'd seen a thousand million sunsets and been disgusted by every single one of them.

"You're not my son anymore," she said. Then she walked towards the door.

"Wait!" Leipfold shouted. Mrs. Marshall spun around with remarkable agility. "It doesn't have to be this way."

"It does," Mrs Marshall said, and only Maile heard her son say the exact same thing at the same time. "I've had it, Mr. Leipfold."

"What if I had an idea?"

"I'll pay your fees either way."

"That's not what I was getting at," Leipfold said. "If you cut off your ties with the boy, it will only make things worse. On top of that, I'd be duty-bound to report his misdemeanours to the police force. He's lucky to have stayed out of jail for as long as he has."

"You do know I'm in the same room as you, right?" Mikey said. But everyone ignored him because he was a junkie, and junkies weren't known for their sparkling conversation.

"Here's what I suggest," Leipfold continued. "Take the boy home. Maile and I will help you, if you need it. Is his father still around?"

"Yes."

"Good," Leipfold said. "You're going to need some backup over the next few days. Here's what I want you to do."

He walked over to Mrs. Marshall and whispered something into her ear. It took him a good couple of minutes to say everything he wanted to say, and Maile watched as Vera's face changed colour from red to green to grey. When Leipfold had finished, she looked frail and old and tired, but she also looked like a woman who'd made her mind up.

She looked Leipfold dead in the eye and said, "Let's do it."

*　　*　　*

A couple of days later, Leipfold and Maile were sitting in the office, brainstorming a plan of attack for their latest case, when they received an unexpected visitor.

It was Mikey Marshall, and he looked totally different to how he'd appeared when last they saw him. The big, black bags beneath his eyes were still there, but they'd lost their purplish hue and now looked like the bags on the eyes of a man who struggled to sleep of an evening, rather than those of a man who'd been injecting God-knew-what into his veins every couple of hours. The track marks on his arms were still there. They could see that when he took his jacket off and hung it on the back of his chair.

Leipfold looked at the man cautiously and asked, "How can I help you, Mr. Marshall?"

The man chuckled. "I think you've done enough, Mr. Leipfold," he replied.

Leipfold backed away involuntarily, and Maile reached into her bag to grab her pepper spray, which was on its last legs and threatening to give out at any moment.

"If you've come here looking for trouble—" Leipfold began, but Marshall cut him off with a gesture. He was still sitting calmly in his seat, the same seat he'd sat in on his last visit, and showing no signs of anger or aggression.

"Please," he said. "Don't worry. I'm a changed man."

"He does look a little better," Maile said.

Marshall spun his head around to look at her. He grinned, and the smile looked genuine, heartfelt. Then he tipped her a wink.

"I'm a lot better," he said. "And it's all thanks to you and Mr. Leipfold here."

Leipfold pinched the bridge of his nose and sighed. "Coffee?" he asked. Marshall nodded, and Leipfold made a fresh round of brews before sitting down again and waiting for him to finish his story.

"My mother said it was your idea," Marshall said. "Don't get me wrong, it was hell. But it worked."

"What happened?" Maile asked.

"She took me home," Marshall said. "And then she locked me in my old bedroom. She'd kept it exactly how it was when I left home, except for one little change. My dad put locks on the doors and the windows. They let me stew it out in there, pissing and shitting and spewing into a bucket that they emptied when they brought food in. It was hell. Horrible, relentless hell. But I came out the other side."

"I'm glad to hear that," Leipfold said. "So you decided to clean yourself up."

Marshall nodded. "Reluctantly at first, you can be damn sure of that. But yeah, I'm getting clean. Thanks to you, Mr. Leipfold."

Maile thought Leipfold blushed, but she couldn't be sure.

He had Celtic skin, pale and freckled, and his cheeks lit up like Rudolph's nose for a number of reasons, from heat and exhaustion to embarrassment and malaise.

"I can't take all the credit," Leipfold said. "You should thank your mother."

"I already have," Marshall replied. "She told me to give you her best."

Leipfold offered the younger man his hand. Mikey Marshall took it and shook it, then climbed abruptly to his feet.

"Now if you don't mind, Mr. Leipfold," he said, "I have to be off. Places to go and people to see."

"What kind of people?" Leipfold asked. He looked shrewdly across at the man, trying to achieve the impossible. He wanted to see inside his head, to figure out what he was thinking and to determine whether the man was likely to fall right back off the wagon.

"Relax, Mr. Leipfold," Mikey Marshall said. "I'm not going to score some dope. I'm going to the airport."

Leipfold's ears pricked and he looked up at him. "The airport?" he asked. "Why?"

"I've got a flight to catch," Marshall said. "I'm going to Italy. My dad says he found me a job out there. It's time for me to turn my life around."

"Good for you, kid," Leipfold replied. "Don't forget to send me a postcard."

Join the Conversation

THANKS FOR JOINING James Leipfold, Jack Cholmondeley, Maile O'Hara and more in the hunt for bad guys, gnomes, geezers and girlfriends.

James, Jack and I would love to hear what you think. Whether you loved or hated the book, please let us know by tweeting @ DaneCobain or by leaving a review on Amazon and Goodreads.

Reviews help indie authors to sell their books, so please do take the time to share your thoughts. I link to my favourite reviews on Facebook and Twitter, so be sure to follow me there and to check out my site for further info. I'll see you soon!

danecobain.com
facebook.com/danecobainmusic
twitter.com/danecobain
youtube.com/danecobain
instagram.com/danecobain

Acknowledgements

WHERE DO I START?

Thanks as always to my loyal readers—you know who you are. Big shout outs in particular are due to Donna Woodings, Carl Woodings, Olga and Alan Woodings, and Heather and Dave Clarke.

Thanks also to Pam Elise Harris, my fearless editor and partner in crime. It's Pam's job to bring me back to reality when I get too carried away, as well as to make sure that my sentences sense do make.

Big thanks too to everyone who's ever read one of my books. There are a surprising amount of you out there, more than I ever thought there'd be when I started writing emo poems and a bad novel at the age of fourteen.

I'll see you all in my next release.

MORE GREAT READS
FROM DANE COBAIN

Driven (Detective Mystery) A car strikes in the middle of the night and a young actress lies dead in the road. The police force thinks it's an accident, but Maile and Leipfold aren't so sure. Putting their differences aside, and brought together by a shared love of crosswords and busting bad guys, Maile and Leipfold investigate. But not all is as it seems, as they soon find out to their peril...

The Tower Hill Terror (Detective Mystery) James Leipfold and Maile O'Hara are back with a brand new case. The Tower Hill Terror is on the loose, a serial killer with a grisly M.O., and Maile and Leipfold must work fast to take him down before another body is found. Meanwhile, Leipfold's cop friend Jack Cholmondeley finds himself working on the same investigation, but the killer is always one step ahead.

About the Author

DANE COBAIN is a published author, freelance writer, book blogger, poet and (occasional) musician with a passion for language and learning. When he's not working on his next release, he can be found reading and reviewing books for his award-winning book blog, SocialBookshelves.com.

If you enjoyed reading this book,
please consider writing your honest review
and sharing it with other readers.

Many of our Authors are happy to participate in
Book Club and Reader Group discussions.
For more information, contact us at info@encirclepub.com.

Thank you,
Encircle Publications

For news about more exciting new fiction, join us at:

Facebook: www.facebook.com/encirclepub

Instagram: www.instagram.com/encirclepublications

Twitter: twitter.com/encirclepub

Sign up for Encircle Publications newsletter and specials:
eepurl.com/cs8taP

CPSIA information can be obtained
at www.ICGtesting.com
Printed in the USA
LVHW102233120522
718523LV00005B/43